Wings of Pegasus

Andromeda Chronicles II

Jay Allan

system 7
publishing

Books by Jay Allan

Flames of Rebellion Series
(Published by Harper Voyager)
Flames of Rebellion
Rebellion's Fury

The Crimson Worlds Series
Marines
The Cost of Victory
A Little Rebellion
The First Imperium
The Line Must Hold
To Hell's Heart
The Shadow Legions
Even Legends Die
The Fall

Crimson Worlds Refugees Series
Into the Darkness
Shadows of the Gods
Revenge of the Ancients
Winds of Vengeance
Storm of Vengeance

Crimson Worlds Successors Trilogy
MERCS
The Prisoner of Eldaron
The Black Flag

Crimson Worlds Prequels
Tombstone
Bitter Glory
The Gates of Hell
Red Team Alpha

Also by Jay Allan – The Dragon's Banner

Join my email list
at www.jayallanbooks.com

List members get publication announcements and special bonuses throughout the year (email addresses are never shared or used for any other purpose). Please feel free to email me with any questions at jayallanwrites@gmail.com. I answer all reader emails

For all things Sci-Fi,
join my interactive Reader Group here:

facebook.com/groups/JayAllanReaders

Follow me on Twitter @jayallanwrites

Follow my blog at www.jayallanwrites.com

www.jayallanbooks.com
www.crimsonworlds.com

Books by Jay Allan

Blood on the Stars Series
Duel in the Dark
Call to Arms
Ruins of Empire
Echoes of Glory
Cauldron of Fire
Dauntless
The White Fleet
Black Dawn
Invasion
Nightfall
The Grand Alliance
The Colossus
The Others
The Last Stand

Andromeda Chronicles
(Blood on the Stars Adventure Series)
Andromeda Rising
Wings of Pegasus
Into the Badlands

The Far Stars Series
Shadow of Empire
Enemy in the Dark
Funeral Games

Far Stars Legends Series
Blackhawk
The Wolf's Claw

Portal Wars Trilogy
Gehenna Dawn
The Ten Thousand
Homefront

Cast of Characters

Andromeda "Andi" Lafarge – An orphan from "The Gut," the worst slum on the industrial hellworld of Parsephon, turned Badlands adventurer. Andi is the captain of the free trader, *Pegasus*.

Gregor – A member of *Pegasus*'s crew. A native of a high-gravity world, a virtual giant towering well over two meters and massing more than one hundred fifty kilograms.

The Jackal – A member of *Pegasus*'s crew. An ex-thief, stealthy and light footed.

Anna Fasarus – A member of *Pegasus*'s crew. A good fighter, with an unknown and shadowy past.

Barret – A member of *Pegasus*'s crew. Ex-Confederation navy gunnery specialist.

Yarra Tork – A member of *Pegasus*'s crew, and the ship's gifted engineer.

"Doc" Rand – A member of *Pegasus*'s crew. A former first aid technician, and now the ship's de facto doctor.

Sylene Merrick – A former member of *Pegasus*'s crew, now retired. A gifted programmer and expert hacker, and Andi's best friend.

Vig Merrick – A member of *Pegasus*'s crew. Brother of Sylene Merrick.

Lex Righter – A gifted engineer on Dannith. Becomes a member of *Pegasus*'s crew.

Durango – A shipyard manager and contact of Andi's on the mysterious series of space stations known as Samis.

Carmichael – A Spacer's District Gangster with Sector Nine connections.

Brewer (only one name known) – Sector Nine section chief on Dannith. Contact of Carmichael.

Aimee Boucher – Senior Sector Nine agent, commander of Badlands operations.

Drusus Olivetti – Sector Nine agent, Boucher's deputy.

Antoinette Bissel, Nicolas Caron, Louis Moreau – Sector Nine agents.

And, ***Pegasus***, Andi Lafarge's ship, formerly known as *Nightrunner*, a Veritas-class light freighter converted into a Badlands free trader.

Chapter One

HWS Effestius
Spacer's District
Port Royal City
Planet Dannith, Ventica III
Year 302 AC

"A quarter of a million, in untraceable platinum. That was the deal. So, where's our money?" Andi Lafarge's voice was hard, like reinforced steel. But she knew something was wrong. The deal had gone south...or it had been a setup all along. She wasn't sure which...and she wasn't sure it mattered.

She'd left the swag behind at least, hidden, so Carmichael's goons couldn't jump her small group and take it. The artifacts weren't back on *Pegasus* either, in the event that the gangster's people made a run at getting past the security protocols Sylene Merrick had left in place when she'd departed the free trader and its crew—and the entire Badlands frontier—for a well-deserved retirement. Sy Merrick had asked Andi if she'd wanted lethal or non-lethal responses to attempts at forced entry.

What a stupid question from someone as smart as Sylene...

If anybody was stupid enough to try to break into Andi's ship, the least she could do was mop up their guts.

But now, she was in trouble, and she knew it. It wasn't detectable in her expression, or in the hard words coming from her mouth, but her stomach left little doubt. She had Sylene's younger brother, Vig, and Yarra Tork with her, good backup by any measure, but she had no idea how many of Carmichael's leg breakers were packed in the back room waiting for some signal. One on one, her people could put the petty mobster's sacks of meat into the ground without working up a sweat. But five to one or ten to one, that just wasn't fair.

"I want to see the goods, Andi. I think that's only reasonable, don't you?" Carmichael clearly thought he was a good actor, but Andi saw right through his façade. Whatever doubt she'd had that she and her people had been set up was gone. Now, her thoughts went entirely to potential options for escape.

Escape, and just how she was going to stare deeply into Carmichael's eyes as she gutted him. She might not get her revenge then and there, on the gangster's turf, but she would get it.

"That wasn't the deal, Carmichael, and you know it. I sent you the vids as agreed upon, and all of Sy's specs. *That* was a bonus. Now, the deal was for you to have the money here and to show it to me before we worked out the final exchange. So, where the hell is it?" Andi moved her hand slowly, very slowly under her jacket. Colfax's was a saloon with a strict no weapons policy, which meant each of her own people only had one gun stashed on themselves.

Except her…she had two. Andi's disrespect for rules had always been profound.

"I had to change the terms of the deal. A quarter of a million is a lot of cash, Andi. You can't be too careful."

"I could say the same about old tech electrical components. I'm willing to bet I could get more than the quarter million if I just move them on the black market." Andi's eyes darted around. She could see the door behind the bar moving slightly.

"I think you'd better tell me where those artifacts are, Andi. There's no need for this to get...unpleasant."

Andi's senses were on fire. She glanced to the side, toward the door. Four men, trying a little too hard to look like garden variety District lowlifes, had walked into the bar. They were making an effort to look like they were having a conversation, but Andi figured they could use some acting lessons. She knew they were there to block the door.

"You don't want to go this way, Carmichael..." Her hand slipped a few centimeters farther under her coat. The pistol was a high-tech plastic model, one design to elude detection, at least by the kind of low-grade equipment in use at Colfax's.

But it wasn't an automatic. She'd only have one shot at a time. She just *might* take out the four guys at the door before they managed to fire back, but that was at best a 50/50 proposition. And if she went that way, she wouldn't be shooting Carmichael...or at the other thugs she had no doubt would be pouring out of the back room.

It was mostly not shooting Carmichael that bothered her. She wanted to put a bullet in that bastard so badly, it made her headache.

"I'm going to give you one last chance, Andi. Where are the artifacts?"

Her fingers felt the smooth plastic of the pistol. Andi didn't have a deathwish. Far from it. But giving in wasn't something that came easily to her. She knew she'd blundered, that she'd walked into a trap, and she was ready to fight her way out, even if that meant a high likelihood of getting herself killed trying.

But she wasn't ready to take her people with her. Vig was young, almost painfully earnest...and in the half a year since he'd been part of the crew, she'd come to appreciate him, even to trust him. And he was Sylene's kid brother. The computer expert and former Nightrunner team member was the closest thing Andi had known to an actual friend since the Marine.

I can't get Sy's brother killed…

"Listen to me, Carmichael…if you want to renegotiate, we can talk." The words came out of Andi's mouth like bitter dregs. There was nothing she hated more than giving in, even partially.

Except watching her friends die.

"There's no negotiation, Andi. You bring my people to the artifacts. Now. I'm a reasonable man. I'll pay you what I think they're worth." A pause. "So, what's it going to be?" As he finished, the back door opened up, and half a dozen men came walking out. They wore civilian suits, fairly high-end ones, and they could have passed for any number of things besides what Andi knew they were.

At least to any whose eyes were less sharp than hers. She could see the subtle bulges in their coats, and from the sizes, she guessed they all had auto pistols. That meant they could spray her people down with a few hundred shots in a couple seconds. Whatever chance she might have thought they had to get away was gone.

Still, she sat silently, staring back at Carmichael with iced venom in her eyes. *You're going to die, you piece of shit. Maybe not today, but I will stare down into your lifeless eyes.*

"You're out of time, Andi…" The impatience in the gangster's tone was unmistakable. "Do I have to kill one of your people to show you I'm serious?" A few seconds of silence. "Krexor, shoot…"

"Okay…okay…I'll take you to the artifacts."

"Now, Andi."

"Yes…now." There was defeat in her tone, though perhaps half of it was performance for Carmichael's benefit. She wanted him to believe she had surrendered, that she had taken his word that he would pay her once she took him to the goods. It infuriated her to think the bastard could believe she was that much of a fool, but it served her purpose. She needed time, and she needed to move things to a place where the advantage shifted back to her side.

She knew better, though, and she realized he'd never let her live, whether she gave up the imperial swag or not. He knew enough about her to understand how foolish *that* would be. Andi had a reputation for holding grudges, and acting on them with considerable…enthusiasm.

She'd done half of Carmichael's job for him, too. The artifacts were stashed in an old warehouse, in a decrepit and half-abandoned neighborhood on the edge of the District. Carmichael's thugs wouldn't even have to worry about the sorry excuse for law enforcement in Port Royal City's most notorious section of town. No one would be around, not at the current hour.

It will be days before they find us—or find Carmichael and his cronies—probably not until somebody notices the smell.

"Alright, Carmichael…you've got a deal. I'll take you there now. I just want your word you'll let us go once we show you." A little more effort to convince him she had truly yielded. *Stupid fool…*

"Of course, Andi. I don't want trouble. I just want what I sent you for."

"So, I have your word?"

"You do."

That and a pile of dogshit on the street will get me a dirty shoe…

"Alright, let's go." Her hand moved away from the pistol, toward the tiny device she had slipped under her belt. She felt her way to the small button and pressed it.

She might have made a mistake coming into the bar, trusting Carmichael as much as she had. But she was still Andromeda Lafarge…and that meant she had a backup plan.

Gregor was out in the street, with Jackal, Barret, and Anna. And every one of them was packing a lot heavier than she and her two current companions were.

She wished she was out there leading them, too, armed

to the teeth. In her absence, Gregor tended to take the lead in potential combat situations. The giant was loyal, and one hell of a fighter, but he wasn't the most subtle tactician she'd ever known. If there was going to be a fight, the best place for it would be at the warehouse, and not out in front of Carmichael's bar, twenty meters from God only knew how many reinforcements he might have.

Gregor had always been ready for a fight, but since he'd lost his arm, he'd been particularly grouchy. And the prosthetic, the one Andi had gotten specially ordered for him, and paid for herself, had twice the strength his own massive appendage had possessed, and he seemed to particularly enjoy the fear the hideous metallic thing caused in his adversaries.

There was nothing she could do but hope for the best. Gregor was a veteran of many missions, if he was also somewhat of a mindless thug in his own right.

He knows what is at stake...

Andi stood next to the table, staring at Carmichael. "So, are we going to do this? Or do you just like listening to your own voice?"

* * *

The street was dark and filthy. Fewer than half the lights spread thinly down the dingy thoroughfare worked, and even with the portable lanterns four of Carmichael's people carried, Andi had to watch carefully to avoid the large chunks of garbage and broken chunks of pavement in her way. She'd chosen the spot just because it was so old and rundown. Few people would want to come to such a worn and forgotten stretch of town, and the last thing she'd wanted was squatters and wanderers poking around her hidden stash of old tech.

But to her sensibilities, as rough and forgotten as the neighborhood appeared, it wasn't so bad. She'd grown up in the Gut, and they didn't make filthy and violent slums any more hideous than that one.

She'd looked and listened carefully, both for reassurance that Gregor and the others had followed…and also concern that the lumbering giant would give his position away. She didn't want to trigger a battle, not yet. The street was narrow right there, but it was wide open. As outnumbered as her people were likely to be, they needed to fight someplace where they could grab some cover. Like the warehouse.

But getting there was dependent on Carmichael's people remaining unaware they were being followed.

"Seriously, Andi…you couldn't find a worse dump to hide this stuff?' Carmichael looked down at his expensive shoes and frowned.

Andi didn't look back, but inside she felt a taste of revulsion. She'd always thought the gangster was little more than a fop, and he was proving her correct.

"Carmichael, if you ever saw where I came from, you'd shit yourself." There was utter disgust in her tone. She knew he was dangerous, but she suspected he'd turn out to be a gutless whiner begging for his life if she ever got him alone somewhere, one on one.

The gangster looked for a moment like he was going to respond, but then he just gestured forward and kept walking.

Andi continued past another four or five buildings, and then she stopped in front of an old structure with a half-crumbling façade. It was a storage facility, or at least it had been decades before. There were faded letters along the masonry just under the roof, but only three or four letters remained legible, not enough to make out the name of the business that had once operated there. All appearances suggested that had been forty years ago, or more.

She stopped in front of a large overhead door that looked like some kind of access point for freight haulers. It was battered and wobbly looking, but it still stood in place, and it barred entry.

"It's in there." Andi gestured toward the door, but she made no move to open it.

"How do you get in?" A pause. "Open the door, Andi...I'm through playing games."

She remained still for a few more seconds. She hadn't noticed the others following for quite a while, which was a testament to Gregor's unexpected finesse. She might have thought they'd abandoned her, at least if she'd known them less well than she did. But she wanted to give them every chance to get there, just in case they'd fallen behind.

"Now, Andi." Carmichael's voice was hard. He waved his hand, and two of his people leveled their weapons at her.

"Okay, okay...this place is an old dump. It's not like I've got AI access or anything." She reached inside an indentation and grabbed a metal bar inside. As she had earlier, when she'd stashed the swag, images flashed through her mind of what might live in that small, filthy crevice. Dannith had a number of really nasty stinging insects and small reptiles. None of them were truly dangerous, at least away from the southern deserts, but rumor had it they hurt like fire when they struck.

She pulled hard, the rusted old manual access latch resisting until she put almost all her strength into it. Then, it jerked free, and she felt a pain radiating up her arm as it slammed into place. She wasn't hurt, but the last thing she needed was a numb arm when she went for her pistol, which she was going to do the instant Gregor and the others showed.

She reached down an put her hands under the now-loose door. Then, she paused and looked back. "It's a little heavy for me alone, Carmichael." Not really true. She'd managed it fine earlier. But she wasn't trying to buy time for her crewmates to catch up then.

The gangster frowned, but then he gestured toward Vig. "Help her," he growled.

Vig stared back with a defiant look, but then a few seconds later, he leaned forward next to Andi and grabbed the bottom of the door. They both pulled, and the thing practically flew up along the tracks that guided it.

"Now, let's go inside…everybody. It's time for you to get those artifacts."

Andi was looking back at the gangster, but she could see movement in the distance, over his shoulder. She knew he wanted them all inside because that was a convenient and private place to murder her and her two companions.

But she wanted to get inside, too. She had a surprise for Carmichael…one she was determined would end with a nice round hole in the lying scumbag's forehead.

"Okay, follow me. It's right in here…all ready for you."

Time for a good old-fashioned gunfight.

Chapter Two

Abandoned Warehouse
Just Outside the Spacer's District
Port Royal City, Planet Dannith, Ventica III
Year 302 AC

"Here it is, Carmichael, just like I said. I'll inventory it with you if you want." The room was full of the remains of several dozen wood crates, half rotten and clearly quite old, but Andi stood over three small plastitech boxes, each of them sealed with an electronic lock.

"Just open those locks, and I'll take it from there. Then, you and your people can go. Come find me tomorrow, and I'll pay you what this stuff is really worth."

Andi felt a flash of anger, one she could barely hold back. It wasn't because the gangster had reneged, or that he was stealing her loot...or even that he was going to kill her and her two companions.

It was because the pompous bastard believed she was stupid enough not to know that, to open her AI-locked boxes for him like some sniveling fool begging for her life, and then to turn around to leave so his thugs could shoot her in the back.

This planet will sit inside the swollen red dwarf its star will become in a few billion years before that happens...

But opening the boxes served her purpose just then.

She knelt down, one hand tapping out the combination codes she'd set, while the other slipped under her coat. She couldn't be sure Gregor and the others were out there waiting for her signal—or for that matter, if Vig and Yarra were following her moves. Yarra had always been more comfortable in the engine room than the battlefield, and Vig was so…young.

Young? He is only four months younger than you.

None of those concerns mattered anyway. They were all dead if they didn't do something.

This was their only chance.

She popped open the first box, pushing it a few centimeters toward the gangster, and then she dove over the other two, dropping to her knees—harder than she'd intended—as she whipped the gun out from her coat. She ducked to the side, behind a pile of old metal girders, firing as she moved. Carmichael yelped in pain, and for an instant, she wondered if she'd killed the miserable son of a bitch. But then she saw the spray of blood around his shoulder as he, too, dropped down behind cover.

Carmichael's men scattered, clearly startled, if not shocked, at her sudden move. Then, she caught the gangster's voice, and she relished at the pain she heard in it.

His words were deadly serious.

"Kill her. Kill them all."

Andi ducked low behind the pile of metal as Carmichael's thugs opened up with their automatic weapons. She gritted her teeth as she listened to the rounds ricocheting off the metal in front of her. The girders weren't perfect cover, and she half expected some of the rounds to find their way through. But she was only pinned for a few seconds. Then she heard more automatic fire, from a far heavier gun.

Gregor with his autocannon.

To normal people, the weapon as a stand-mounted job,

usually operated by a crew of two. But the giant wielded the thing like a rifle, and the sound of the heavy slugs slamming into the walls was music to Andi's ears.

Not to mention the cries of Carmichael's goons as at least half a dozen of them went down under the relentless fire.

But there were still a lot of them left, and even with Gregor and the others, her people were still outnumbered.

She crawled to the end of the pile or girders, and she scanned the room. She picked out one of Carmichael's people turning toward the direction of Gregor's fire, bringing his rifle around. She reached out, struggling to aim in the difficult position, and she fired three times, as quickly as the small pistol could manage.

She missed twice, but the third shot took off a piece of the gangster's head, and he dropped like a sack of cement. She could feel the smile forming on her face, but there was no time for celebration. The fight wasn't over, and she'd just given her position away to anyone paying attention.

She didn't think much of Carmichael's men individually, but there were more than a dozen of them left, and they all *had* to realize they were in a fight to the death.

She scrambled forward, struggling to get up onto her feet as she pushed herself out from behind the steel and stumbled over toward a concrete half-wall about two meters away. She heard the fire coming her way—the rounds ripping through the air behind her, fortunately—and she spun around as she reached the wall, staring out over it as her pistol fired again and again, almost as if it were on some kind of autotargeting routine. She took down at least two more of Carmichael's people when one of them spun around and opened up on her with one of the compact submachine guns. It wasn't a particularly hard-hitting weapon, but at a range of five meters, it didn't have to be. She reacted, dropping down behind the wall…but too late.

She felt the pain along her neck, and for an instant, she

thought she was dead, that the thug had taken her down. But she quickly realized the bullet had only grazed her neck. It was throbbing, painful…but it was localized.

She took a deep breath without any real trouble, and she righted herself, preparing to lunge back up. But the fire was still coming in, and she stayed down, pinned, her mind frantically trying to figure out what was going on. She heard the sounds of her people yelling, shouting out to each other as they battled the enemy—and a couple of high-pitched shouts that had her stomach tied up in knots—but she was stuck, and there was nothing she could do.

Not until her adversary's clip emptied.

She waited three or four more seconds…and then the fire stopped.

It could be a trap, she thought to herself, but she'd been doing her best to get a feel for the number of rounds fired, and in an instant her mind bet that the weapon's magazine was indeed empty.

The stakes of the bet were high. Her life.

She leapt up, swinging over the half-wall and racing forward, her eyes scanning furiously for her target. She spotted him, just as he was slamming a new clip in place.

He saw her, too, almost at the same instant. He started to bring his own weapon back up to bear…but he was just an instant slower than Andi.

She fired, and then again, but the first shot had been enough. She put the bullet right into her enemy's left eye, and he fell back, dropping the submachine gun to the ground as he did.

Andi dove for the weapon, grabbing it and executing an almost perfect combat roll. As she came back up to a prone position, her finger started to tighten on the trigger.

But the enemy was gone. All of them.

She could hear them scrambling out of the building and into the street. She guessed none of them would have made it, save for the fact that Gregor was standing against the wall, struggling furiously to clear a jam in the massive gun he'd used to cut down swaths of the gangsters.

Her legs tensed, and she started to race forward, to follow her enemies and gun them down in the street. She'd wounded Carmichael, but not mortally…and she wanted the piece of shit dead. She took two steps, determined to finish the fight…and then she stumbled to a halt.

Yarra was on the ground no more than two meters from where she stood. The engineer was lying in a pool of blood, one that grew in size as Andi watched.

"Doc!" She screamed so loudly, her throat felt as though a hot blade had cut across it. But *Pegasus*'s medic was already there, and he dropped to his knees and began frantically working on Yarra.

"Gregor, Jackal…get outside and make sure they've really had enough." Andi didn't' think Carmichael had the stomach for more, not when half his men were down, and his own shoulder was a bleeding chunk of meat. It was his style to pull back, to wait for a chance to strike when the odds were more in his favor. A time Andi knew would almost certainly come.

But she wasn't going to take any chances. IF Carmichael found some hidden courage, if he sent his people back in, she wasn't going to let her people get caught by surprise.

"On it, Andi." She heard the giant's deep voice, but her eyes and her attention were already back on her stricken shipmate. For a second or two, she panicked, and thought Yarra was dead, but then she saw the engineer's chest move up with a shallow breath.

She could tell it was serious just by the amount of blood, and also by the frantic nature of Doc's efforts. She knelt down beside her friend, oblivious to the wetness soaking through to her knees as she did.

"Doc…"

"I don't know yet, Andi…but distractions aren't going to help. Go out and see how Gregor and Jackal are doing…or go stand in the corner. You can't help here." The medic's voice was raw, ragged. He was clearly scared, and Andi wondered whether he really wasn't sure, or if he was just trying to lie to himself that there was a chance. Doc was skilled at patching wounds—the result of long experience along the wild frontier of the Badlands—but he wasn't a real doctor. If Yarra had serious internal injuries, he didn't have the skills or the equipment to save her.

Andi hesitated, staring down at her stricken friend, as though her gaze alone offered some kind of medical treatment. Then she turned abruptly. Doc was right. She wasn't helping. She started to walk toward the front of the building when Jackal ducked back in.

"They're gone, Andi. Gregor's up on the roof. He can see anybody coming at us from either direction. All's clear so far."

Andi just nodded. She was proud of her people, of the way they operated as a unit. She'd inherited some of that from Captain Lorillard, of course, just as she had the ship itself. But she'd made a difference herself, and she'd put the Marine's teachings to good use.

She didn't have time to think of that, though, and her mind was focused on her wounded friend. Aside from worry for Yatta, all she felt was rage, a fury she could barely contain. Part of her wanted to run out into the street, chase that bastard Carmichael to the ground, and put a bullet in his head then and there. But it wasn't time for that. Her people needed her. Yarra needed her.

Another time...

"Doc..." She'd held back as long as she could, but she needed to know *something*.

I think I've stopped the bleeding. I've got her pumped full of painkillers and coagulants, and I'm giving her the pack of artificial blood I had in my pack. But that's not going to be nearly enough...and she's going to need a lot more than I can do here. Maybe more than I can do at all.

She needs a hospital…or at least, we need to get her back to the ship.

A trip to the hospital would trigger a lot of uncomfortable questions. But that didn't matter to Andi, not then. She was ready to do whatever she had to do for Yarra, and damn the consequences.

But the hospital in Port Royal City is too dangerous. Carmichael will be out for blood, and as much of a horse's ass as he is, he's got a lot of connections. One switch of an IV pouch, an ambush on her people coming in and out would be the end. She couldn't leave Yarra unprotected, and she couldn't get her people in with any weapons. The hospital was out, at least until she was able to deal with the gangster once and for all.

The ship. It's the only choice.

"Do what you can to get her ready to move. We'll make a dash for the ship. *Pegasus* is our best bet right now."

She'd finally started to get used to the new name. *Pegasus* had been born from *Nightrunner*'s past, and the name change had done a considerable amount to cut down on the heat bearing down on her people, from the authorities, of course, always a thorn in the side of a Badlands prospecting team, but mostly from Sector Nine. The Union spies that infested the Spacer's District, and all the other ports along the Badlands border, were deadly dangerous. They paid good money for artifacts, though getting caught dealing with them could turn moderate harassment from the navy into something far more dangerous. The Union was the enemy, if not quite officially at present, and three wars in eighty years were reason enough for naval patrols to react harshly to prospectors selling their swag to Sector Nine.

"Okay, Andi…I've got her as ready as she's going to get. We'll have to carry her—and the less she gets jostled around, the better. Those wounds are barely patched up, and she can't afford to lose any more blood. Another liter, and we'll lose her before we even get to the ship."

Andi looked up, her eyes fixing on Jackal. "Go back out,

and tell Gregor to get back in here. Then, stay up there, and keep an eye on the street until we get moving."

She gestured toward the front of the building, but Jackal was already turned around and heading back out. She spun back toward Doc. "Gregor's the best bet to carry her. And she won't slow him down at all."

Andi wasn't even letting herself think about how much unwanted attention they'd get when they got near the spaceport. She didn't care.

Her eyes moved over the crates with the artifacts, all her people had to show for three months of hard work and more than one close escape. They were torn apart, riddled with what looked like hundreds of bullet holes. She moved toward them, but she stopped herself. There was no point. She knew the stash was a total loss without pawing through the shards of obliterated cases.

Besides, as much as greed, an almost uncontrollable lust to rise above the hell into which she'd been born, drove her on, as far as Andi Lafarge was concerned, her people came first. Always.

They were all that really mattered to her, and just then Yarra needed her. They all needed her. Getting back to the ship alive would be reward enough, at least just then. The last thing they had time to do was fish through the wreckage hoping to find a piece big enough to be worth something.

It was time to head back, and damned any District toughs or checkpoints that tried to give her trouble. If someone got in their way or gave them any crap, she still had rounds left in her gun.

Chapter Three

Free Trader Pegasus
Port Royal Spaceport
Port Royal City, Planet Dannith, Ventica III
Year 302 AC

"I've got her in the med unit, Andi, and the medical AI is managing her care. But *Pegasus*'s med suite is limited. She's badly hurt, and she's going to need treatment. *Real* treatment."

Andi knew exactly what Doc was saying. There was a streak of cockiness that ran through her crew, and most of them had a difficult time admitting when they couldn't do something. And that was exactly what *Pegasus*'s medic was saying.

Doc wasn't a real doctor, he wasn't even a formally trained medical technician. But he was what Andi had, what Yarra had, and that was going to have to be enough.

"Doc...we can't take her to the hospital. I wouldn't be surprised if Carmichael's got people watching the ship even now. We'd never be able to protect her...and that son of a bitch knows going after her will be a good way to get to me. We can't risk it."

"I can't help her, Andi. I just don't have the skills. And, even if I did, *Pegasus* doesn't have the equipment we need."

A pause. "She's going to die if we keep her here, Andi."

The words hit like a hammer. Andi had a way of convincing herself she could make anything work. But she was helpless to save her friend.

She turned abruptly, her stress driving the move, and she winced. Doc had bandaged up her own wound, though she'd pushed him away the first few times he'd tried. It had proven to be a bit worse than the graze she'd thought it was. The bullet had penetrated her arm, and it was still in there. She didn't have time just then to let Doc go rooting around looking for it. It was annoying, but between the patch job and the painkillers, it hurt a lot less than it had.

Except when you move like a lunatic...

Her mind was racing, searching for a solution. Then one came to her, a desperate one.

"Durango." She muttered the name, to herself more than to anyone.

Her thoughts drifted to the seventh planet in the system, and the extensive network of stations positioned around it, to the shadowy figure who'd managed *Nightrunner*'s repairs, and the ship's illegal—but well executed—name change. The Samis shipyards operated under the radar, avoiding unwanted attention. She hadn't thought it through before, but now she realized how Durango and his associates maintained their status.

They must bribe a hundred people, no, probably more—navy, law enforcement...mob leaders...

The Samis shipyards, and the other facilities orbiting the seventh planet offered services for people who needed discretion.

And there is a medical facility there.

No one had spoken since she'd uttered the name. Now, she spoke again, and asked the only question that remained as far as she was concerned.

"Can she make it that far? To Samis? Can we get her there in time?"

Doc didn't answer right away. He didn't answer at all. He just nodded, an affirmative response of sorts, but one that didn't particularly inspire confidence.

Andi wasn't sure what to do, and flashes of previous times, when Captain Lorillard had faced seemingly impossible situations, and led them all through to the other side, danced around the fringes of her mind. *She* was in command now, and she realized Lorillard had left her more than the ship. He'd left her responsibility. Responsibility for his people. *Her* people.

She knew the faces staring at her were waiting for her to decide, to *lead* them. And the stubbornness and grim determination that had driven her survival back in the Gut, that had taken her from that industrial hell into a new life, kicked into gear.

"Barret, get down in engineering." *Taking Yarra's place…*

She turned toward the others. "We're taking off as soon as we can. We're going to Samis."

* * *

"Samis control, this is the Free Trader *Pegasus*, requesting immediate landing clearance. We've got a medical emergency aboard. We need transit to the infirmary to meet us at the landing slot." Andi paused. She didn't really know the protocol for approaching the mysterious renegade base. She'd only been there once before. But she figured knowing somebody was probably the best way to get in. "Please advise Durango that I am requesting a meeting as soon as he is available." She'd had a sense the shipyard manager was more highly placed than he pretended in the operation of the network of orbital stations around the frozen planet. Hopefully, dropping his name would get her people in again.

"*Pegasus*, you are cleared for immediate approach, on vector A9. Land at bay seven. Medical transport and a security detachment will be waiting for you."

Andi nodded gently. Durango's name *had* seemed to help...maybe he *was* one of the real powers behind the installations at Samis. It would be helpful to have a contact so highly-ranked on the mysterious facility.

She was less than thrilled with the last bit about a 'security detachment,' though.

"Acknowledged, Samis control." Andi reached out and took the controls, easing *Pegasus*'s thrusters, pushing the almost-stationary vessel forward. Her screen shifted its picture suddenly, showing a schematic of the station, with a blinking 'seven' next to one location.

Bay seven, I presume...

It had taken some serious computing power to penetrate *Pegasus*'s defenses sufficiently to take control of her screen that way. *Are they trying to tell me something? To behave? To keep my mouth shut when I leave? Both?*

She was a bit angry, too. She didn't like anyone messing around with her ship—and *Pegasus* felt completely like hers now, though it had been less than a year since she'd first taken the helm as captain.

She eased the ship forward, biting back hard on the simmering anger. Durango had been one hundred percent straight with her, both on the repairs he'd conducted on the ship and as broker in the disposal of the old tech artifacts that had paid to put *Pegasus* back into operational condition. And she needed help. Yarra needed help. Andi knew she didn't have the luxury of being angry, nor of asking any questions.

She watched as the station appeared on her screen as a visual, and then as *Pegasus* approached a row of massive hatches, all closed save one. She tapped the throttle to the side, pulsing the maneuvering jets to bring the ship on a direct line to the bay. The AI could have landed the ship—and she suspected Samis control could have as well. But sitting at the controls herself made her feel somehow better.

She'd brought Yarra this far, and it was on her to see it through, get her friend the help she needed.

It was also a way of asserting her own control, even if, as she suspected, it was mostly illusion.

She hit the deceleration thrusters, slowing the ship to a crawl, and she eased *Pegasus* into the bay, sliding into the stabilizer brackets with a smoothness that sent a message to those on the station watching.

At least she hoped it did. She hated feeling as powerless as she suspected she was just then.

There were a series of loud clangs, as the large supports connected to *Pegasus*'s hull, holding the ship firmly in place. A few seconds later, a docking column extended toward the ship's airlock and locked into place. Then, a chime sounded, *Pegasus*'s AI confirming that conditions outside the airlock were safe.

Andi got up, turning and leaning down over the comm unit. "Barrett, get up here and meet me in the airlock. We'll go out and make sure everything is okay." *And what the hell are you going to do about it if they're not?*

She had the urge to go to the weapons locker and grab some heavy ordnance. But instead, she unhooked her belt and dropped the holstered pistol she still carried onto her seat. She knew better than to go into Samis station armed. The station was no District dive, someplace with creaky sixty year old detection equipment she could game to sneak a few guns past.

She walked down toward the airlock, and she began the opening sequence, even before Barret got there. She wouldn't go so far as to say she *trusted* Durango, but he'd been straight with her before and, besides, she'd already bet all their lives on him anyway. If she'd brought *Pegasus* into some kind of trap, Barret standing next to her—or every weapon in Pegasus's arsenal—weren't going to make a damned difference.

The inner door slid open immediately, and she stepped

inside, *Pegasus*'s gunner, and now makeshift engineer, running up a second or two later. Andi reached out and tapped the controls—she could have just as easily ordered the AI to open the outer door—and she stood there for a moment, looking out on one of Samis's docking bays, cold gray and empty, save for the portable med pod surrounded by two white-coated medtechs, and behind them, the somewhat weary-looking and bedraggled figure of none other than Durango himself.

"Andi...it is a pleasure to see you again. I hope you've taken good care of our handiwork. That old rustbucket of yours was in sorry shape when you got her here last time."

Andi fought back a smile. She'd have managed one for Durango, if she didn't have a grievously wounded shipmate, and if Carmichael's treachery hadn't cost her a small fortune in lost loot. She had enough in her reserve accounts to pay the docking fees, and most, at least, of the medical expenses, but somewhere in her mind, behind the worry for Yarra and the others who were wounded—not to mention whether she really *could* trust Durango—another thought bounced around.

She was on her way to dead broke.

Again.

"The ship's fine, Durango, but some of my people need help." She turned toward Barret, ready to send him back to tell Doc to bring Yarra out, but before she got out a word, a motorized gurney came rolling down the small ramp. It moved past her, Doc walking just behind it.

Durango motioned toward the medtechs, and they moved up, adjusting the mobile stretcher and carefully moving Yarra into the pod. Without a word to anyone, they activated the pod, and the top door slipped shut as the whole mechanism began to move.

Andi felt the urge to chase after the pod, but Durango's voice stopped her. "She's in good hands, Andi. We've got top shelf med facilities here. We get a fair number of folks who need discretion, as you know, and sometimes they need more than their ships fixed up." A brief pause. "I take it the rest of your people in need of care are walking wounded. If you bring them out, they can follow along. We'll have them patched up in no time."

Andi turned and nodded to Barret. He raced up the ramp and came down again a moment later, leading every member of the crew who'd suffered anything more than a cut or scrape in the fight. She watched as they walked off—in some cases, limped off—and then she looked back at Durango.

"Thank you." It was all she could think to say. Andi didn't like needing anyone, certainly not anyone outside her inner circle.

"You're welcome. We like to think we have a good relationship with our clients. Discretion is a two-way street, Andi, and as far as I've heard you haven't uttered a word to anyone about what we did for you. If that's an example of the way you operate, I believe we can have a long and fruitful relationship.

Andi almost snorted. Durango didn't have any real idea what made her tick. She was a lot of things, a killer when need be, a pirate by many standards...but Andi Lafarge knew how to keep her damned mouth shut. Someone could make her talk, probably, but there wouldn't be much left of her by the time they managed it.

"As long as that remains two ways, Durango…"

"Of course, Andi. Discretion is our primary service." A pause, as Durango looked at Andi and clearly saw the worry in her eyes. "Try not to be too concerned about your friend. If you were able to get her here alive, I would be very surprised if our medical staff couldn't help her. I am sure you want to run right over to the infirmary, but I can assure you that would serve little purpose. I am sure she will go into surgery almost immediately, and you will be sitting pointlessly for hours. Perhaps we can use that time more productively."

Andi wasn't sure if Durango was worried about payment—and perhaps he had some cause to be—or if he had something else he wanted to discuss. He portrayed himself as a shipyard managed, but there was more to him than just that, she'd have bet almost anything on it. She had no idea what, but there was something her Samis contact was hiding.

"Of course, let's go and have a chat." Andi wasn't exactly comfortable, but she found herself wanting to know what Durango had to say.

And how much trouble it was likely to mean for her and her people.

Chapter Four

Samis Station Three
Orbiting Ventica VII
Year 302 AC

"Your shipmate is out of surgery, Andi, and she is doing well. She was very badly hurt, however, and she will require more treatment and a lengthy recovery period...and possibly more surgeries. But she is out of danger, and she will survive."

Andi had watched as Durango scooped up his headset when the call came in, rather than putting it on the speaker. Her natural suspicion flared up, and for an instant, she suspected some kind of treachery. Then, she realized Durango had probably not been quite as certain Yarra would survive as he'd led her to believe. He'd wanted to hear it himself first if she had died, and the flash of anger Andi felt at the well-meaning deception was quickly washed away by her relief.

She was angry again, at the deception this time, but that only lasted a passing instant, and she realized Durango's massaging of the truth had been a mercy as much as a way to manage her. And the news that Yarra was going to live overcame any remaining bad feeling.

Though, she wondered about that 'long' recovery, and

just how fully recovered Yarra would be when it was over.

"Thank you again for all your help, Durango. This is the second time you've done exactly what you said you would, and I trust you understand what a minority of the human race that places you within."

The shipyard manager—and something more, Andi suspected—nodded and smiled. "Thank you, Andi. I believe that you, too, are trustworthy...which is why I want to tell you about a prospective mission. I've been retained to find a ship and a crew to undertake a...difficult...operation."

"And you couldn't find anybody else desperate enough to take it on?" Andi smiled, but she was only partially kidding.

Actually, she wasn't kidding at all. And she *was* desperate, something she'd tried to hide from Durango, an effort that had obviously failed. Of course, asking him to wait on doing a full refuel on *Pegasus* until Yarra's medical bills came in had been a dead giveaway. Andi Lafarge was a lot of things, but a deadbeat wasn't one of them. If half a load of fuel was all she could afford, she would make do with that.

"I'd normally joke with you, Andi, but not this time. It is a dangerous mission, so much so that several other crews have turned it down. When you hear the details, you may want to pass on it as well. But there's one thing about it that's not risky at all...the payday. You'll get a hundred thousand credits just for going, even if you come up empty. All you've got to do is take some verified video to prove you were there, and the cash is yours. And if you find what my client is looking for, it's worth half a million to you and your crew. Confederation physical credits, too. Pure platinum eagles."

Andi had always been told she had a hell of a poker face, but she was sure she'd given away her reaction at what she'd just heard. By the time she paid for her people's medical expenses and put some fuel into *Pegasus*, she'd be hard pressed to buy breakfast. Half a million credits—even a hundred thousand—seemed like a vast fortune to her just then. And a mission with no risk, at least none of coming up empty and limping back truly broke, without even the ability to reprovision the ship, was just what she needed. She was an adventurer, a gambler in her gut, but she also knew not to bet what she couldn't afford to lose. Sitting in some spaceport on Dannith, worrying about Carmichael and his people, without enough to pay for fuel or even docking fees didn't seem like an attractive proposition. If Durango's deal was legit, she could get her finances in order, and guarantee her people a nice payday.

Assuming they made it back, of course.

"I want the hundred thousand upfront." It was a bold thing to say, audacious almost to the point of insanity. She had a good reputation as far as Badlands prospectors went, but she was also fairly new to running the show on her own, and she still traded on Captain Lorillard's bonafides as well as her own, more limited track record.

Translation: No one in their right mind was going to hand over a hundred thousand to her on a promise to go search for whatever artifacts the client wanted.

But she didn't need a hundred thousand, not really. Just enough to get *Pegasus* properly fitted out…and maybe a little insurance in case she turned out to be wrong about Durango. If she got back with *Pegasus* all shot up and out of fuel again, and then she got stiffed…well, hanging the shipyard manager's skin on her wall wouldn't exactly solve the problem of having a battered ship and no coin to get it fixed.

Durango smiled. Apparently, he liked audaciousness. "You know that's not going to happen, Andi…but if I recommend you to my client, I might be able to convince him to front you ten thousand. That will cover fitting out the ship, plus the special equipment you'll need, and still leave a decent bit left."

"Twenty." Andi stared at Durango with cold eyes.

"Ten, Andi...and I said *if* I recommend you to him. He's a good client, one I've dealt with many times. And, he's not too forgiving of failure. I need your word, Andi—and I *mean* it. If you take this job, you will get it done, or at least you will come back here able to convince me, and whoever else you have to, that you did your *damned best* to get it done. I suspect you're a dangerous one to doublecross...let's just say we're cut from the same cloth on that one." He stared at her with an intensity she hadn't seen before. For an instant, she wanted to turn him down, to cut and run and limp away with her people more or less intact and *Pegasus* half full of fuel. But she knew she didn't have a choice. Dannith was far too hot just then to go prospecting for another job, and she couldn't wait long for something either.

It was a tense decision, a dangerous one...but in reality, it was no decision at all.

"Alright, ten...and you do a refuel and quick refit of *Pegasus* on the house."

Durango looked back at her for a few seconds, his face an emotionless mask. Then he started to laugh. "Alright, Andi, you're one hell of a negotiator...even if you are the next thing to penniless and hiding here with a price on your head on Dannith."

That was a new bit of information, but one she couldn't call unexpected. Her people had killed a lot of Carmichael's men, and she'd managed to wound the bastard himself. She wondered if Durango knew how much the tightfisted gangster was offering for her.

Actually, it was helpful in one way, too, just another brick in the tentative wall of trust she was building with Durango. He could have grabbed her the instant she'd landed, or just put a bullet in her head, and collected the bounty.

"Yeah...I've got unfinished business with Carmichael." A pause. "So, we have a deal? I especially want the positioning jets checked out and tuned up. If you're sending me into the flaming shithole I suspect you are, we're going to need every bit of maneuverability we can get."

"Yes, we have a deal. But you've gotten all you're going to get, so stop negotiating." A few seconds of silence. "I'll throw in the full diagnostic on the secondary jets...but that's it. And I need your word, Andi. I mean, I've got to hear it. Now."

"You have my word, Durango. When I say I'm going to do something, I do it." That was mostly true, or at least it was when she was dealing with people she trusted. She'd lie to a pile of filth like Carmichael without a second thought.

That was the least of Carmichael's problems. Forget lying to him. When she got back, she was going to finish the job she'd started. She was going to kill the bastard.

"Good." Durango stood up and reached out his hand. "Let's shake on it...and come back here tonight. I'll have your money ready."

Andi stood as well, and she gripped his hand. She liked people who kept their deals...and especially ones who were so prompt with their payments.

*   *   *

"She's got a lot of guts, that one...but she's pretty young for something like this, isn't she?" A door in the back had just opened, and a shadowy figure stepped out from the next room. Andi had left less than a minute before. The man was tall, and his voice was deep, commanding.

"She's good." Durango sounded a little uncomfortable, and he twitched in his chair a few times.

"You're worried about her. You have some doubts about sending her and her people to Aquellus...and I don't mean the kind of doubts I've got, about whether she can get the job done." A pause. "You like her."

"She's a good kid. I know 'kid' is a strange thing to call a ship captain, but she *is* awfully young. I checked her out thoroughly last time, though, and she's legit. She's been through a lot. A mean a *lot*. She's from Vulcan City on Parsephon. From the Gut. She pulled herself out of there, and made it all the way to Dannith. She deserves better than to end up face down, floating dead in some Aquellian ocean."

"The Gut, eh? Worst shithole in the Confederation. A scandal, and a blight on what we like to think we stand for. So, she made it out of there? That means she's tough, for sure, and it makes me a little more confident. But Sector Nine's after this prize, too, Durango, and they're ahead of us. That's a lot, even for a wildcat from the Gut, to handle."

"She's dealt with Sector Nine before, too, and she came out on top. I know. We fixed up her ship, and I can tell you firsthand, she and her people made it back after one hell of a fight. I wasn't sure at first we could even repair the thing." He was trying to hide the emotion in his voice, but he suspected he wasn't managing it as well as he would have liked. "I'm telling you, she's the best we're going to get to make this run. Maybe the best out here overall, though it will take some time to decide that. I'd bank a year's pay on Andi at least doing everything possible to complete the mission. I'm more afraid she and her people will end up dead out there than I am they'll bolt and come back here with their tails between their legs."

"They're tools, Durango, don't forget that, assets we use when we need them...and ones we expend when we have to in order to accomplish our objectives. Don't get emotionally involved. You have to stay focused, or you'll lose yourself. The artifacts we suspect are out there are worth a fortune. I'm more concerned about her realizing the value and keeping it all for herself. If she finds out what that stuff is really worth, we're going to have to pay her more than half a million, I'd wager, a damned sight more."

Durango shook his head. "No, I don't think so. She shook my hand and gave me her word. You may laugh at me, but I believe her. Even if she finds out the haul is worth half a billion or more, she'll honor the deal she made. You just watch."

The man shook his head slightly, but then he stopped. "I've never known you to have too much faith in people, Durango, so we'll go with your gut on this one. It's not like we've got a choice, anyway. None of the other major prospectors are desperate enough to take this job now…so Andi Lafarge is what we've got." He paused for a few seconds, and then he continued, "We can't let Sector Nine find these artifacts, not with tensions so high with the Union. There's going to be another war, and probably soon, and if this Andi Lafarge and her crew are the price we need to pay to help keep the Union from winning that conflict, then it's a cost we have to accept." There was a grim finality to the man's tone.

Durango hesitated for a moment, but then he nodded grudgingly. He didn't speak right away, but when he finally did, he said simply, "I just think she's one of the good guys, deep down under that rough exterior and all the bravado. I'll send her, you know I will, but I'm rooting for her to make it." A pause. "And, I'm going to make sure she's got everything she might need, all the gear that might come in handy, and a bit more thorough a checkup than she's expecting on that old ship of hers."

Chapter Five

"What is all this?" Andi stood in the bay next to *Pegasus*, pointing toward a pair of cargo lifts as she spoke.

"Some equipment you might need on this trip." Durango paused, catching the concerned look in Andi's eyes. Then he added, "It's all on me…as are your ship upgrades."

"Upgrades? I thought you were just going to check things out and refuel her."

"Yes, well, I thought some additional items might be of some aid on the trip. First, we pressure coated the hull. Aquellus is a water world, and you may have to operate in one of its seas. Anything that keeps out the vacuum of space should keep out water, of course, except that, if you have to function at any significant depths, the pressure becomes a consideration. *Pegasus* is a sturdily built old ship, without question, but the coating will increase hull integrity by fifty to sixty percent. That should allow you to function one and a half kilometers below the surface, even two, two and a half in a pinch. We also installed baffles around the engines, which will aid your maneuverability in the water. And we stocked your emergency kits with a special sealant in case you get any breaches in the hull. It's stronger than the usual stuff, again, just in case pressure becomes a serious problem."

"Thank you. That is…appreciated." Andi's thanks sounded genuine, but it was still clear she was uncomfortable with the idea of prowling around some alien world's oceans. And the fact that Durango was springing a whole bunch of free equipment on her could only inflame her concerns.

She won't worry about the oceans so much if she runs into Sector Nine out there. Few things drove away concerns faster than deadlier problems.

"There's something else…something I probably should have told you before." *But I didn't want to risk you're backing out on me.* "There's a chance, a small chance…" *If close to one hundred percent can be called small.* "…that you might run into a Sector Nine team out there."

Andi was clearly trying to hide her fear and her concern…but it slipped out anyway. So did the fiery rage that shone from her eyes. He wasn't sure if she was feeling hesitancy to mix it up again with the Union spy agency…or a thirst for Sector Nine blood.

Probably both.

"Sector Nine…" Her words dripped venom. "You checked out the weapons systems, too, I hope."

Durango had dealt with all manner of frontier brigands, but something in Andi's voice gave him a chill. "Yes, of course. All fully operational. We added a bit, too. You've got a dozen torpedoes now. *Pegasus* doesn't have tubes, of course, but we managed to rig an ejection system in the cargo hold. It makes targeting a little tougher for sure, but the torpedoes are self-guided anyway, so it's not that much worse in the end." A pause. "They pack a *punch*, Andi, far more than your lasers. They've got fusion warheads, and against the kind of craft you're likely to encounter out there—even Sector Nine ships—you won't need a direct hit.

Anything within a couple hundred meters will be devastating, and you can cause significant damage from as far out as a kilometer in space…and a lot farther out in an atmosphere."

Andi was nodding, but Durango could see she was still processing it all. He knew her well enough to guess that her mind was recomputing the projected danger of the mission. And very likely revising the total sharply upward.

Still, half a million was a good sum, though he'd have gone to a million if she'd really pressed him. The fact that she hadn't testified to just how preoccupied and desperate she'd really been.

"Thank you, again. Let's hope we don't need those." Her tone suggested she assigned exactly a zero probability to that. "But it seems like you're trying to tell me you're sending us right into a fight."

"No, Andi…not at all." He paused. He didn't like lying to her. "But better to be prepared than not prepared. We've uploaded all the specs and data sheets we have on the facility. We can't be sure about much of it, but we've had half a dozen expeditions searching for it, and every clue they've managed to find pointed to Aquellus. We're as confident as we can be that it's there."

"Half a dozen missions?" Andi stared quizzically, but she didn't ask anything further. Her discipline only increased Durango's opinion of her, and inflamed his regret at sending her into such a dangerous situation. He wanted to believe *Pegasus* would succeed and return, but he felt his initial estimate of eighty percent—a number born of far more hope than cold analysis—melting away like a block of ice on a hot day. He was down to 50-50, and struggling to hold there.

She is good…don't forget that…

"Yes, half a dozen. Seven actually, though none of those had the pre-mission data you do, or the armament. We've got a considerable investment in finding the place. Your data files will open automatically when you get to Aquellus, and you'll know more than. I'm sorry for the secrecy, but it wasn't easy getting the data we have, and we have to be careful with it."

"Of course. I understand completely."

She might understand, but she's edgy about it, that's clear enough. Good…if she wasn't scared, she'd be a fool.

And no fool is coming back from this mission.

"You had a chance to see your shipmate again?"

"Yes, she seems to be doing…very well."

Durango understood the hitch in Andi's response. Yarra *was* recovering, but as he'd warned Andi, it was going to be a long process, and in the interim, the truth was, *Pegasus's* engineer looked like death warmed over.

"It's a relief to know Yarra is here and not in some hospital in Port Royal City. She'll be…"

"Safe here? Absolutely. Samis has understandings with all the factions on Dannith. We're neutral ground, and everyone will respect that." A pause. "It's been thirty years since anyone's violated our status, and almost no one even remembers that poor bastard's name."

Andi nodded, looking reasonably satisfied. A few seconds later, she said, "If we don't come back…"

"You'll still earn the hundred thousand…and I'll see that your shipmate gets it. But you'll be back. I wouldn't be sending you if I didn't believe that." A stretch of the truth, certainly, but a statement with a kernel of fact in it.

"One more thing…" Andi paused. Clearly, she didn't like asking for help. "I have some experience knocking around the engineering space, as does my shipmate, Barret. But if we run into any real trouble, Barret's our best gunner, and we'll need to be ready to deal with any battle damage."

Durango could see the pain in Andi's face at the thought of replacing Yarra, even temporarily.

"You need an engineer." Durango was silent for a moment. "I'd try to get one of my people to go with you, but you really need a ship's engineer and not a shipyard technician. It's a different skill fixing a ship with bits and pieces of parts in the middle of nowhere and having a fully-stocked warehouse at your disposal." Another pause. "I know someone, Andi, someone good. Really good. But there are two problems."

"Solvable ones?"

Durango shrugged. "Well, first, he's on Dannith, down in the District, though I suspect you can manage to sneak in and out without alerting Carmichael and starting a full-fledged war down there.

Andi stood stone still. Durango didn't question her confidence in her ability to get in and out of Port Royal City without Carmichael finding her. The challenge would be doing it and resisting the urge to try to find her enemy herself. She had an iron will and good self-control, Durango was sure of that. But she had one hell of a temper, too.

"I'll manage. Carmichael's an imbecile." A pause. "What's the second problem?"

Durango hesitated, just a few seconds. Then he said, "Well, he's an incredibly gifted engineer, he really is…but he has a little bit of a drinking problem." Another pause while he tried to get a read on Andi's reaction. Her face was like stone, impassive, unreadable.

"I can tell you where to find him. His name is Lex Righter."

* * *

"Are you sure? All of you?" Andi stood on *Pegasus*'s bridge. The small space was crowded when the three stations were occupied, and now it was packed with all of her people. "This mission is likely to be a rough one. I don't know everything I'd like to…but there's some chance we might run into Sector Nine again while we're out there. You all know what that means."

Andi had been worried about the mission since the moment Durango had opened his mouth about it, but she'd gotten even more nervous when she'd inspected the torpedoes he had provided. They were military grade. Hardcore, the kind of thing a battleship might carry, or at least a cruiser. She decided nothing the 'shipyard manager turned up would surprise her, but she didn't even want to guess what they'd cost.

Or how illegal it was to have them in *Pegasus*'s hold.

Concerns like that quickly gave way, though, to the question that drove her to call her people to the bridge. *How the hell dangerous* is *this mission?*

"I mean it." She'd waited for a few seconds, but no one had spoken up. "I won't think less of anyone who wants to stay behind. Durango has agreed to let you stay on Samis until there's less heat on Dannith." She almost wanted some of them to stay. She'd likely need every hand she had to get through what was ahead, but she also knew, from firsthand experience, what she would feel like if one of them—or more—died following her. She didn't fool herself. They were only going on such a dangerous and uncertain mission because she'd crewed up with Carmichael, and they'd lost their goods from the last expedition. It was her fault they were so desperate, at least that's how she saw it.

And those who came now would be following her toward a deadly threat.

"I'm not going anywhere except right here, Andi. And I don't think anyone else is, either. We're with you…all the way." Vig Merrick's voice was loud, his tone strident. He was full of the kind of instinctive confidence—cockiness—that bubbled up as a side effect of youth.

You're almost as young as he is…

She was in years, maybe, but not in experience. She'd seen things as a child in the Gut, things that would make combat veterans break out in a cold sweat.

"Vig's right, Andi…you can't possibly think we're going

to let you go out there without every one of us at your back." Gregor's voice boomed loudly, the ducts running along the ceiling almost rattling from the impact.

Andi appreciated the support, but she was concerned that Vig's and Gregor's comments would silence anyone who'd been considering staying.

Who are you kidding? None of them would stay. They're following you, going because you're going. If they get hurt—killed—it's on you. The captain left you the ship, but he left you something more, something hard to bear sometimes.

"Thanks, all of you. Really. It means a lot. And if we can pull this off, it's a big payday…without the risk of having to fence contraband to untrustworthy people like Carmichael." Her failure with the District gangster had taken money out of everyone's pocket, and it was the reason they were about to jump into a shadowy mission with so little in the way of specifics.

The fact that there had been no one more reliable than Carmichael who could handle the kind of stuff they'd brought back was irrelevant, as was her realization that she had done all she could to ensure the success of the transaction. At least in moments of self-flagellation.

"We're ready, Andi. Let's get going…there's some imperial swag out there with our names on it." More of Vig's youthful enthusiasm.

"We'll get started soon enough, but first, we've got a stop to make." A pause. "We're going back to Dannith, to the District." She'd been cocky with Durango, but in truth, she figured getting in and out without alerting Carmichael was roughly a coin toss. He was a fool in some ways, but his connections snaked all through Port Royal City and the spaceport.

But rushing out into the Badlands—into a possible fight with Sector Nine—without an engineer aboard seemed like a worse bet. Maybe a lot worse.

"The District? But…"

"I know, Jackal…I know. But there's somebody there we need to pick up, somebody we'll need for this mission. Yarra's going to be in the hospital for a good bit, and somebody's got to be down in engineering keeping the ship running." Her mind was already racing, trying to figure out just how she could bring *Pegasus* in without it showing up in the docking records.

Translation: Who she could bribe?

She looked down at the floor, and in her mind's eyes, she saw the bag of coins sitting in the ship's secure safe. The ten thousand Durango had given her upfront.

And she wondered how much of that it would take to slip into Port Royal City for long enough to find Righter…and to somehow convince him to join the crew.

Chapter Six

O'Rourke's Saloon
Spacer's District, Port Royal City
Planet Dannith, Ventica III
Year 302 AC

Andi stood just inside the door, her eyes scanning the room. For an instant, she thought she must be in the wrong place, but her memory had always been razor-sharp, and she was sure this was where Durango had told her to look.

This is a worse shithole than Carmichael's dump...

Andi had seen her share of dive bars in the District, but O'Rourke's was a strong candidate for the worst of them all. She could see from the scratches and gouges on the walls—and the patched together look of the furniture—that O'Rourke's saw its share of blood on the floor.

Probably every night.

No big deal. You've seen enough places where they sweep up the eyeballs at night...and every one of them looks like a resort next to the Gut.

Still, her hand moved slowly over her coat, her fingers running over the outline of the pistol holstered under her shoulder. O'Rourke's didn't even make an effort to keep out weapons, a concession to reality she found strangely comforting.

She walked up to the bar. There were about a dozen people at the large wooden slab, most sitting, with a few standing behind waiting for drinks. There were at least another twenty at the rickety tables spaced out across the room. A quick glance confirmed that most of them were in at least a reasonably advanced state of inebriation.

Andi stopped about a meter short of the bar, and she scanned the room. She had a basic description from Durango, but in one way or another, it fit about a quarter of the bar's patrons.

"What'll it be?" The bartender's voice was raw, harsh…with an implied, "If you're not drinking, you're leaving."

"You have any Quillian brandy? Or maybe a nice Port?" Andi wasn't much of a drinker, and when she did partake, it was usually an expensive brandy, or something else of quality.

"You kidding me? What is this, some kind of joke?" Joke or not, the bartender was clearly not amused.

"I'll take a whiskey…straight. If you've got a clean glass back there somewhere, I'll pay extra for it." She'd have stacked her tone up against the bartender's any day, but then she put the reins on her attitude. She'd have enjoyed seeing the surprise on the barkeep's face when she kicked the shit out of him, but drawing attention to herself while she was in the District could cause all kinds of problems. Not the least of which was wasting the thousand credits it had cost to slip *Pegasus* into the spaceport and buy six hours of silence.

The bartender didn't answer, but he returned about half a minute later with a glass about a third full of brown liquid. Andi had no doubt the liquor was the worst kind of rotgut, but the glass did look fairly clean.

She threw a coin on the table, a five-credit piece. It was at least ten times the value of the drink. "Thanks," she said, moderating the hostility in her tone. "That's for you. Just point me toward a guy named Lex Righter."

The bartender laughed, and then he handed her the drink and scooped up the coin, slipping it in his own pocket. "So, Righter's into you, too? Looks like there's already a line, and from the look on Mekel's face over there, I don't think your man's got any coin. Looks like he's gonna get another beating. Unless Mek's sick of his shit and ready to take the loss once and for all." The bartender looked her over for a few seconds. "I'd just finish your drink and get the hell out of here. A pretty little thing like you's got no business tangling with Mekel and his guys…or dealing with a useless drunk like Righter."

"Thanks for the advice." For a few seconds, she was concerned Righter had gotten himself into one of the Spacer's District syndicates, but one glance told her this Mekel was just a two-bit loan shark and hustler, plying his trade in the worst dives on the fringes of the District.

Nothing she couldn't handle…and if they surprised her and gave her any real trouble, she had Gregor waiting outside.

She gulped down the whiskey like an experienced drinker. It was the kind of street cred that mattered in a place like O'Rourke's, but her primary intent was to minimize how much of the battery acid she had to taste. Then she slammed the glass down hard and walked across the room.

The man the bartender had pointed out was standing, or something as close to that as he could manage, but even as she walked toward him, one of the men around him hauled off and punched him in the face. He collapsed hard, but the two thugs flanking him grabbed hold and yanked him back up.

"I've had it with you, Righter. You're a deadbeat and a drunk…you ain't worth shit to anybody. So, nobody's gonna miss you. Nobody's gonna care when they haul your body out of the alley in a couple days." The man who'd punched Righter turned toward the others. "Let's get him out of here. We can't beat out of him what he ain't got, so we'll just make an example out of him to show what happens when people stiff me."

"Lex, is that you?" Andi walked up toward Righter. She tried to make eye contact, to make an effort to communicate that she was going to help him. But she quickly realized he was too drunk to even know what was going on.

"I don't know who you are, little girl, but get the hell out of here while you still can." The man turned toward Andi, and he glared at her with undisguised menace.

"So, that's what a two-bit gangster wannabe looks like when he's trying to seem tough." The words came out while she was still formulating her plan.

Ok, direct and blunt it is…

"What the hell did you say?" The man was enraged, and he reached inside his jacket. But Andi was far too quick for him.

Her arm swung around, the bottom of her palm crashing into the man's face just under the nose. He howled in pain, and he staggered back a few steps. Andi would have preferred to just shoot the bastard, but even in a sewer like O'Rourke's, firing first and killing three people was difficult to explain. She had to provoke them, pave the way to take them down in justifiable self-defense.

Or whatever passed for it.

The two men holding Righter let him fall, and they reached inside their overcoats, pulling out weapons.

Two Mallincrofts…better guns than I'd have expected these minor leaguers to carry…

She slipped to the side, changing her position, just in case one of them was faster than either of them looked. As she moved, her own hand came out, fingers wrapped around the worn grip of her pistol. She heard a crack, the first shot, and she saw her attacker was well off-target. She knew that could change, of course, but the bastard wasn't going to get a second shot.

She almost fired. She could have dropped them both in an instant, but even self-defense was poor legal protection in a place like O'Rourke's. If Mekel was a regular in the place, and it looked like he was, half the patrons would swear she'd shot first…and the police in the District didn't ask too many questions. They'd arrest the easiest target—if they didn't just shoot her first—and finish the paperwork as quickly as possible.

Better to keep things non-lethal.

That's easier said then done, when it's one-sided…

She knew the loan shark's men would kill her, so she had to disable them first.

She leaned back, putting most of her weight on her back leg, even as she watched the closest gangster bringing his pistol around toward her.

Her leg darted out, a kick so fast it seemed lie a blur. Her boot struck the man's hand, sending the gun flying across the room and, from the sickening crunching sound, breaking at least a couple bones. The man doubled over and dropped to his knees. But Andi was already on his companion.

Her hands lashed out, a series of rapid punches, one after the other, and thug number two dropped backwards to the floor, his face a mask of fresh blood and his own pistol skittering across the floor.

Then, she turned back to the loan shark. He had a gun out, but Andi did as well…and while, he was still fumbling to take aim, hers was ten centimeters from his face, aiming right of the center of his forehead.

"Drop it." Then, a second or two later. "Don't make me kill you."

The man let the pistol fall from his grip and drop to the floor. He seemed to be trying to hide his fear, but he was doing a singularly poor job of it.

"What does he owe you?"

The man looked back, surprised at Andi's question.

"Three hundred," he said after a long pause. "Plus interest."

Andi's eyes were locked on the loan shark's, moving only for an instant every few seconds to check on the two downed henchmen.

"Okay," she said, "I'd bet you're lying to me, but I'll take you at your word." Her hand slipped into her pocket and she pulled out five platinum coins. "Here's five hundred. That'll cover what he owes you...and the wear and tear on your men." She tossed the coins toward the loan shark, and they landed on the floor just in front of him. It was a bit of satisfying disrespect, but mostly, Andi had no intention of getting close enough to take any chances. She doubted the man could have taken her, or even moved quickly enough to stop her from putting a bullet between his eyes, but she wasn't taking chances.

"Go ahead. Pick it up."

The loan shark looked suspicious, but after standing motionless for a short while, he leaned down, scooping up the coins as his gaze remained locked on Andi's.

Andi turned her head for an instant. The bar was silent, half the patrons trying to look like they weren't watching, and the rest just staring openly. "This is a straight deal...we got no beefs here." She looked back at the loan shark. "We even?"

The man hesitated, but then he just nodded.

"Good...so all of you can get back to swilling your drinks, and you...Mekel...you can grab your men and get the hell out of here. Lex..." She pointed to the engineer, still sitting in a stupor on the floor about a meter away, and still apparently oblivious to all that had transpired. "...is my problem, not yours anymore. Right?"

Mekel nodded, looking a little angry that Andi had embarrassed him in one of his regular haunts, but far more scared. He looked down at the coins in his hand, and then he waved toward his two men, and they all moved toward the door. Andi watched them go, and as she did, she saw another man racing out through the doorway into the street beyond. A hint of recognition quickly flamed into full blown recollection.

One of Carmichael's lieutenants.

She almost ran out after him, but she knew she was too late. The streets outside were a twisting, mazelike mess, with a hundred places to stay out of sight. And getting into a gunfight on a crowded street wasn't exactly conducive to maintaining a low profile.

She looked down at Righter, still blissfully ignorant of all that had happened. She tapped at the small control in her pocket, the small comm unit that would call Gregor. An instant later, the giant came racing in, looking ready for a fight.

She put up her hand, a gesture to calm the big man. "It's alright, Gregor. This is Lex Righter down here." She lightly kicked the almost motionless figure. "I think you're going to have to carry him. And we need to get out of here before the police come." She paused. "Or anybody else. One of Carmichael's goons was in here…and I didn't notice him in time. We've got to get back to the ship. Now!"

Gregor nodded, and then he leaned down and grabbed the almost-unconscious Righter, throwing the fairly large man over his shoulder like he weighed nothing.

"Let's go,' Andi said, waving toward the door and then following Gregor out into the street. She'd put her gun back in the holster, but her hand remained close to it. She figured they could get back to the ship…and if they really got lucky, manage to lift off before Carmichael send fifty District thugs after them.

They moved quickly down the street, trying not to draw attention to themselves. That was a heavy lift, of course, for a man the size of Gregor, especially when he was carrying someone over his shoulder. But all sorts of strange things went on in the District. They got a few glances, but nothing more.

Andi stopped when they reached the entrance to the spaceport, looking around in every direction before she waved Gregor on. The giant paused for an instant, and then he turned toward her.

"You said we were going to recruit this guy, Andi, not kidnap him."

"Yeah, that's what I said. But plans change, you know that well enough. We need an engineer…and if I'd have left him back there, he'd be lying dead in the alley by now, so it's fair trade as far as I'm concerned."

That all made sense to Andi, but she still wondered how Lex Righter would feel after he slept it off and woke up on a ship a few hundred million kilometers from Dannith.

Assuming they could get aboard and get the hell out before a firefight erupted all around them.

Chapter Seven

Docking Berth G4-111
Port Royal Spaceport
Planet Dannith, Ventica III
Year 302 AC

Andi felt a wave of relief as her eyes locked on the familiar form of *Pegasus*, sitting just where she'd left it, in the middle of the docking berth. Jackal and Barret were standing around just below the ramp leading up into the ship, but the others were nowhere to be found.

Inside, I suppose.

You hope.

Andi had left strict orders for everyone to remain close to the ship, but she'd feel better when she new for sure. With any luck, she'd get aboard and manage to take off before the shit hit the fan, but looking for an errant member of the crew would be a schedule buster for sure.

She managed to convince herself luck would come through, that they'd manage to escape without a fight.

That hope lasted about three seconds.

She spun around at the sound of the first shot. There were shadowy figures approaching. They were pretty far away, still, four or five men on foot, and coming up behind, rapidly overtaking them, was a vehicle. It was a light, open transport, but Andi immediately spotted the heavy semi-portable mounted on the back.

Shit.

"Gregor, get Righter inside…and start the launch prep. Barret, you go with him. You're the closest thing we've got to a flight engineer right now. At least a conscious one."

"Got it, Andi." The giant looked unhappy at the prospect of leaving her behind when enemies were approaching, but he lumbered up the ramp anyway.

"Yes, Cap." Barret nodded and raced up after Gregor.

Andi dropped down behind one of the landing gears, a large metal construct that offered her some kind of cover. That was all well and good against small arms, but the semi-portable was another matter. That thing could even damage *Pegasus* if it managed to score a hit in the right place.

She pulled out her pistol, ducking behind the landing strut as another half dozen shots rang out. She was about to try to aim the tiny gun when Anna Fasarus came scrambling down the ramp, her arms wrapped around three heavy assault rifles. She tossed one to the Jackal, and handed the other to Andi as she took position next to *Pegasus*'s captain, on the other side of the landing gear support.

"Thanks for the heavy artillery…I think we're going to need it." Andi jammed the pistol back in the small holster and extended the rifle in front of her, just around the strut. The vehicle was out in front of the men on foot now, and she could see one of the occupants positioning himself behind the semi-portable.

Andi stared down the rifle's sights, moving the weapon around as she tried to adjust to the vehicle's movement. The range was still long, the shot a tough one. She fired, once, then again, missing both times.

But the third shot took the gunner right off the back of the vehicle.

That'll buy us a few seconds, at least.

Andi knew her people were good in a fight, but when

that big gun really opened up, all bets were off.

"C'mon, guys…get moving up there. We're running out of time." She was talking softly, to herself, but some part of her believed her people up in the ship could feel what she was saying.

They know we don't have time to waste…

She fired three more rounds, and then she switched the gun to full auto. She had to keep that semi-portable under fire, pin anybody trying to get up there to man it.

Easier said than done.

The rifle Anna had given her had a spare clip snapped in place against the butt, but she'd go through both of those with a few seconds sustained automatic fire.

She managed to drop another of the vehicle's crew, but then the attackers managed to get the shield deployed, providing some cover to the gunner…just as a second armored transport came racing up from behind.

That's a lot of firepower to deploy in the open…

She knew Carmichael had influence, but if he was able to clean up after the kind of display she was seeing, he had more pull then she'd thought.

"Alright, let's pull back…we've got to get this ship up, ready or not."

She knew, in her gut, even before she did in her head, that her enemy had gotten to someone in flight control. *Pegasus* wasn't going to get launch clearance…and that meant blasting off against orders and making a run for it. Past any system patrols, and even naval ships if there were any nearby.

Damn…

"Anna…you first. Jackal, we're going to give her covering fire on three." She took a deep breath.

"One." She ducked back behind the support as the semi-portable opened fire. The rounds coming in were much louder, almost deafening as they echoed off the metal of the ship's hull.

"Two." She glanced up, checking *Pegasus* as she did. The heavy rounds were leaving small dents in the hull, but the attackers hadn't managed to target a vulnerable spot.

Not yet…

She tightened her hands on the rifle.

"One…Go, Anna!" She opened fire, spraying the vehicle with the forty rounds remaining in her first clip. The bullets were too weak to penetrate the vehicle's shield, at least at the current range, but the attack was violent enough to distract the gunner.

And that bought Anna enough time to race up the ramp and onto the ship.

"You next, Andi…I'll give you some cover." Jackal slammed his second clip into place, and he brought his rifle back to bear on the closing enemy.

"No way, Jackal…you're next, and that's a damned order." The command structure on *Pegasus* was a somewhat hazy thing. The entire crew respected her place as the captain and the ship's owner, but they were far from a military unit in terms of organization. Or obedience.

"No, Andi…you're more…"

"Dammit, Jackal, if you argue with me, we'll both get scragged. Now get ready…empty your rifle on two and get up there on three."

"One," she shouted, practically daring him to argue with her.

She stared ahead. The lead vehicle was close, and the sound of the heavy bullets slamming into the ship was working her last nerve. She could see a piece of a secondary antenna laying on the ground a few meters away. It wasn't vital, but it was cold proof that the enemy fire *was* a danger to her ship.

"Two." She sucked in another deep breath and her legs tensed. She was going to lay down some covering fire for Jackal, and then she was going to race up right after him and hope for the best.

Then, a blast of fire slammed right into the support in front of her, and she stumbled back. It was too late, she realized suddenly. The first vehicle was within point blank range, and the other one was coming up right behind. Even the men on foot were in firing range, and fire ricocheted all around. A chunk of metal landed about five meters behind her, another piece of *Pegasus* torn off, an unidentified one this time.

Andi didn't give up. It wasn't in her. But she knew it was over. There wasn't enough time, not before those heavy guns managed to damage something vital. It wouldn't have to be a critical hit. Anything that prevented the ship from lifting off immediately was as good as a death sentence, to her certainly, and probably to all her people as well.

She was about to swing around, use up the last of her ammo—and use it well. If she was going to die, she was going to take as many of her enemies with her as she could. Her body tensed, and she started to lunge around the edge of the support…when a voice blared through the outside speakers. "Andi, get down!"

She reacted instinctively, ducking low behind the strut, just as a searing wave of heat hit her.

It was almost unbearable, and she could feel her skin burning. There was brightness, too, so intense that even after she closed her eyes, the lids glowed orange. For an instant, she had no idea what had happened. But then she opened her eyes again, and she saw the two vehicles, or what was left of them. One was a burning hulk, and the other even less, more a scattered field of twisted wreckage. And the men on foot were just gone.

The lasers.

Of course…Barret fired one of the lasers.

Those weapons were light ones by the standards of space combat, but they were made for just that purpose, for fighting over the vast distances in the depths of space. On a target less than thirty meters away, they were destruction incarnate.

They were also illegal to fire in port. More than illegal. Absolutely, utterly forbidden. Andi didn't even know what the penalty would be, but it certainly eliminated any chance at all of getting clearance to lift off.

Or to come back…ever.

Pegasus was going to have to make a break for it, and run the gauntlet toward the transit point. Her ship shouldn't have had a chance to escape from the patrols, but then, of course, *Pegasus* had a few…unauthorized…modifications.

They *did* have a chance. Probably.

But they had to go immediately, before the authorities showed up, and she had to decide if she'd open up on Port Royal cops and spaceport security teams.

Andi turned and raced up the ramp, her hand reaching out and slapping on the controls to close the door as she passed by.

Yes, they had a chance…but she didn't dare to try to put any numbers to it.

*   *   *

"Free Trader *Pegasus*, you are ordered to cut all engine thrust immediately and prepare for boarding." The message was the third one, repeated almost verbatim in the same officious tone.

Andi ignored it, just as she had the other two. She was committed. *Pegasus* was making a run for it, and she was reasonably confident she could outrun the pursuing patrol ships.

Assuming she could evade any shots if they opened fire.

Any doubts about that 'if' were quickly washed away as the energy readings on the scanner shot up, two enormous spikes that could only mean one thing.

The pursuing vessels had fired. And missed.

"Two lasers, Andi...some pretty bad shooting, too." Barret had been a naval gunner before he'd...retired...and become a Badlands adventurer. Andi knew he was right, but she also knew the navy looked down on the system patrol crews, considering them amateurs. Barret's disdain was no guarantee there wasn't someone on one of those ships who could actually shoot.

For that matter, neither was a pair of misses. *Pegasus* had some devilish evasion routines, courtesy of Andi's prior collaboration with Sylene Merrick, and a difficulty to score an initial hit didn't mean the gunners were incompetent. Andi fancied *Pegasus*'s routines could evade naval gunners as well, at least for a while. That wasn't a guess she wanted to risk testing, though.

It was a long way to the transit point, and even with *Pegasus* redlining its reactor, it would be at least ten minutes before her ship pulled away and out of firing range.

She knew the tactically correct thing to do. Barret was a crack shot, and she doubted the patrol crews were prepared for the armament *Pegasus* actually mounted. Her guns were nothing like the ones listed on her manifests—or transmitted by her beacon, more of Durango's handiwork.

But she wasn't ready to open fire on Confederation ships.

She knew she'd taken the step into full blown outlawry, but that didn't mean she was going to gun down Confederation spacers.

"Andi, I can take out those..."

"No, Barret. We're not firing on them."

A pause. "I might be able to disable them without causing critical damage."

"Can you guarantee no casualties?" Andi already knew the answer. The question was as much a repeated answer to her gunner, as a request for an answer.

"No, of course not, but..." Barret's voice dropped off. Andi knew his request had been an instinctive thing, and not something he'd really considered. She couldn't imagine her ex-navy gunner blowing up legitimate system patrol craft. Odds were, at least one of those ships had a navy veteran or two onboard.

I might be an outlaw, but I'm no traitor…

"Let's push the engine output." She had to do *something*. Even those clowns at the controls behind her would hit if she gave them ten minutes with no return fire.

"We're already at one-ten."

"Then go to one-twenty…and get down to engineering. With our new engineer still sleeping it off, you're what we've got. Keep that reactor from Scragging, whatever it takes. We're looking at maybe fifty minutes to transit, and that's a long time this deep in the red zone."

"Andi, there's no way I…" He stopped suddenly. "Okay, Andi…I'll manage. Somehow." The gunner, now wearing his hat as a makeshift engineer, leapt up and raced off the bridge, even as Andi felt the added acceleration kicking in. *Pegasus's* engine output was well beyond the levels her dampeners could handle, and Andi guessed everyone onboard was feeling an effective 2g, maybe 2.5g.

Barret wobbled a little on his feet as the force hit him, but his years of naval training served him well. He righted himself and slipped through the door and down the ladder to the lower level.

"They're falling behind, Andi." Anna Fasarus struggled to her feet, moving from the third station to the newly vacated second as she reported.

"They're still in range, though." Andi's hands were gripped around the controls, jerking around almost randomly, throwing some extra push into *Pegasus's* evasive maneuvers. She didn't like running, she was a fighter by nature, but there was no other choice, not just then.

Not unless she wanted to start gunning down Confederation spacers…and if she did that, she would not only despise herself, she would probably provoke the patrol into following *Pegasus* into the Badlands.

Maybe the navy, too. The military didn't particularly respect the patrol crews, but she doubted they'd react well to someone who killed them.

So, running is all you can do…

Her eyes moved toward the main scanner. There were three naval ships in position around the base orbiting Dannith's largest moon. She'd been worried since she'd broken out of orbit, afraid she'd see the energy blooms indicating those ships were preparing to pursue. The vessels were small by naval standards, but they were vastly larger and more powerful than *Pegasus*…and their weapons outranged those of the patrol vessels by at least twenty thousand kilometers. She'd never outrun the navy ships, nor would she escape from their fire.

But they were still just sitting there. Clearly, an outlaw making a break for it was less than a top priority. She was surprised at first, but then she decided she shouldn't be. The navy patrolled the Badlands frontier, and while they weren't above occasionally boarding prospector ships and arresting their crews, they didn't particularly care to take orders from Dannith's civil authorities…and that fact gave Andi a chance at the margin she needed.

It was a touch of arrogance that just might save her life. All her people's lives.

She looked back at the display. Forty-one minutes to the point. And maybe eight until *Pegasus* pushed past the patrol ships' range.

She leaned back, her hands still hard on the controls.

It was time to see just how long eight minutes could be.

Chapter Eight

Free Trader Pegasus
Approaching Transit Point Frontier-1
Ventica System
Year 302 AC

Andi's eyes were burning, the long trail of an escaped tear making its way slowly down her face. She wasn't crying—it would take more than a few system patrol boats to bring her to that particular pass—but the smoke in the air was acidic, and with her hands tight on the controls, she couldn't wipe it away.

It had seemed almost like a joke, a nasty prank the universe had decided to play on her. *Pegasus* had *almost* been out of range. She'd dared to hope her ship *was* out of range. Then, a shot, the last one, taken at the very edge of long range, scored a hit. For a terrible instant, she thought her people had been caught, that *Pegasus* had been crippled, and that they'd end up in a Dannith prison for the next twenty years. But Barret had quickly stripped those fears away. The shot had taken out a cooling unit, and released a burst of caustic, but not especially dangerous, coolant into the ventilation system. But that was all.

The backups had come online immediately, and *Pegasus* hadn't lost any noticeable power or acceleration. In fact, just about the only real effects were red and swollen eyes across the ship.

"Everybody, stay strapped in. The life support system is fully operational, and it should have the air cleared in a minute or two. We should be out of reach of those patrol ships, and it doesn't look like we're notorious enough for the naval units to respond." *Thank you for that.* "We're heading right into the transit point, and we're going to keep blasting the engines at full the whole way. So, sit tight, and in a few minutes, we'll be back out there. Back in the Badlands."

Andi sighed softly. She'd addressed the immediate situation, but she hadn't even touched upon the unspoken shadow hanging over them all. A blood feud with a local gangster had been bad enough, a dangerous situation certainly, if the kind of thing they'd dealt with before. She suspected all her people figured she'd eventually find a way to get to Carmichael and kill the fool…which was exactly what she'd planned to do.

But shooting up the landing bay and making a break for it from the system patrol boats was something else entirely. She'd bribed her way out of minor problems with the law before, but this time it looked very much like she'd pulled herself, and all her people with her, into a hole too deep to dig out of. They were full blown outlaws, now, wanted criminals. She'd never thought of herself quite that way before, not really. But if *Pegasus* returned to Dannith, the best she could hope for was immediate arrest and trial…and conviction meant jail, not to mention the authorities seizing her ship.

And she couldn't come up with any scenario that didn't end in conviction. After all, her people *had* opened up with the ship's lasers in the middle of the spaceport.

She just *might* slip back to Samis undetected to collect the reward if her people completed the mission. *Assuming Durango doesn't just turn us over to the authorities and avoid the need to pay for whatever swag we're bringing back.*

I'll think about that later. We've got to make it back before that's a problem, and if I don't stay focused on this mission, we'll solve our legal problems by getting captured now...or wasted in some imperial ruin.

She stared at the display, at the strange image of the transit point, sort of a deep black void, but something else as well, something no one had ever been able to adequately describe. *Pegasus* was close just then, close enough for visual contact. And then, in an instant, the ship was inside.

The experience of a transit was something else no one had ever managed to express to anyone else, especially to someone who'd never experienced it. A jump *did* take time, that had been more or less proven through experimentation, and the duration of a transit varied with the distance traversed, from less than a second, to the highest recorded duration of 11.23 seconds. But the apparent time to a traveler varied enormously, even in multiple trips through the same point. Andi had jumped out of Dannith and into the Badlands more than a dozen times, and no two had seemed the same, at least not in the faded and sporadic memories one retained of such trips.

The transit felt like a long one to Andi, and she wondered if her own stress and tension affected her interpretation. She tried to think about it, to look back at other transits to create some kind of correlation. But in-depth thought was all but impossible during a jump, and her mind simply wandered uncontrollably. Images of the Gut, of the Marine, of her mother...of friends and comrades, both with her and lost, swirled around in a seemingly random witch's brew of memories.

And then, suddenly, she was back to normal. More or less...it took a few seconds to truly adapt to the return to normal space.

Pegasus had crossed the border. They were back out in the Badlands.

* * *

"Shut the hell up, and listen to me. You have no idea how much trouble we went to—how much we still have to deal with—just to get you, and to pull your ass out of the mess you were in. I don't care who broke your heart, or how life disillusioned you, or what else drove you to the bottle and to the wretched waste of skill and talent you've obviously become, but I can tell you one thing. That's over now."

Andi glowered at the wretched form in front of her, the disheveled—and stinking—man she'd saved from almost certain death. The one she'd gone back to Dannith, with exceedingly troublesome complications, to find. She tended to believe Durango—he'd never lied to her yet, not that she'd caught, at least. But she found it hard to believe the pile of human debris sitting in front of her was a man who could fill in for Yarra.

Righter looked up at her, his expression half anger and half destitution. "I didn't ask you to come find me, and I damned sure didn't ask to be loaded on this scow and dragged out...wherever the hell we are. So, why don't you just take me back to Dannith right now...and in the meantime, somebody give me a damned drink!"

Andi grabbed him hard and pulled him from the chair, throwing him to the deck. She hauled off and gave him a hard kick to the ribs, and she stared down as he whimpered in pain. "It's time for you to understand your new reality. You're in the Badlands now, Righter. There's no law here, no cops, no security...assuming any of those would give a shit about a piece of garbage like you in the first place. *I* am the law here. If I order my people to throw your stinking carcass out the airlock, they'll do it." Gregor was standing off to the side nodding, looking very much like that command was his greatest fantasy just then. "And no one will ever find your frozen corpse, much less pin it on us. So, take all that into consideration before you speak again." Her expression practically dared him to argue with her.

Righter looked utterly miserable, but he kept his mouth shut.

"Welcome to *Pegasus*, Righter. You're going to live in the cargo hold for now, where a reeking pile of slime like you belongs, sleeping on the metal deck until you dry the hell out. And, if you find something, some coolant or engine lubricant—or anything else you decide might be some kind of intoxicant—I'm going to beat the hell out of you for the trouble you cause. There may not be many things you think are worse than not having your alcohol right now, but you can count on this. *I* am one of those things."

She paused and stared into his eyes with a look that said she'd just as soon kill him as make the kind of effort she'd just described. Then she said, "And when—if—you begin to resemble a human, and to smell like one too, we'll start treating you like one. *Pegasus* isn't the worst ship to serve on, Lex. When you've got a better grip on yourself, ask some of the crew. When we get back from this voyage, we'll let you off the ship and you can go back to your miserable excuse for an existence, freed for the moment from the debts that had you this close..." She held her fingers a centimeter apart. "...from ending up face down in a District alley somewhere. That one is on me, call it payment for services you will render. But if you decide you want to stay and try to live like a human again, well, we can discuss that, too."

She turned toward Gregor. "Take him to the hold and lock him up...and make sure there's nothing there he can drink."

* * *

"I   need   you   to   deliver   this   message   to Brewer...immediately." Carmichael sat behind an enormous desk, staring coldly at the pair of his men standing there, nervously. He knew why they were edgy. Andromeda Lafarge. She was nothing but the captain of a prospector ship, and yet somehow, she and her people had managed to kill more than twenty of his men in two encounters, and they'd put as many more in the hospital. It was infuriating, and as pompous as the gangster was prone to be, he had to acknowledge, the crew of the *Pegasus* had badly damaged his organization. He could recruit more muscle, of course. He had already begun that effort. But he'd have to be careful for some time. His rivals, even his allies, were men and women unlikely to allow opportunity to slip past them…and his weakness was their opening. And it was only exacerbated by the humiliation of being bested by Andi Lafarge and her ragtag crew of pirates.

"Yes, Boss." One of the men leaned forward and took the data chip. "We'll see to it immediately." The two thugs turned and raced out of the room, leaving Carmichael alone. He took a deep breath and considered his situation. He'd dealt with Brewer before, and the Sector Nine operative had always done what he'd promised. Carmichael needed help, and Brewer could provide that. Not all the gangsters in the District knew the agent's true identity, of course. Very few did. But they all knew he was a powerful man, one with considerable force at his beck and call. Not many would want to cross him by moving against Carmichael, at least as long as Brewer extended his protection to his sometime ally.

District mobsters were a strange lot, and some would readily deal with anyone who could further their interests, even representatives from the Union's feared spy agency. Others exhibited a strange form of patriotism, even as they flagrantly violated the Confederation's laws.

Carmichael fell firmly in the first category, his moral ambiguity allowing him to do just about anything that seemed to be in his personal interest. And, that was about to pay dividends once again. Andi Lafarge had gotten the better of him twice now. But he'd scored a win of sorts against her, as well, one she knew nothing about.

He knew all about *Pegasus*, the true history of her vessel, and how she got it. And he had no doubt, Sector Nine would be very interested in knowing that the old *Nightrunner* was still in operation, with a brand new name, and Jim Lorillard's hand-picked successor at the helm.

Yes, Brewer would find that information very interesting, and very likely of considerable value. Certainly, enough to throw some support Carmichael's way until he could get back up to strength...and probably enough extra to leave him a sort of marker he could call in one day. Andi and her people had done serious damage to the Union's spy organization, and killed a number of their agents.

Sector Nine lived up to its reputation, for cruelty as well as efficiency...and as far as Carmichael knew, one of the agency's central tenets was never to let a wrong against them go unpunished.

It might even be a double win for him. He wanted Andi Lafarge dead so badly, it made his head pound. But he'd tried twice and failed. Just maybe, Sector Nine would get there first...and get rid of the troublesome Lafarge for him.

I'd like to have my own people kill her...but I'm willing to drink a toast over her bullet-riddled corpse no matter who pulls the trigger...

Chapter Nine

Sector Nine Stealth Ship Phantasia
Approaching Planet Aquellus
Olystra System
Year 302 AC

"We're picking up drive trails, Commander, but no sign of *Vysaria* or *Celestra*. Increasing active canners to maximum power."

"Very well. Report anything out of the ordinary, Drusus, even if you think it is of no account." Aimee Boucher leaned back in her chair, her mind crisp, focused. Aquellus was going to be a tough nut to crack, she'd known that all along. At least three freelance crews, typical Dannith prospector trash she'd hired to have a go at the imperial facility suspected to lie under the planet's oceans, had perished in the effort. But *Vysaria* and *Celestra* were Union ships, Sector Nine craft crewed entirely by agents. Boucher had been brought up in the ruthless political system of the Union, and she was prepared to sacrifice whomever she had to in order to complete her mission. But it still hurt to lose her own people, especially since it made her look bad.

Bring us into orbit, Drusus, and I want all scanners on full. If there's something in this system, someone else looking for what we seek, or even some ancient imperial defense system, I want to know the instant there's a power spike large enough to brew a pot of coffee. Understood?"

"Yes, Commander, of course."

Drusus Olivetti had been her choice to serve as her second. Indeed, she'd hand-picked everyone on *Phantasia*. Her responsibility for the casualties suffered to date, and of the potential loss of the two ships she'd come to check on, was at least arguable. She'd been following orders, and she'd been saddled with many of the agents who'd been sent out. But she was in charge on site now, given the job—and the responsibility for success—directly from Gaston Villieneuve. The head of Sector Nine, and member of the Presidium, had a reputation for rewarding success...and an even stronger one for punishing failure. She had imagined returning to Montmirail victorious, with the sought after artifacts in hand.

She'd also considered the alternative...and she wondered if she wouldn't be better off dying in the effort than returning empty handed. She'd sent her share of enemies and victims to Sector Nine's fearsome cells, and she had no wish to join them, nor to hear the laughter of those ghosts that had come before her as she suffered the torment failure had earned her.

"Put the Foudre Rouge on alert as well. I want a squad ready to go down on a moment's notice. Full aquatic gear. And I want those drive trails tracked. If those ships entered the atmosphere, we should be able to tell where they went." Not necessarily true, she realized. Trails in atmosphere dissipated far more quickly than they did in space. But she didn't need much, just a basic entry course. *Phantasia*'s computers could take it from there and give her the two or three most likely points at which the two vessels had penetrated the ocean surface.

"Yes, Commander."

Boucher held back a sigh, and she sat still, appearing calm on the outside, even as her tensions built inside. She didn't like the ghostly region of space the Confeds called the Badlands. It seemed like a haunted graveyard to her, filled with world after world devoid of human habitation, where untold billions had once lived.

She didn't like the lack of knowledge she suffered from either. She knew there was something valuable on Aquellus, at least analysis of reams of intel and data suggested there was. But she didn't know what she was looking for, and while Villieneuve must have known, he hadn't deigned to share that information with her.

She didn't need to know, of course. *Any* imperial artifact was exceedingly valuable and worth taking, and if she found whatever had caused all the fuss, she suspected she'd realize it. Still, it made her edgy. Worse, perhaps, the fact that reports suggested the Confeds had the same intel meant Confederation Intelligence would show up at some point.

Or, at the very least, they would send someone.

Boucher was ready for a fight. *Phantasia* was larger and more powerful than the converted freighters and other ships Badlands adventurers tended to use. There was almost a full platoon of Foudre Rouge soldiers onboard, plus a carefully gathered crew of technical experts. If the Confeds *did* send some ship out to Aquellus, and if it arrived before she had finished her work, she would simply destroy it. She'd dropped scanner buoys at all the transit points, and she intended to keep *Phantasia* in orbit, and on full alert, throughout the mission. She had enough landing sleds to ferry her people down, all of them custom-outfitted for submersible operation. So, her people could search for…whatever they were looking for…and her ship could blast any interlopers into plasma before they even got near the planet.

She'd considered any possibility, and her confidence held firm. Success would propel her to the very highest ranks of Sector Nine, even to the deputy director's position. Many had long assumed Ricard Lille would claim that spot, that

Villieneuve's only real friend was an unbeatable candidate. But Boucher knew Lille, she knew him well. Sector Nine's preeminent assassin had no interest at all in power, an oddity among those in the Union's espionage and political sectors. Ricard Lille was a dissolute, almost emotionless machine. He indulged in all manner of debauchery, women, drink, mind-altering substances...but only when he was off the job. When he was in the field, Lille was the most focused person she'd ever seen. And he only *truly* enjoyed one thing.

Killing.

Boucher would never challenge Lille in any way, nor was she naïve enough to imagine their yearlong stint as lovers would delay the assassin from killing her, even for an instant, if circumstance pitted them against each other. But she couldn't take from Lille what he didn't want, and if she managed to reach the deputy's seat, she would make certain to show the killer the proper respect. And give him what he truly wanted. More people to terminate.

Don't get ahead of yourself. There's a whole planet down there, and almost every square meter of it is under water. You're a long way from success...and there are a lot of dangers between here and there.

She almost shivered as she sat in her chair. She wasn't afraid of any Confeds that might come blundering into the system. She could handle them. But old imperial installations made her skin crawl, and one sitting thousands of meters under the ocean was even worse.

"I want those scanning reports, Drusus. What the hell is taking so long?" A pause. "I want to know where those ships went. Now."

* * *

"How do you feel?" Andi's voice was soft, almost sympathetic, completely unlike the tone she'd used every time she'd previously spoken to Righter. The engineer had suffered badly for days, banging on the locked hold doors incessantly, and screaming piteously. Fortunately, the doors were nearly soundproof, and Andi had just turned off the comm and left her passenger to his own miseries. It was the only way, at least to her mind. Righter had to overcome his demons to be worth anything—to her, or to himself—and the first step toward that was getting him clean.

That had taken two weeks, during which time she'd given him nothing but water and some basic ration biscuits…and had the hold powerwashed at least half a dozen times. She had to get a new engineer out of all the effort, and a damned good one at that. Nothing else would be worth the final cleaning job the hold was going to need.

"Strange…I don't think I've been truly sober—and not on something—for three years now." Righter had already told her of his history, his days as a working engineer, and his fall from grace into utter degradation. He'd had bouts with alcoholism more than once in his life, but the last one had been the worst.

And it would have been the one that killed him if Andi hadn't come along, something he had begun to realize.

Andi had asked him what triggered the most recent fall, and it had taken everything she had to keep her eyes from rolling back when he told her it had been a girl. She'd almost felt it coming, and she'd hoped against hope it would be something better, a real reason, at least, to wallow in a filthy stupor for three years.

Still, despite his weakness, and the revulsion she felt toward it, she had a feeling the man knew his engineering—another checkmark on the list of Durango's reliable tips. And since *Pegasus* was almost to the Olystra system, and whatever awaited it there, it was time to put those skills to the test. She'd have preferred to give Righter another few weeks, maybe even some more time in the hold, wallowing in his own filth, just to impress on the now-sober man just how miserable his life as a morbid alcoholic had been. But she was out of time. Durango had been straight with her about the possibility of Sector Nine activity…and Andi took "possibility" to mean certainty. If Sector Nine showed up— or if they were already there, ahead of *Pegasus*—there would be a fight, no doubt. And Andi wasn't going up against Union ships without someone down in engineering who really knew what they were doing.

Barret had been a reasonable substitute, but he was also her best gunner, and in a fight, she needed him on the bridge.

That left Righter, in whatever wobbly state of sobriety he'd managed to achieve. He would stay sober, that much she was sure. She'd locked up everything on *Pegasus* that could cause intoxication, including medications and two or three industrial chemicals. Righter wouldn't get drunk, and he wouldn't shoot up either.

But that didn't mean he couldn't fall to pieces under the stress of combat.

"So, you know why I brought you here, both for your own good, and also to serve our needs. That loan shark was going to finish you off. I got there just in time. You may feel that you were kidnapped, but if I hadn't taken you, you'd be dead right now. So, consider that."

"I have, believe me." His tone was soft, almost compliant. It was clear his initial resentment had faded, and some realization that Andi had indeed saved his life had set in. "But I still don't know how you found me, or even knew who I was."

"Do you know a guy named Durango?"

Righter let out a quasi-laugh, the first genuine sign of amusement she'd seen in him. "I should have known. Yes, of course I know Durango. I used to work for him. Before I screwed it all up."

"Well, whatever you did, it didn't damage his opinion of your engineering skills. He told me you're a wizard with spaceship engines and power plants. And it just so happens that we need someone with those exact skills. I won't promise you more than this mission, Lex..." Andi had switched to his first name, hoping the more familiar tone would help integrate Righter into the crew. "If I did, you'd know I was lying anyway, and who the hell knows if you'd even want to stay longer. You're going to have to stay sober for the long haul, that's for sure, and that means back in port where there's a bar on every corner as well as out here where I've locked everything up. But whether you stay or not, we're looking at a healthy payday for this mission, and you'll get your full share. Stash it away, or drink every millicredit, that's your call. But if you keep it together, we'll have a talk about what comes next. And if you don't, you're likely to end up dead out here with the rest of us." A pause. "So, what say you? You're stuck here anyway. Do you want to ply your trade, and make some coin?"

Righter looked back at her, silent for a moment. Then he said, "Well, I could be angry about being dragged all the way out here, but I guess you did save my life. I'd pushed Mekel about as far as I was going to, I don't have to believe you to know that. There's not much point in sitting around being mad...and I'd wager we've got a better chance of getting back to Dannith if I help." He paused, and a thin smile formed on his lips. "So, I guess you can count me in."

Andi felt a wave of relief. His decision only made sense, of course, but she was honest enough with herself to question whether she could so quickly overcome the anger at being abducted...and treated as roughly as Righter had been.

And she knew one thing for sure. She needed someone down in that engineering space. Someone damned good.

Righter stared at her, the barest grin still on his face. "I've seen enough of that cargo hold of yours, so maybe now you can show me what kind of engine room this ship's got."

Chapter Ten

Union Landing Craft G72-X111
Upper Atmosphere
Planet Aquellus, Olystra III
Year 302 AC

"We're on course, Commander. Scanners on maximum. We're hanging onto that last trail, but barely. The AI's been crunching it, and we've got four possible routes down, with a combined probability estimate of ninety-six percent." Nicolas Caron was strapped in the pilot's seat, as much because it was a vacant chair as anything else. He *was* technically flying the ship, of course, but he had the AI fully engaged, and he was mostly just watching. He could fly the thing himself, if he had to, though he was by no means an expert. But with no enemy, no incoming fire, no detectable malfunctions, there wasn't much reason to take over.

And it was taking all he had to follow the rapidly dissipating drive trail. He was going to lose it any second, but each passing instant tightened his course and narrowed the range of choices. With any luck, he'd hang on long enough for the AI to single out one course as a clear favorite. That wouldn't be a guarantee, of course, but it would be better than chasing after four disparate vectors.

"Very well, Agent Caron. You are to proceed in

accordance with the operation plan. Deploy floating relay stations before you submerge, and depth-neutral boosters wherever necessary. I want you to remain in contact, no matter how deep you go. We've had far too many unexplained disappearances here, and that stops now."

"Yes, Commander Boucher." That all sounded good to Caron, but he was a damned sight less certain about it than Boucher sounded, back up on *Phantasia*'s dry and well-protected bridge. The landing craft was durable, built to endure combat landings and the g-forces common in such operations. But they could only take so much pressure, and that limited how deep they could go, safely at least. How much farther they would press things if the need arose would be Boucher's decision, of course, and that made Caron sweat a little. He wasn't so sure about the utility of the comm buoys either. They'd extended communications range down a kilometer under the surface, maybe more. But if his people had to go deeper than that, they'd almost certainly be cut off and on their own. That would put him entirely in charge, and as much as he relished the idea of getting Boucher off his back for a while, the prospect made his stomach flop a bit, too.

That wasn't all that was eating away at his composure. He glanced at the small screen showing the rear cabin. The Foudre Rouge were back there, strapped into their seats. The clone soldiers always gave him the shakes. Something about the way they sat there, seemingly without any emotion at all, as they descended toward some alien ocean that had swallowed up every previous expedition. They didn't seem quite…human.

He knew they were clones, but that didn't explain everything. He'd heard stories about the training programs, about the harsh discipline and difficult conditions the Union's soldiers endured. It was supposed to make them the ultimate soldiers, utterly invincible. They *were* effective in combat, there was no question about that, though their archenemies, the Confederation Marines, had gone against them toe to toe in three wars, and they'd matched them every step of the way, perhaps even gained a slight upper hand.

Still, he was glad to have the muscle. Sector Nine agents got combat training, too, but it was intended for a different kind of use. If there were imperial security systems still active down there—and that was the only way he could explain the disappearance of the previous expeditions—he'd need the kind of raw firepower a squad of Foudre Rouge could deploy.

The landing craft shook as it skipped on the thickening atmosphere. Aquellus was a habitable world, its atmosphere eminently breathable, if its pressure was a little heavier than most humans found comfortable. The people who'd lived there, before they'd all died in the Cataclysm, had no doubt adapted over the years and generations of life there, but Caron had ordered all his people equipped with breathing gear. It wasn't terribly likely they'd end up exploring any of the handful of small landmasses on the surface, but there was no harm in being prepared.

Of course, they'd need the breathing gear anyway, since any action would likely take place underwater. Even if there were imperial facilities down there, he had no idea how they'd fared over the years. Once habitable corridors and chambers could have flooded centuries before, or ancient air pumps and life support units could have failed. In any event, his people would debark with full underwater survival suits.

"Two kilometers to sea level. Scanners still detecting intermittent drive trails. The AI has calculated a course with sixty-four percent probability." Antoinette Bissel sat next to him at the controls. She was another agent, just like him, but she had actual naval experience, three years serving as the political officer on a heavy cruiser. It didn't make her a battle-tested admiral, but it did give her a surer hand with the controls, and with the scanner array.

Caron nodded. That was good, getting the choice narrowed down to a clear favorite, but sixty-four percent wasn't enough. "Push the scanner power levels up, Antoinette, just a touch past specifications." Union equipment was no match for the Confederation's, at least not in terms of durability. Union ships rarely dared to try to match their enemies' sometimes reckless tactics in redlining reactors and weapons. But he only needed a little more, just another few seconds of data. If the trend continued the way it was going, he'd know with a reasonable likelihood where the last ships to come to Aquellus had come.

As those vessels had disappeared without a trace, he had mixed feelings about following their courses so effectively. But if failure was dangerous in the Union, outright cowardice was manifestly fatal. If he broke off and ran, he doubted he'd get back to Montmirail to face any kind of trial. Boucher would more than likely blast his landing craft out of the sky…and write off any innocents trapped onboard as collateral damage.

So, forward…chasing after the ghosts. Just stay focused, and make sure you don't become a ghost yourself…

* * *

"You've got some stuff down here I didn't expect to find. These old converted freighters usually barely run, but half of this looks almost military grade." Righter's voice blared through the comm, and Andi smiled. *Pegasus* was a special ship, in more ways than one. Captain Lorillard had begun the process of upgrading the vessel, and Andi had continued it with such zeal that she constantly found herself almost out of cash for the amounts she poured into the ship. *Pegasus* was tougher than any outsider would expect, and she was a *lot* faster. And her weapons suite was an order of magnitude above the single light laser turret most free traders carried.

And that doesn't even take the torpedoes into account…

She knew the weapons Durango gave her were powerful, and she hoped she didn't have to use them. That was both because she didn't want to run into an enemy tough enough to warrant it…and because she was far from sure Barret could effective target with weapons he basically had to drop out of the cargo bay.

"Now you know why we needed a good engineer, Lex. Take a close look around down there, because we're counting on you to be at one hundred percent if we get in the shit…and you're stuck on here with us, so you'll want to be at your very best. If *Pegasus* doesn't get back, none of us get back." It was blunt, but nothing save the hard truth.

"That's a fact, Captain." Righter's voice was different, lighter than it had been. Andi understood, at least to a point. Righter hadn't become the skilled engineer Durango said he was without being deeply interested in the subject matter. Yarra had always spent hours down in engineering, even when she wasn't needed there, and it looked like her temporary replacement was cut from the same cloth.

"Let me know if you need help down there." Andi had almost sent someone down to watch Righter. He was almost a stranger, after all, and trust came slowly to Andi, and with great difficulty…if it came at all. But she needed Righter, and every instinct she had on people management told her he needed to feel like part of the crew if he was going to do his best. And fight off his demons. That was in all their interests, since every one of their lives could depend on getting a damaged system back online a few seconds quicker.

"Will do, Captain."

Andi cut the line, and she turned and looked over at Barret. She knew what her comrade was going to say before he even got the first word out.

"Don't say it, Barret. I know…but we need him. With Yarra in the hospital on Samis and you stuck up here at gunnery in a fight, a simple overload could end up being fatal. We need someone in engineering, someone who knows what he is doing. I didn't choose to trust Righter. I don't have any choice but to trust him…not if we're going to have a go at this mission." *And we don't have a choice about that, not a real one.*

Barret just nodded, a grudging and wordless acknowledgement that Andi was right. A few seconds later, he said, "Approaching the transit point, Andi. AI calculates insertion in seventeen minutes, forty seconds."

"Maintain course and velocity." She stared at the display, and her hands tightened on the armrests of her chair. She was edgy, more than she usually was. At first, she'd written it off to everything that had happened on Dannith, on worries about how she was going to clean up *that* mess. But then she realized she wasn't just concerned about trouble on the mission. She expected it. Bad trouble.

Sector Nine…

Andi detested the Union intelligence operation with righteous zeal. But she also feared it, something far more difficult for her to face and to accept. She'd changed her ship's name to lay low, to escape Sector Nine's wrath for what she'd done the last time they'd tangled. She'd bought a new beacon, a highly illegal act that had only been possible with Durango's assistance. She'd told herself such precautions were smart, tactically correct. But in moments of true self-reflection, she'd admitted to herself that fear had been at play at least as much as any other motivation.

Now, they're out there. Maybe on their way now. Maybe even there already, waiting for us…

She swallowed hard, pushing back against the cold feeling trying to spread through her body. *Keep it together, Andi…don't lose your shit now.*

"I want evasive routines queued up before transit, Barret."

"Andi? You think someone's waiting for us just past the point?"

"I don't think anything, but we're not taking any chances. We're going to be ready for whatever is there. If its nothing, what do we lose? A few minutes of data upload?" Andi had run into hostile ships in the Badlands before, but she had a feeling they were heading into the deadliest battle they'd ever fought. She knew very well her people just might lose, that her ship might be overwhelmed.

But they weren't going to die because she was unprepared. *Pegasus* and her crew wouldn't pay the ultimate price because their captain was too young, too inexperienced. Like she knew some outside her tightly knit group had whispered.

No way…

"And I want the forward lasers ready to power up as soon as we emerge."

"Yes, Andi." She could tell she was unnerving Barret a little, but there was something more, something that helped prop up her courage.

She could see his faith in her, his absolute commitment to follow her orders, to trust her completely. To trust her with his life.

She couldn't fail him, nor any of the others.

She wouldn't. Whatever it took.

Chapter Eleven

Sector Nine Stealth Ship Phantasia
In Geosynchronous Orbit
Planet Aquellus, Olystra III
Year 302 AC

"Commander, we're receiving a pulse from the scanner buoys positioned at transit point three."

Boucher's head snapped around. She'd taken great care to cover for every contingency, but she hadn't really expected anyone to show up, at least not so soon. She cursed to herself under her breath. She'd just sent the first expedition down to the surface. She'd lost contact when they'd descended into the watery depths, past the extra range the surface buoys had provided, but that had been expected. It was a waiting game, and she wouldn't start to worry about them for at least eight or ten hours.

But if we've got visitors...

Her best chance to catch a signal from the landing party was to remain in geosynchronous orbit, directly above their submersion point. But if she had to deal with another ship, orbit was the last place she wanted to be.

"All scanner input on my screen." She stared for a few seconds as the data scrolled down the display. There had been something, almost certainly, but there wasn't enough of a reading to identify what had transited. It could as easily have been a chunk of rock or an icy comet that had come through by chance.

"Launch a spread of probes, Drusus. If there's something out there—I mean something manmade—I want to know exactly what we're facing."

"Yes, Commander." The bridge was almost silent save for the clicking of the aide's keyboard. Then, *Phantasia* shook four times in rapid succession, as the long-range probes blasted out and accelerated toward the outer system.

"Probes away," Drusus added, somewhat needlessly.

Boucher sat silently for a minute, perhaps two or three. It would be at least an hour before the probes got far enough out to send back any meaningful data, longer even for their comm signals to reach *Phantasia*. She hoped the scans would prove the buoys had issued a false alarm, that she and her people would remain unmolested long enough to complete their mission. Whatever imperial defenses remained operational were more than enough to worry about...the last thing she needed was some Confed ship full of greedy prospectors. She could destroy any ship likely to come to Aquellus, she was sure enough of that. But any fight would draw her away from the planet, and leave the landing party unsupported.

"Drusus, team number two is to prepare for launch at once." She hadn't intended to send more of her people down, not until she'd heard from the first group...or become sufficiently concerned at the lack of communications to assume something was wrong. But if she ended up having to pull *Phantasia* away from Aquellus to engage an approaching ship, the second team was the only backup her vanguard would have for hours.

"Yes, Commander. Flight deck confirms launch prep initiated on landing sled number two." A few seconds later: "Agent Moreau also acknowledges. Estimate time to full launch readiness, fourteen minutes."

Boucher turned and almost snapped out a reply. Fourteen minutes wasn't the kind of response time she wanted, but she pulled back on her angry response. Her people were on edge, and it made sense to pick her battles. It would be hours before any ship—if there even was a ship out there—could come close enough to Aquellus to compel *Phantasia* to engage. That meant fourteen minutes, even an hour and fourteen minutes, would serve her current needs well enough.

She leaned back in her chair, trying to ignore the growing intensity of her headache. She tried to tell herself it was nothing, most likely some kind of natural phenomenon. The absence of any further contact data supported that conclusion. But her gut resisted the call to relax, and something she couldn't quite pinpoint was telling her there *was* a danger out there.

Whatever it was, she would make sure of one thing. She would be ready for it.

* * *

"Andi, we just picked up...something. It was very quick, a short energy burst, but it was definitely there. Almost like..."

Andi swung around abruptly, her eyes boring into Barret's back as her comrade hunched over his workstation. She could see the tension in his neck and shoulders, and she realized instantly he was concerned. She'd learned to trust Barret's old navy instincts, and she saw no reason to change that practice just then. "Like what?"

"Like some kind of comm burst. I couldn't get a fix. Honestly, we didn't get enough of a reading even to be sure I'm not hallucinating. But it just reminded me of..." He paused for a second or two. "...of an exercise we did when I was posted on *Renown*." He reached out, his hands moving in a blur over his controls. Then: "Andi, you may think I'm crazy, but I think there's a scanner buoy out there. I know it doesn't make any sense, but…"

"No, it makes perfect sense." Andi was generally suspicious, usually verging fairly close to paranoid…but that didn't mean her concerns weren't right more often than they were wrong. "Cut all power…engines, reactor, scanners, everything. Go down to minimums for life support."

"Yes, Andi." Barret flipped a series of controls, and *Pegasus* lurched once as its thrust cut out. An instant later, the dampeners dropped as well, and Andi felt the familiar sensation of weightlessness. She reached out almost instinctively and snapped her harness into place.

"Activate the port side positioning jets…we've got to change our vector, at least as much as we can without sending up a flare to anyone who's watching."

"Andi…I'm not *sure* that was a scanner buoy. I'm not even sure I think it was. It could have been any one of a number of things."

"Like what?" Andi had the advantage, of course. She knew Sector Nine was in play, that they were a far greater danger than she'd let on to her crew. Barret's passing suspicion had become her operative assumption that Union forces were already at Aquellus.

And now they know we're here, too…

Maybe, maybe not. If we run silent, sneak up on the planet, maybe they'll figure an asteroid came through the point.

Pegasus's vector was good, close to the approach course toward the planet. That was a lucky break. She'd have to use the positioning jets, but the compressed gas nozzles were hard to detect at long range, even for sensitive scanning suites.

They're also weak. You're going to have to navigate this one perfectly if you want to get to Aquellus.

She knew one thing for sure. She'd have to fire up the main thrusters to decelerate, and when she did that, *Pegasus* would pop up on every scanner screen anywhere near the planet. Then it would be a dead run for the one place her ship had a chance to hide.

Deep in Aquellus's oceans.

She sucked in a ragged breath. She'd known the mission was a dangerous one. Durango hadn't even tried to lie about that. But the fact that Sector Nine had gotten there first drastically escalated the risk level. Andi had always had a strange sort of confidence, a belief she could get through anything, a positive outlook that somehow existed alongside her pessimism and suspicion.

If there's a Sector Nine ship here, it's probably in orbit.

She needed a way to draw that vessel out, away from the planet. She had to open the way, to give *Pegasus* time to slip past and make a run for the ocean.

She unhooked her harness and stood up, holding onto the armrest to steady herself in the zero g environment. "You've got the con, Barret. I've got an idea…and I need to have a chat with our new engineer about making it a reality."

*   *   *

Still nothing.

Boucher sat, almost stone still, her eyes fixed, as they had been for hours, on the scanning display. She was looking for something, anything, that suggested some kind of ship had transited into the system. But there had been nothing at all.

It was frustrating. If the scanners picked up a vessel, or even some readings that suggested one was out there, that would be definitive. But she couldn't prove a negative. There would be no solid report that there was nothing out there. The chance of a potentially hostile ship lurking in the system declined with every passing minute, every flash report from the probes showing nothing but clear space.

Just what a skilled captain lurking out there would want.

Phantasia was a large and powerful ship by the standards of the craft that typically prowled the Badlands, but Boucher was well aware of the dangers of being caught unaware, regardless of armament. If she returned to orbit, if the ship was attacked from a superior position, while her people were focused on operations down on the planet...anything was possible. Even defeat at the hands of an inferior enemy.

She couldn't divert her attention fully to the two landing parties she'd launched, not until she was sure whatever had caused the initial alarm had been a natural phenomenon.

There was an irony to it. The more time that passed without any contact, the likelier it was her ship was still alone in the system. But if that turned out to be wrong, it also meant whoever was in a vessel out there was extremely competent, a dangerous adversary, regardless of *Phantasia*'s greater resources.

"I want all scanners to remain at full power. The ship will hold position sixty thousand kilometers from Aquellus orbit."

"Commander, we won't be able to receive any transmissions from the landing parties unless we return to orbit." Drusus rarely questioned her orders, but she understood that she must seem paranoid to her subordinate, almost obsessed with the idea of a phantom ship out there. The odds of a real threat were dropping steadily, in every calculation...everywhere except in her gut.

Part of her could *feel* something out there. She knew it was ridiculous, and she scolded herself for harboring such considerations.

But she wasn't ready to reenter orbit. Not yet.

"I understand that, Drusus. Maintain position and scanner power."

If there was something out there, she damned well was going to find it.

* * *

"Do you think you can manage it? We've got a decent

supply of spare parts, but you'll still have to figure out how to make it work. And we don't have much time." Andi stood over a long cylindrical shape in the cargo hold, gripping one of the zero grav handholds and looking at Lex Righter. She realized she was speaking softly, almost a whisper, a pointless affectation. *Pegasus* was on silent running, of course, but that had nothing to do with actual sound.

Silent running. It was a foolish term, one with no real meaning in the vacuum of space. Andi had heard that it traced back centuries—millennia—to the days when submersible craft detected each other by searching for sounds. But the meaning was clear enough, if the words themselves were inaccurate and outdated.

"I don't know…" Righter was looking down at the six meter long object. He'd opened a small panel on the thing, and his eyes darted over the wiring inside. "These are pretty sophisticated units…not something I'd expect to find on a ship like this." He paused, seemingly concerned he'd somehow insulted *Pegasus* or Andi or something.

Andi didn't take offense. The large torpedoes didn't belong on *Pegasus*, and the things had probably cost more than her whole ship was worth. But Durango had given them to her precisely because he'd suspected—known?— that she would encounter Sector Nine at Aquellus. Now, she had to figure out how to use them effectively.

"We don't usually carry ordnance like this, Lex…" She'd continued using the engineer's first name, and she'd made a conscious effort to show him kindness and respect, somewhat of an offset for the rough way she'd handled him at first. "…they're special for this mission. We don't have a launcher, obviously, so we're going to have to figure the best way to roll these things out of the cargo hatch if we get into a fight." Though Andi had wondered what the things might be worth on the black market, assuming she made it back to see.

And that Durango didn't want any unused units returned.

"I think I can handle most of what you want, but the ECM mods worry me. I'm an engineer, and I know my way around most of this pretty well, but I'm not a software expert. You're going to need some significant changes to the basic attack program in these things, and I'd say it's about 50-50 I can manage it."

Andi felt a twinge, and thoughts of Sylene Merrick, *Pegasus*'s old computer expert, and one of her closest friends, passed through her mind. Sy was Vig's older sister, but she'd been retired a year or more. Her often uncanny skills were no more than past chapters in *Pegasus*'s—*Nightrunner*'s—history, and they were sorely missed.

"That will have to do. I've faced worse odds." *That* was definitely true. Andi had come through scrapes where the chance of survival had seemed far less than one in two. Plus, she suspected Righter was underestimating his ability...and even if he couldn't get the changes completely correct, there was still a chance the plan would work. She didn't need to deceive the enemy for any extended period. Just long enough to slip in and make a run for the planet's surface.

"I'll do my best." Andi could hear the emotion in Righter's voice. The resentment, most of it at least, was gone. She'd handled him sternly, but she had also saved his life, and it seemed he had realized that. But there was definitely fear. Andi couldn't argue with that. She was scared, too. Any sane person would be afraid.

"That's all anybody can do...but we don't have much time, so..."

"I'll do it as quickly as possible." Righter had already dropped down to his knees and crouched over the open access panel. "These aren't just military...they're state of the art. How the hell did you end up with them?"

Andi just looked down at the engineer and smiled. Some questions were better left unanswered.

Chapter Twelve

Free Trader Pegasus
Approaching Planet Aquellus
Olystra System
Year 302 AC

"It's ready, Andi...at least as ready as it's going to be."

Andi nodded as Righter's voice came over the comm unit. His tone was full of caution, even uncertainty, but she grasped at what she could. He'd started calling her 'Andi,' and that further supported her feeling that the engineer did not bear active resentment for the way they had met. Righter was stuck on *Pegasus*, of course, so his efforts to make the torpedo modifications she'd requested could have been solely in the interest of self-preservation. But increasing familiarity suggested a growing comfort level...or a degree of sophisticated manipulation she suspected was beyond the engineer's range of such things.

"Very well...and, thank you again, Lex. You're the only one on this ship who could have even given it a legitimate try." A pause. "Is Vig down there? Did he set up the drop rig?" *Pegasus*'s cargo hold had not been built for ejecting weapons into space. She'd sent Vig down there with vague instructions to put some kind of makeshift bracket together, a way to hold the torpedo near the outer doors until she gave the order to drop it.

"I'm here, Andi. My job was a lot easier than Lex's. It's a makeshift kind of thing, but I'm pretty sure it will work."

'Pretty sure' wasn't the kind of thing Andi wanted to bet all their lives on…but it was the best she was likely to get, so she took it.

"Good, Vig. Nice work, both of you. Now make sure everything else is well-secured, and get the hell out of there. We're going to launch that thing in less than ten minutes."

"Everything's bolted in place, Andi. It's all secure."

She tried to gauge the level of certainty in Vig's voice. For a few seconds, she considered going down and checking herself. She was going to bring the atmospheric pressure in the bay down to fifteen percent. That was enough to minimize any damage from explosive decompression, while still providing the outward force to carry the torpedo into space. But if *anything* was loose down there, she would not only lose whatever it was, but also leave a trail of debris that could only lead the enemy toward *Pegasus*.

"Doublecheck, Vig…I mean it. We need to be sure." She found herself surprised when the tension in her legs subsided, and she slouched back into her chair. She trusted Vig.

At least as much as she trusted anybody.

She turned toward Barret. "Keep an eye on the scanners…and especially when we open the hatch." *Pegasus* had escaped detection so far, and her ship had made its way across the system, coming close to achieving the needed vector corrections with the positioning jets. But Andi was going to have to burn the main engines, both to complete the course modifications and to decelerate as the ship approached the planet. She'd be firing the engines at full power, maybe even a bit more…the unavoidable result of waiting for the last minute. There was no way the Sector Nine ship she was sure was lurking out there, could miss that.

Unless the torpedo works, and they're out there chasing shadows.

And if this doesn't work, they'll be on us just as we come into orbit.

"I'm watching, Andi. I don't think I've taken my eyes off this thing in twelve hours." An exaggeration, perhaps, but Andi realized the statement had been at least close to literal truth. Barret's eyes were likely very sore and tired. She could tell how much they burned by the number of times he'd rubbed his hands over them.

She leaned down over the comm unit again. "Lex…go back down to engineering now, okay? If Vig needs help in the hold, Gregor can handle it." Andi was going to need massive engine power on an instant's notice. It was always a risky proposition to ramp up reactor output too quickly, and having the ship's engineer in place could be the margin that saved all of them in a pinch.

"I'm on the way."

Andi nodded, and she took a deep breath. Then she looked over at the display, and the small chronometer counting down in the lower corner.

Four minutes…then we'll see if we can pull this off…

Of course, her plan would only get *Pegasus* down into the planet's atmosphere, and with luck, under its uncharted seas where it had some hope of eluding the enemy scanners. Getting out would be another thing entirely.

But she'd worry about that later.

* * *

Boucher's eyes were fixed on the large screen at the end of *Phantasia*'s bridge. An instant before, there had been nothing, and now the readings were pouring in, powerful thrust, significant energy output…and a moment later, the first estimated mass readings.

Twelve thousand tons…just about the mass she'd expect for a Badlands prospecting ship.

Her first reaction had been to break out of orbit, to make a run directly at the ship and blast it to atoms before it could escape. But something was wrong. How had the vessel gotten so far in-system?

Boucher had always had a keen sense for danger. If the vessel she was tracking was only a converted freighter, she doubted it could have come so far undetected. And, even if it had coasted in with its power systems at minimal output, why was it blasting its engines so hard just then? Deceleration would be necessary to approach the planet and land, but the course she saw on her screen was heading away from Aquellus.

She had been on the lookout for adventurers, even for the armed pirates that sometimes preyed on prospecting vessels. But now something else occurred to her.

Confederation Intelligence…

Sector Nine considered itself superior to its rival, sometimes to the point of unbridled arrogance, but Boucher was more cautious. The Confederation spy agency had suffered under a series of poor leaders, and it perennially had to struggle with the Senate to maintain its funding levels, but she suspected their newest chief, Gary Holsten, would prove to be a far more dangerous adversary than those who had come before. He was still hampered by lower budgets and susceptible to political interference, but there was something about him, at least from the dossier's she had seen, something that told her he would handle all of that with considerable ability. Sector Nine benefitted greatly from its second role of keeping the Union population in line, a service it provided for its political masters…and one that ensured a continued stream of generous budgets.

Most of Sector Nine had regarded the news of Holsten's appointment with derision, calling him a spoiled and decadent child of wealth who'd bought his appointment, but Boucher wasn't so sure. There was something about him that seemed different, at least from the data to which she had access, and she was concerned about who he might have sent to Aquellus.

"Prepare to activate engines, Drusus. Set a course toward the new contact." Whatever that was out there, she *had* to do something. She wasn't going to rush right at the thing…she just wanted it to look like she was. "And get the two attack ships ready to launch." *Phantasia* carried a pair of modified two-man fighters augmented with bombing kits. They gave her a strike capability without exposing her ship to counterattack. If that contact was just a prospector's vessel, the bombers would obliterate it.

And if it was something more, something truly dangerous, she would know before *Phantasia* was close enough to be in danger.

"Engine room reports ready for full thrust on your command. And the bomber crews are en route to the bay. They'll be ready to launch in six minutes."

"Very well." She sat stone still, her eyes still fixed on the display. Her mind was racing, trying to think of anything else she could do. Most likely, she realized, that *was* just some adventurer's ship out there. The sources of leads on Badlands artifacts weren't the most reliable, and despite Sector Nine's efforts to instill fear into those they bribed, it was notoriously difficult to keep such things secret for very long.

Especially after several previous expeditions were sent…and vanished.

Ghost stories spread quickly in places like Dannith's Spacer's District.

She wasn't going to take any chances. Whatever that was out there was dangerous. That might be a gut reaction devoid of much supporting evidence, but her instincts had done well for her so far. She wasn't going to abandon them now.

* * *

"Andi, we've got to decelerate now. Another ninety seconds, and we won't have time, not before we reach the planet."

No, Barret, we won't. At least not at normal reactor output.

"Maintain silent running." She leaned over the comm. "Lex, are you in position?"

"Yes, Andi."

"I'm going to need every watt you can get out of that reactor when I call for it...and that means pushing well past redline."

"Understood. I'm ready."

She looked back up, her eyes finding the display. There was a ship in the system, and it was a threat. Any question of that was long gone. The mass readings suggested it was larger than *Pegasus*, by a factor of at least three. She'd managed to draw it out of orbit with her ruse, but not far enough. Not yet, at least.

Whoever is commanding that thing is cautious...and probably smart, too...

She had to wait for the ship to move, to close with the disguised torpedo. She needed more distance, more time.

But she didn't have it.

Andi had hoped the enemy ship would advance right at the contact she'd created, blast toward the torpedo that was very likely showing up in their scans as a converted freighter, at least if Lex Righter had managed to program the ECM correctly. She'd even dared to imagine it would get close enough to be damaged or destroyed when the warhead detonated, though she'd have settled for simply pulling the ship far enough from Aquellus. That wouldn't help when they were on their way back, trying to get past that vessel, but that was a concern for later.

One problem at a time. There was no point in worrying about escape, not yet. First, they had to survive long enough for that to be an issue.

"Andi…" Barret again, the tension in his voice ratcheting up with each passing moment.

She looked at the small screen on her workstation, at the AI's running calculation. It would take one hundred one percent of regulation output to decelerate in time to enter orbit…assuming she gave the orders immediately.

But the enemy was still too close.

"Not yet." Her response was sharper than she'd intended. She was sure what she had to do, and she trusted her timing. But that didn't make her immune to stress.

She watched as the number on the monitor clicked up, a tenth of a percent at a time. One hundred one point five.

Point six.

She looked up at the main display, staring, almost willing the Union ship to fire its engines. Then she saw it. Two smaller contacts, moving from the main ship.

Shuttles? Fighters?

The enemy ship was large in comparison to *Pegasus*, but it was no carrier. Still, it could have a launch bay, or even a few ships docked externally. Getting those kinds of details would require active scans, and that was out of the question, at least until *Pegasus* dropped its silent running and made a break for Aquellus.

And by then, it would be irrelevant.

One hundred two…

Andi's hands tightened, almost into fists. She would wait as long as she could, but she was running out of time. *Pegasus* could manage 102.5, maybe even 103, but if she had to push the reactor and engines harder than that, she risked a meaningful chance of malfunction.

And just about any equipment failure right then meant almost certain death.

Her palms were wet inside her fists, the sweat building up, seeping through her fingers. She had to remind herself to breathe or she just sat there holding her breath. Andi was a stone-cold gambler with a grim poker face. But she was out of time, and she knew it. And that ship's not going any farther. They're going to wait and see what those small craft find.

"Alright, Lex, let's…"

Her eyes darted back to the display. The Union ship *had* increased its thrust, a little. It wasn't the move she'd hoped for, but just maybe it would be enough.

It was the best chance she was going to get.

"Full thrusters now, one hundred three on the reactor." She'd intended to warn the others, to make sure they were strapped in, but she realized she'd been too focused on the display, and she'd forgotten. It didn't matter. If she failed, they'd all be dead…and if they made it, a few scrapes and bruises were a small price to pay.

She felt the ship shaking as the reactor flared up almost immediately to full power levels and beyond. The pressure slammed into her, the full 12g at first, before the dampeners came back online and cut the effective force to about 2g.

She winced in pain from the initial shock of acceleration. She guessed she'd just pulled a muscle, but there was some chance she'd cracked a rib. It didn't matter. She was going to do what she had to do, and she would never stop, not while she had the slightest bit of strength left.

"Approaching planetary orbit, Andi." She could tell from Barret's voice, he too, was in some degree of pain.

"Stay on course." She'd already calculated the insertion vector, but even as she uttered the command, her fingers moved over her controls, increasing the descent angle. *Pegasus* had a jump on the Union ship—and she was still only assuming the vessel was a Sector Nine asset—but that was far from a guarantee. Every second she could shave increased their chances of making it.

But it's going to get hot out there…

The planet's heavy atmosphere was going to exacerbate the problem. *Pegasus*'s hull was tough, but she was about to put the reinforced alloy to the test.

"Andi, the enemy ship is reversing thrust. It looks like they're trying to come around."

They're coming after us.

Andi knew the Union vessel couldn't catch *Pegasus*, not before her ship slipped beneath the waves, but she had no idea what kind of armament the thing mounted. They didn't have to reach *Pegasus*'s position. They just get into firing range.

And she had no idea what that was. The thick atmosphere would attenuate fire, but the ranges involved would be vastly smaller than those typical for space combat.

"Active scans, Barret...now!" *Pegasus* wasn't hiding anymore, and Andi wanted to know what was going on with the torpedo. The screen flickered to a second or two, and then three icons appeared.

The torpedo was in the center of the screen, moving at close to 0.01c. The two fighters were closing. Andi felt a burst of excitement. The ECM *was* working. They still believed they were chasing a ship.

And that's keeping them from joining the mother ship in going after us...

It wasn't everything, but Andi suspected the two attack craft would have had an easier time in the atmosphere than the larger vessel, and she was glad to see them out of the chase. *Pegasus* was fully streamlined for planetary landings, but she doubted the Union ship was. The actives scans were giving her a closer look, and her first educated guess was the vessel was landing-capable, but also that it would handle like a pig in thick air like Aquellus's.

Every advantage helped.

"Moving below close orbit level, Andi. Forty seconds to upper atmosphere."

Andi reached out and put her hand on the controls. The AI had brought *Pegasus* this far, but she was going to take her ship through the heavy atmosphere herself. She glanced over at the screen, at the enemy ship moving back toward the planet. In open space, the enemy would already be firing, but the Union vessel would have to get closer to hit *Pegasus* in the atmosphere.

Hopefully, a lot closer...

Andi pushed the throttle forward, further deepening the angle. The sooner she could get under the cover of the Aquellian ocean, the better.

Pegasus shook hard as the ship raced down into the upper atmosphere, the air pressure and wild gusts buffeting the vessel hard. The hull temperature started rising almost immediately. Two hundred degrees, three hundred.

Andi held tightly to the controls, trying to offset the increasing turbulence. The air pressure was rising steadily, and the hull temperature passed five hundred degrees.

Then, she saw a flash on the scanner.

She told herself there were a hundred things it could have been, but that wasn't true. She knew exactly what had happened.

The enemy ship had opened fire.

The laser pulse had been badly attenuated, its power reduced to a fraction of its original levels...but she knew it wouldn't take much to wound *Pegasus*, not while the ship was navigating the thickening atmosphere. The slightest hull breach, or even a material weakening of a section of alloy, could prove fatal to all aboard.

Her instinct was to initiate evasive maneuvers, but it just wasn't possible. It was taking all she had, and all her engines could manage, to keep *Pegasus* on course through the thickening air. The carefully executed shifts in lateral thrust so common in space combat wouldn't work in an atmosphere.

She checked the altitude...ten kilometers from sea level. Her eye moved toward the screen displaying input from the exterior feeds. The hull was glowing a bright orangey-red, and a quick check showed the temperature exceeded twelve hundred degrees.

Pegasus's hull was an alloy of titanium, tungsten, and half a dozen other metals. She had no idea of the proportions, or how much of the high-melting point tungsten was in the mix. She could only guess at the metal's endurance. *Maybe eighteen hundred...two thousand if we're lucky.*

The hull was at fourteen hundred already, up almost two hundred in the past twenty seconds, and she had both hands on the controls, trying desperately to stabilize the ship, even as the vastly strengthening air currents buffeted it. The altitude was down under five kilometers, but now the pursuing enemy ship was entering the atmosphere as well. Andi had been right, the Union vessel handled like a pig, even in the lighter air pressure of the upper atmosphere. Still, there were barely twenty kilometers between the two vessels now, and that was almost nothing in terms of space combat.

But the atmosphere changed that whole dynamic. The thick air around *Pegasus* was almost like armor plating, and the seemingly powerful lasers of the pursuing ship zipped past the hull, not much more powerful at the current distance than a strong flashlight. Still, *Pegasus*'s hull was compromised and far more vulnerable than it usually was. The last thing she needed now was any laser impact striking her tortured ship. An extra hundred degrees could be the difference, the extra push that turned a section of the hull into liquid...and started a landslide of damage that destroyed *Pegasus.*

Three kilometers. Hull temperature fifteen hundred.

It was going to be close. Andi could feel her hands trying to move, to pull back on the throttle. She had to reduce the ship's descent angle, no matter how close on her tail that enemy ship was. She wasn't going to make it otherwise.

But if she slowed down too much, the enemy might just score that fatal hit.

She gritted her teeth and held the angle. If she had to bet on something she couldn't control, she'd rather place her faith in her ship than count on some Union gunner continuing to miss.

"C'mon, baby...I know it's hot out there...but we're close now."

So close...

"Andi, we've *got* to slow down. At this speed and angle, that waterline's going to be like solid concrete."

She nodded. She knew Barret was right...but she could also see the Union ship closing. Its fire coming closer and closer with each volley.

She had to keep going. She'd pull up at the last second to minimize the impact, but she couldn't afford any more time than that.

Two kilometers.

The hull temperature was eighteen hundred. She felt her stomach twisting into knots, and she knew any instant, the overheated metal could fail. At *Pegasus*'s speed, a half-meter breach would be enough to tear the ship apart in a matter of seconds. Aquellus's heavy air would stream in with unimaginable force, and that would be the end.

One kilometer. A laser blast ripped by, less than twenty meters to port. It was still severely weakened, but the scanners picked up energy levels almost twice those of the last volley. One hit like that would be enough, at least with the alloy so close to its melting point. There wasn't a spot on the hull that could endure that impact, not just then.

The ship was shaking hard, bouncing all around, despite her best efforts to hold it on course. It was hot on the bridge—close to fifty degrees, and the sweat was pouring off her in waves. Her shirt was plastered to her back, and she slid around on the slick, wet leather of her seat. But she stayed focused, her eyes fixed, her soaking wet hands somehow holding onto the controls.

Her board showed a dozen system failures, mostly burnouts. She ignored them all. There was nothing she could do, nothing but bring her ship down into the waves below…in one piece.

Five hundred meters. She pulled back hard on the throttle, trying to level off the ship's approach. But there was no response.

She pulled again, harder. Still nothing.

Two hundred meters.

She popped open the emergency controls, and pulled back on the small switch inside.

Then she tried again, knowing it was her last chance.

"Come on, baby…for me…"

She felt a wild lurch, as *Pegasus* responded, almost as if answering her plea. The ship's approach angle lessened as the thrust blasted from the engines…but it was too late. The ocean surface was just ahead.

Andi took a deep breath, wondering if it would be her last…and then *Pegasus* slammed hard into the water. The ship skimmed along the surface for a few seconds, bouncing up twenty or thirty meters and then coming down again. Hard.

A spray of water flew across the bridge as a gash opened in the hull, and Andi could hear the hissing of steam from outside as the white hot alloy met the far cooler water. She struggled to maintain control, but it was a hopeless effort. The ship bounced along across the waves for another few hundred meters, tortuous creaking sounds announcing damage being suffered all around her. Then, *Pegasus* flipped up in the air, and came down hard, capsizing almost immediately.

Andi felt her harness bite into her shoulders as it held her in place, upside down and looking at the bridge's ceiling, now below her. Her stomach twisted into a roiling mass, and she felt the bile rising up, spitting out of her mouth as she tried to reach for the controls.

There were at least two more leaks on the bridge now, and more, she suspected elsewhere. She knew she had to get out of her chair, try somehow to save her ship. But her hands clawed ineffectually at her harness, and then, a few seconds later, *Pegasus* jerked hard, its tail jutting up toward the Aquellian sky, as its bow slipped beneath the waves of the planet's vast sea…and then the ship slid down, plunging into the deep blue depths.

Chapter Thirteen

Samis Station Three
Orbiting Ventica VII
Year 302 AC

"You've been in a stupor for weeks now, Durango. I know you like her, or at least you respect her. But there was no choice. We couldn't send a navy ship, not without Senate authorization. And involving the politicians would have tied our hands even more." Gary Holsten almost grunted. The new head of Confederation Intelligence stared across the room at his operative, a man known to the adventurers of the frontier as someone who could fix their ships, and maybe get them a job, all on the down low. None of his many and varied clients and contacts knew he held another position, one as an operative for Confederation Intelligence.

Or that Samis had been conceived, funded, and built by the spy agency. Not even the vast multitudes who crewed the stations and provided the vast menu of quasi-illicit services they provided, had any idea they were working for Gary Holsten. He most common assumption was that Samis was owned by a secret consortium of underworld organizations, and that rumor suited Holsten just fine.

Holsten had actually come very close to doing the very thing he'd just described. He was still reasonably new to his post, and disregarding direct Senate orders was still something of a reach for him. He'd spent considerable time preparing his arguments, and he'd even ordered his ship to prepare for a trip back to Megara, but then he asked himself a simple question. *What will you do if they say no? Let the Union gain the upper hand, build enough of a lead to win the next war?*

"She may be a good captain, and an admirable person in her own way, Durango, but remember, she *is* a criminal. Don't forget that. She's dealt in Badlands contraband who knows how many times…one of those, at least, with you." The irony that Andi had committed one of her crimes dealing with his own people wasn't lost on Holsten, but he was trying to make a point, not engage in a debate on principles. "And she shot up the Port Royal spaceport on her way out to the Badlands. I was able to intervene and prevent any immediate naval pursuit—and she proved adept enough to evade the system defense yokels—but she's not exactly an innocent. Nor is she the child she looks like, the helpless young girl she can pretend to be. Not with her background."

"I know all of that, sir. But I still wonder if there wasn't another way." The shipyard manager and old tech fence—and Confederation spy as well—looked morose.

"There wasn't." A pause. "Durango, you've been at this game for two years now. You were one of my first recruits after taking over the agency, and even before that, you worked on Samis without knowing it was a Confederation Intelligence front. You know what we do, and you know why we do it. I don't take Andromeda Lafarge's life lightly, nor those of her people. But four billion Confederation citizens died in the last war with the Union. And three billion in the one before that. We've still got eight old Confederation worlds under Union control, billions more living in a totalitarian nightmare. Andi Lafarge and her people could be the most commendable group we've ever encountered, but would it matter? Can their few lives match up to the stakes here? You saw the intel as well as I did. If the artifacts we think are on Aquellus are actually out there, it could move AI technology forward by a generation or more. We've got the edge in that now, by the slimmest margin. What do you think would happen if the Union leapfrogged us in that area? They've already got twice the worlds we do and half again as many hulls. Do you want the navy fighting the next war unable to target Union ships as well as being outnumbered? Do you want to see this rogue paradise here on the Badlands border turned over to Sector Nine? Do you want to see some Union commissar sitting in the ruins of the Senate Compound, sending people to death camps? I'm not fan of our esteemed leaders and their corruption and arrogance. But neither of us believes they are remotely comparable to the psychopaths that run the Union."

"Of course not. I know why we do what we do." There was realization in Durango's tone, but still some doubt. "But I volunteered, didn't I? You recruited me, gave me the speech about defending what was important. We didn't do that with Andi. We just lured her in, even took advantage of her situation by dangling some money—and medical care for her injured friend—in front of her. How could she have refused?"

"How are we hurting her? By saving and protecting her wounded friend? By repairing her ship and offering her a large reward for completing the mission? This is what she *does*, Durango, whether or not we're involved. She takes leads—buys them—from some of the most disreputable types imaginable, and then she plunges into an area of space almost unknown to us, far from any protection, any help. She chose a life of danger, we didn't lure her into it. She managed to get into a fight with Sector Nine before we were involved, so how different is this? If anything, she's far likelier to survive with us helping her, whether she knows about it or not. She'd has three million credits of torpedoes in her hold. You think she'd have that on a mission she picked up in some Spacer's District bar?"

Durango knew Holsten's words were nothing but the truth. But he was still uncomfortable. And worries.

The two men were both silent for a moment. Then, Holsten spoke again. "If it helps you, I find it difficult, too. I haven't met Andi Lafarge, and all I know of her is what you've told me, plus what is in the mission reports, but it is hard to send people into danger, and even harder when they're people we like and admire. But it's our duty to overcome such doubts, to do what we must to preserve what little exists in the galaxy of freedom. We're behind the enemy on this operation, Durango, and Andromeda Lafarge and *Pegasus* are all we've got. As much as they're at risk in this, so is the Confederation itself. If Andi fails, the ramifications go well beyond her death and those of her crew. The lives and futures of billions could be at stake."

Durango nodded. Holsten had swung somewhat to the dramatic, but his words hit all the harder for the fact that he'd told only the hard truth. Durango wondered if he'd feel better if he'd been able to tell Andi what was truly at stake, if he'd been able to recruit her openly to serve the Confederation.

Or would that have been worse for her? She sees that there is freedom in many places, no doubt, and prosperity. But she was born into abject poverty, in a place with little effective liberty. She found her way out...into a profession where she is harassed by the authorities, pushed into virtual outlawry. Would she have felt better knowing she was serving a Confederation that had largely failed her at every turn? Or is she better off just thinking she was there for gain, to make a profit for herself and for her loyal crew, probably the only people in the galaxy that actually mean anything to hers?

"I understand, sir." A pause. "I just...I just hope they make it back. Andi doesn't fit any normal definition of a solid citizen, not by a longshot. But there's something about her. I think she has a real future, something beyond

Badlands prospecting…and I hope we haven't cut that off at the root."

*   *   *

Carmichael twitched nervously in the chair. It was a hard bench, and he wondered if it had been specifically designed to be uncomfortable. The way Sector Nine approached things, he figured that was a likely prospect. He knew why he was there, why he had been for almost half an hour. Brewer was sending a message. Carmichael understood, but he still bristled with barely contained rage. The gangster sent such signals to people, he didn't receive them.

But as much of a bully as he was by nature, Carmichael was scared to death of Sector Nine. It was treason to deal with the Union spy agency, of course, but fear of being caught and prosecuted was far down on his list. He knew just how Sector Nine operated. The Intelligence outfit generally rewarded those who served it well…but those who failed were treated harshly. And, they rarely hesitated to discard someone—in the most sinister definition of that term—when it served their purposes, or when an asset was no longer deemed valuable.

Carmichael knew Sector Nine well enough, mostly because he owed his modest criminal empire to the agency. He'd cooperated with the Union spies for years, helping them hire prospecting teams to follow up on leads…and ensuring that any finds resulting from such operations ended up securely in their hands. It made him a traitor, at least most people would see it like that, but it had also made him rich.

"I thought we agreed not to meet in person again, at least not unless there was an emergency." Carmichael hadn't noticed the man slipping into the room. The figure standing in front of him was nearly two meters tall, with sandy hair and a nasty facial scar.

Brewer.

"There is something of an emergency."

"To you, perhaps, Carmichael, but do you think I concern myself with petty disputes among District...operators?"

Carmichael stood up, trying to equalize the dynamic of the discussion, but falling short in the shadow of the near giant standing in front of him. "The damage I suffered was not at the hands of a competitor. It was a Badlands prospector and her crew, one who has long been a thorn in my side."

"Again, Carmichael, I fail to see how this involves me. I assisted you in building your organization so that you would be able to aid me when I needed it...not so you could rush to me for help every time you encounter a problem."

"I am not here, Brewer, because she is a problem for me..." A lie, of course, but one with *some* truth in it. Carmichael was hoping Brewer would help him rid himself of Andi...but he knew his adversary was also Sector Nine's enemy. "...I am here to help you solve a problem or yours, or at least to settle a score. I understand your organization believes strongly in dealing with its enemies in a permanent way. I thought surely you would be interested in assistance in that area."

Brewer stared back, his face mostly a mask of emotionlessness, but Carmichael could see the agent was interested in what he had to say.

"Do you remember a certain captain named Lorillard.? He commanded a ship called *Nightrunner*. Would it intrigue you to know his handpicked successor, a woman I also believe is of interest to you, was now the captain of that vessel, since renamed *Pegasus*?"

"You are sure of this? You know where Andromeda Lafarge is...and you are certain the vessel *Pegasus* is *Nightrunner*?" Brewer let his guard down further, and Carmichael was sure he'd hooked his prey.

"I am sure."

"It was this *Pegasus* that fought with your people in the spaceport?"

"Yes."

"Do you know where that ship is now? My sources inform me the vessel lifted off after creating a considerable ruckus, and then outran the system patrol to escape into the Badlands. Where was Andromeda Lafarge headed? Do you have any information on her whereabouts or intentions?"

Carmichael was silent for a moment, then he shook his head and said, "No, unfortunately I do not. I was able to trace some of her recent movements. *Pegasus* fled Dannith after my first…unpleasant…encounter with Captain Lafarge. The ship was gone for a short while, and then it returned unexpectedly, after bribing someone at landing control to hide her ship's identity. I do not know where she was in the time between her initial departure and her return. If was not long enough for a trip to the Badlands or, indeed, any other interstellar voyage. Perhaps, she was simply hiding out somewhere in the system…or…"

"Samis." Brewer's tone was one of certainty. "She must have gone to Samis. There is no other place within five systems she could have replaced *Nightrunner*'s beacon and replaced the ship's old identity with a new one…one that checks out in records systems. That means she has a relationship with someone there. Perhaps her ship needed more repairs, or…"

Carmichael stared at the tall man. "Or?" The gangster didn't know much about Samis, nor the mysterious owners of the outer system facility. But there were rumors, dozens of rumors actually, many contradicting each other.

"Or…something else. It is possible there are more reasons Captain Lafarge would have gone to Samis than simply to hide or obtain repairs."

Carmichael could see Brewer knew more than he did, or at least that the Union operative had some idea of what

Andi Lafarge might have been up to on Samis…and he looked concerned about it.

More concerned than Carmichael had ever seen the normally self-assured spy.

"Very well, Carmichael," Brewer finally said. "The information you provided might indeed be of some value. And it will serve your purposes, too. Andromeda Lafarge has been a thorn in our side for far too long, one we will now remove…and in doing so, solve one of your problems as well. This, I trust, will make us even on this particular transaction."

Carmichael smiled. "Yes, Brewer, it will. I can rebuild my organization, negotiate truces with my rivals until I regain my strength…as long as I don't have to worry about Andi Lafarge." Carmichael hated himself for being scared of Andi. But that didn't change the reality that he *was* afraid of the outlaw captain. Very afraid.

"You won't have to worry about Captain Lafarge for long, Carmichael. She will have to return to Dannith at some point…and we will be waiting." The spy was silent for a moment, his mind clearly somewhere beyond Dannith. "Unless we find her before she comes back."

Chapter Fourteen

Sector Nine Stealth Ship Phantasia
Olystra System
Year 302 AC

"Contact number two has crashed into the sea, Commander. Their descent angle was critically steep. It is likely they were destroyed on impact."

Boucher frowned. I wouldn't assume that, Drusus, and you shouldn't either. The vessel is almost certainly damaged, but we cannot be sure it is not salvageable without further inspection." A pause. "Prep team three for immediate launch. They are to descend into the Aquellian sea and locate that ship...or its remains. They are to exercise extreme caution, and to approach only if the vessel is destroyed or critically damaged. If the ship appears to remain functional, they are to break off at once and report."

"Yes, Commander."

"Load navigational data into the landing sled's AI, including trajectory and speed of impact with the ocean surface...and bring us back to high orbit as soon as team three is away." *Phantasia* was a large ship, barely streamlined enough for atmospheric operations. The vessel handled sluggishly in air, and Boucher wasn't about to test it out in the even more difficult underwater environment.

Besides, there was still another contact in the system, one her attack ships were about to engage. And she'd lost radio contact with the bombers once *Phantasia* had entered the atmosphere. It was time to see what was going on up there.

She sat quietly as the final lander prepped for launch, and then she watched as the sled blasted its way out of the launch bay and into the rough air currents above Aquellus's planetwide sea. She waited a few seconds after the lander had cleared *Phantasia*, and the she turned toward Drusus, about to repeat her order about returning to orbit. But the aid spoke first.

"Commencing ascent to orbit, Commander. Thrust in three, two, one..."

Boucher felt the force of the ship's engines, and then the rocking as the vessel pushed its way up through the planet's atmosphere. *Phantasia* shook hard, its partially streamlined hull vulnerable to the strong wind gusts buffeting it, even as the vessel rose above the zone of the heaviest air pressure.

The ship continued, the image on the screen moving from light blue to a darker shade, and finally to black as the border of space loomed ahead.

"Continue out of orbit, Drusus. Clear the planet and locate the attack ships. I want an immediate status update."

"Yes, Commander." A moment passed, and then Boucher felt the dampeners kick in, replacing the feeling of 3g acceleration with the sensation of Montmirail-normal 1.07g.

A few seconds later: "We've got the bombers, Commander. They're moving in on the contact now."

Boucher could already see the image on the display, the two attack ships approaching the enemy contact. She stared at the readings for a few seconds, and her eyes locked on the data stream scrolling down the side.

Something isn't right...

The scanners had pegged the contact as a ship, one of a mass comparable to a typical Badlands prospecting vessel, not unlike the one she'd chased down to the Aquellian sea. But the data flow was wobbling, and the AI's assignment of certainty had dropped from eighty-nine percent to sixty-one.

And it was still falling.

Her eyes darted down to her own screen, her hands moving over the controls. Then she saw it, the problem the AI was reviewing. It was minute, the kind of thing she'd never have noticed herself, nor even detected with her own senses. But the AI had confirmed and reconfirmed the inconsistency. The ship, what she *thought* was a ship, had entered an area on the extreme fringes of the system's asteroid belt. And it wasn't exerting the expected gravity on the surrounding interplanetary particulate that it should have been. The differences were minute, the gravitational force exerted by something the size of a ship almost undetectable.

But almost undetectable wasn't undetectable. And the effect, the infinitesimal pull on the dust clouds and small bits of rock, was far less than it should have been. By a factor of a hundred or more.

"Call off the attack ships...now!" But even as the words came out of her mouth, she could see it was too late. The contact dropped its cloak an instant later, revealing it to be a *much* smaller ship.

No...not a ship...

The contact's thrusters fired up, bringing it around, directly toward her approaching bombers. The g force readings were high, impossibly so for an occupied vessel, and they confirmed what she'd feared. That was no ship. The 80g or more of acceleration her scanners were reading proved that.

A robot craft? A probe?

Her heart sank as realization set in.

"I said get those ships out of there!" The anger in her voice was directed at Drusus, but it was her frustration infuriating her, not her aide. Drusus had already sent her orders, but the bombers were eight light seconds away. No known force in the universe could speed the transmission of her command.

And eight seconds might prove to be too long.

She knew what was going to happen, even as she watched in growing horror. Fifteen seconds later, she watched the bombers suddenly push their engines to full power, struggling to come about, to escape the thing. They had received her command, and she knew she was watching the events of eight seconds earlier.

The bombers struggled to pull away from the contact—and she was sure by then it was a weapon of some kind—bearing down on them with rapidly increasing velocity.

She felt the urge to shout out another command, but the pointlessness of it held her back. She'd already ordered the ships to break off...and they were already doing so. Direction wasn't the problem.

Time was. And she had no commands that would alter that unstoppable force.

She watched the weapon—and the data streaming finally allowed the AI to offer a likely identification, some kind of torpedo, a big one—her eyes glued to the screen as it closed rapidly with her fleeing attack craft. The last few seconds dragged out, each one seeming like minutes to her, even hours.

Then she saw a flash on the screen, almost certainly the weapon detonating. She could tell immediately, the explosion had been a massive one, far more powerful than she'd expected. Whatever payload that warhead had carried, it was massive. Then she saw the AI's preliminary calculation.

One point six gigatons.

That's not possible...

As she looked, she could see immediately that one of her ships was gone. Just gone.

The other was moving along, clearly damaged, its data feeds wild and irregular. She turned toward Drusus, about to order *Phantasia* to close, to move to retrieve the crippled bomber, but then she hesitated. There was nothing else on the scanner, but that didn't calm her concern. There were a hundred ways to hide something in a solar system, and a weapon that powerful was a deadly threat not just to small attack craft, but to *Phantasia* itself.

She remained still, silent, even as the urge to move toward the stricken ship beat at her defenses. But then, the bomber spared her the torment. It didn't vanish as the other one had, consumed in thermonuclear fury, but its vector stabilized, its engines clearly dead, its power levels down to dead zero.

Its life support complete offline.

Boucher knew the two crew onboard were dead, or that they were dying just then and would be gone long before *Phantasia* could reach them. She was a Sector Nine section chief, immersed in the Union philosophy of the relentless pursuit of power. She didn't mourn for the four crew lost. They were expendable enough. But the loss of combat power, of her entire mobile attack capability, *that* concerned her.

And it upped the stakes.

It wasn't just the bombers. It was a starkly cold realization.

That torpedo had been solidly military grade, a weapon far more powerful than anything she possessed, if somewhat difficult to employ without surprise.

It was more than just the hardware, though. It was a question she found deeply troubling.

What the hell is some Badlands prospector doing with state of the art military ordnance?

* * *

"I think we've found something, sir." Antoinette Bissel turned from the scanner board and looked at Caron. "It's faint, and…different…from anything I've seen before, but it's definitely some kind of energy reading."

Caron leaned forward, more an expression of the tension he felt than anything else. He looked at the small screen in front of him, now displaying a wave pattern. It was an energy reading, he was almost sure of that, but Bissel was correct. It didn't match any known patterns. He didn't have to figure it out, he just had to decide if it marked the location of the imperial facility supposedly located nearby.

"AI confirms that it's not natural, and that means…"

"Yes." He interrupted Bissel. He'd seen the AI report just before she'd spoken, and a twinge of fear had accompanied his realization. He'd found what he was looking for, almost certainly…and that meant it was time to push forward into the remnant of an almost forgotten time. And a place where several previous expeditions had disappeared. "Increase active scanner pulses. We've got a basic location, so let's see if we can narrow that down some. There's got to be some kind of base or facility down here. Let's find it." *And whatever it is, if we're picking up an energy wave, it's still operational, at least partially.*

The ghostly feeling of long-dead imperial sites was difficult enough to endure. Caron had been at a few surface digs, walked along the ruins of long-dead cities. But two kilometers under the sea, and a base still showing some kind of power generation…it was all he could do to hold back the shakes threatening to take him.

He looked at the scanner screen, even as the first data came in from the pulses his small craft was sending out. There was nothing further…yet. Only sharp rock formations, towering undersea mountains that formed small shelves of flat terrain almost two kilometers below the surface. The more or less flat sections of rock clinging to the mountains were surrounded by massive chasms sinking into the murky blackness to almost unimaginable depths. He'd ordered a series of scans when the ship had first descended, but the deepest undersea valleys defied the range of his equipment. More than fifty kilometers was all he'd been able to ascertain, at least in the deepest spots, and still without a discernible bottom.

"Bring us toward that energy wave, Antoinette. Stabilize our depth at two kilometers, and increase active scanners gradually." Caron didn't really imagine a full-scale imperial security system was actually still operational, but he wasn't going to be careless. Three missions had been lost, and though none of those vessels had possessed the resources *Phantasia* and its crew did, nor the fully combat ready Foudre Rouge the current operation possessed, Caron wasn't about to lose his caution.

"Yes, sir...moving toward the readings now, speed twenty meters per second."

Caron nodded. The ship was moving forward, even as the water currents pushed it around, requiring constant adjustments. The engines were on minimal power, but even so, the heat from the engine was leaving a plume of steam rising up before the colder water above began to condense the vapor back into liquid. The whole thing was making movement difficult, and Bissel was busily adjusting the course every few seconds.

Caron looked at the screen, his eyes focused on the energy readings. For the first moment, they looked unchanged, but then he could see the power level rising as the sled moved forward. They were getting closer, and with each hundred or two hundred meters, the energy wave grew in power. It was still less than he'd expect from a truly operational facility, but it was well beyond minimal levels...and certainly enough to support some degree of defensive array.

"Stay locked on the power readings...and get some active scanner pulses bouncing off those rock formations. The facility's got to be there somewhere."

"Yes, sir." A few seconds later: "Scanners show solid

rock ahead, all results…no, wait. We've got something. Eight degrees off our current heading, depth sixty meters above."

"Bring us in directly at those readings." Caron stared at his own screen, confirming what Bissel had just told him. Then, he flipped the comm channel to the rear hold. "Lieutenant, get your people ready. I want your suits checked and rechecked, and all weapons prepped for action."

"Yes, sir!" The officer snapped out his response. Caron cut the line before even acknowledging. Like so many Sector Nine agents, and even spacers in the fleet, he found the Foudre Rouge unnerving. The clone soldiers fought well, there was no denying that, and they followed orders to the letter. But they still made him uncomfortable.

"We're closing on the nearest detectable cavity inside the rock, sir. It looks big."

"Maneuver us as close as possible, and then bring the ship down. The Foudre Rouge will deploy out the rear hatch."

"Yes, sir."

Caron sat quietly as Bissel lowered the thrust levels further, and activated the forward positioning jets to bring the ship almost to a halt. The small craft crept forward, moving at less than one meter per second, and with a flip of a switch, Bissel turned on the forward lights.

Caron stared out the windows, his eyes staring directly at the deep gray of the rock wall just ahead. It looked very much like a mountain, though it was buried deep under the sea. There were sharp drop-offs all around, descending into the terrifying blackness. Caron had never been particularly nervous around bodies of water, but the almost unimaginable depths of the Aquellian ocean was starting to get to him. He looked at his screen again, transfixed by the data feed from the bottom of the ship. The lights were powerful, but they didn't extend very far into the murky darkness two kilometers below the surface. Caron found himself wondering how far down it went, how many kilometers—dozens of kilometers—of dark water lay under the landing ship before the true sea bottom.

The answer was irrelevant, of course. The sled could handle the pressure at the current depth, perhaps even another half kilometer down. But not long beyond that, its hull would collapse, and its occupants would be crushed in an instant. Caron had served in space enough times to understand deadly environments, but somehow, he found the almost bottomless water more terrifying than any dangers he could remember.

"Bring us down on that ledge, Antoinette...and feed the scanner readings to the Foudre Rouge." He figured the best way to find a way in was on foot, the squad of soldiers in the back of the craft debarking, and searching the rock shelf just ahead.

He sat, watching, as Bissel brought the ship in slowly—painfully slowly. Maneuver in water was very different than in space, or even an atmosphere. And one mistake, one gash torn in the hull by a chunk of jagged rock, and the landing ship would be ripped to pieces by the immense pressure.

Seconds passed, turning into a minute, then two. Finally, Caron heard a soft thud, and he realized the ship was down on the rock. An instant later, Bissel confirmed that with a brief report.

Caron tapped the comm unit again. "Lieutenant, confirm status."

"All personnel suited up and ready, sir."

"Very well...prepare to disembark." Caron reach down and hit the controls, pumping water into the hold and equalizing the interior and exterior pressure. A few seconds later, a green indicator came on, and he pulled a large lever.

He could hear the grinding sound as the rear hatch opened slowly...and perhaps half a minute later, he could see Lieutenant Javais's Foudre Rouge climbing out of the ship.

It was time to find the way in, to discover what lay in the haunted depths of the old base.

And to find the imperial artifacts all reports suggested were still waiting inside.

Chapter Fifteen

Free Trader Pegasus
Somewhere in the Endless Sea
Planet Aquellus, Olystra III
Year 302 AC

Jets of water were flying all across the bridge, shorting out systems and soaking Andi and Barret to the bone. She didn't know what was going on elsewhere in her ship, but her gut told her conditions were no better anywhere else. *Pegasus* had come down hard, and her ship was sinking. It was dying.

Unless she could save it. Along with herself and her crew.

The ship was upside down, or close to it, at least. Andi's harness had kept her in her seat, but Barret had apparently unhooked his, and he'd fallen to the ceiling, now serving more or less as a temporary floor. He was lying on his side below her and off to the side. He appeared motionless at first, and she felt a wave of fear that he was dead…but then she managed to catch a glimpse of his chest heaving with a series of shallow breaths.

She looked all around, unsure what to do. She had to get to the hull breaches, she realized, and patch them somehow. She had the tools. The bridge had a well-stocked repair kit, including one of the patching guns Durango had given her to repair hull damage. It was a temporary solution, but it was instant-drying and strong enough to hold out the vacuum of space, and according to the Samis shipyard manager, to hold back the sea as well.

She guessed Durango had been legit about that, but truth be told, she had no idea of the relative forces involved, how much harder it was to keep out the ocean at two kilometers depth. She would hope for the best. That was all she could do.

But how could she get to the tool chest? It was bolted to the floor, now hanging above her, but if she could get to it, maybe she could pry it open, and allow the contents to fall to the ceiling below. That risked damaging some of the tools, of course, but it was the only way she could think of that offered any chance at all.

How am I going to get over there?

There was no way to move across the floor now hanging above her. She'd have to drop down and make her way back up the port side wall. That seemed difficult—she deliberately avoided the word 'impossible'—but it was her only chance.

She looked down at her shipmate. Barret had clearly been injured by the fall…but Andi was ready for the drop. She would come down in a more controlled manner, one that would allow her to reach the ceiling without injury.

She hoped.

She listened for a few seconds, her ears scanning for any signs her other comrades were trying to get into the bridge. But there was nothing. That could mean they were busy patching holes elsewhere in the ship.

Or it could mean…

She forced that thought out of her mind with brutal force. There was no time to think about such things. Not just then.

She gripped the harness tightly, even as her one hand

moved toward the buckle and released it. She dropped hard, about half a meter, and then she hung there, her grip on the heavy material of the harness holding her above the ceiling below. She let her hands slide down as far as possible, getting as close to the to the bottom as she could before she let go. She was down within a meter and a half, perhaps a bit less. That was pretty close. It was still going to hurt, but she figured she had a good chance to avoid any major injury. At least if she managed the landing roll well.

She stared across the bridge, toward the main display. Most of the screens were dark, their mechanisms damaged by the water still spraying around the bridge. But the main panel was still operating. And the AI had helpfully put up a depth marker before it, too, had shorted out.

Three hundred meters. *Pegasus* was already three hundred meters down. Andi had no idea how deep the ocean was below her ship, but the only thing she could do about that was hope for the best. *Pegasus* could stand a good deal of pressure, but at some point, it would exceed the vessel's endurance. That would be the end, unless the ship hit bottom soon enough…or something killed them all before the pressure did.

Like drowning.

The water on the ceiling was six or eight centimeters deep already, and the intensity of the water coming in was rising. The depth was increasing the water pressure and widening the holes in the hull. Andi had been dangling for perhaps half a minute, trying to find the best way to drop. But she was out of time.

She let go and fell to the bridge ceiling, a drop that took less than a second, but seemed like an eternity. She landed in the water, sending a splash all around as her feet hit the hard metal of the ceiling. She felt a jarring in her ankles, and up her leg, and a good deal of pain. But a few quick moves told her she hadn't suffered any kind of serious injury.

Her urge was to race over to Barret's side, to check his

condition and see what aid she could provide. But she had
to deal with the ship first. It would do Barret no good if she
saved him only to drown, or to be crushed like a grape by
the immense pressure.

She scrambled across the ceiling, now the bridge's
functional floor, and even as she did, she felt the surface
moving under her feet. It took her a second to realize what
was happening, and then she cursed under her breath.

Pegasus was rolling again, and before she could reach
something to grab onto, she slid across the ceiling and
slammed into the port side wall. She heard another thud,
and she winced as she realized her wounded comrade had
been thrown against the wall, too.

She shook her head, trying to remain clear. She'd hit
pretty hard, and the cumulative effects of bruises and
scrapes were getting harder to ignore. She seemed to have
avoided any serious injuries, but it still took just about all the
will power she could summon to force herself up to her
feet, and to begin making her way across the slant of the
wall. The incline was about thirty degrees, and far from
stable, and the walls were smooth in most places, with little
to grip or grab onto to steady herself. Worse, even as she
made her way, the wall under her feet pitched around, the
angle changing as the water currents and increasing pressure
outside battered her tortured ship.

Still, the last pitch had actually helped her, putting her
closer to the tools she needed. She scrambled a few more
steps, and she grabbed onto the chest bolted to the wall, just
as *Pegasus* pitched again.

Her fingers ached, but they held on, keeping her in place,
and she popped open the lid, giving herself half a second's
relief that it hadn't jammed shut.

She grabbed what she needed, before it slipped and slid
down the wall, and then she swung her head around,
looking over at Barret. He was still unconscious—and still
breathing—but he'd landed on his side. The water level had

risen considerably in the short time it had taken Andi to get to the tool chest. She figured she had three minutes, maybe four, before it rose enough to drown her friend.

She scrambled along the wall, rushing toward the closest leak. She had the patching gun in her hand, but she was far from certain it was still functional. It had a full compartment of the strange plastic-based compound that Durango had assured her would patch any gashes in the hull—as long as they weren't too large—but she didn't know if it would be enough. There was supposed to be a canister with more of the material in the chest, but she couldn't have carried it with her, even if she'd grabbed it before it had slid away.

You'd never have been able to reload in time anyway. This is what you've got. If it works at all.

She reached out, grabbing onto the nearest handhold. It wasn't an ideal position, but it was close enough. She gritted her teeth as she swung the gun around, shoving it into place and struggling to hold it there under the pressure of the water pouring through. It took her time, more time than she had, but she managed to wedge herself between the handhold and the breach, and keep the patching gun steady enough to pull the trigger.

The thing pushed back hard, and her arm ached from her shoulder to her hand. It slipped, spraying a clump of the patching material onto the wall about a quarter meter from the breach. She watched for an instant as it expanded, increasing its volume by a factor of ten. That was supposed to allow it to fill up a gash in the hull, but the misfire had resulted in nothing more useful than a large blob of instantly hardened, pinkish-gray material on the wall.

She shoved her arm hard, ignoring the pain shooting up to her shoulder, and she forced the thing back into position. Then she fired again, holding the gun steady with all the strength she could muster.

She wasn't sure at first if she'd managed to get the spray where she needed it, but then she could feel the flow of water decreasing…and an instant later, stopping entirely. She paused for a second or two, staring at her handiwork. It was a mess, a wild and irregular mass of hardened high-tech plastic. It was a scar on *Pegasus*'s bridge wall, an eyesore on the normally streamlined and smooth metal.

But it was holding. The wild jet of water that had been ripping into the bridge had stopped, and as far as Andi could see, there wasn't the slightest trickle still coming in, just the residual wetness all around.

That's one…if it holds.

She looked around behind her. There were two more breaches, and they were in difficult places. She looked back down, checking on Barret again. Patching the one gash had bought her some time, maybe another minute or two, but a cold realization was setting in. She wasn't going to make it, not in time.

And if she tried to move Barret, or to find some way to prop him up above the water, she wouldn't have time to patch the holes and try to right the ship before she sunk too deeply to recover.

Before the growing water pressure crushed her beloved vessel like a discarded can.

She scrambled across the wall, back toward the floor, now pitched up at almost a ninety-degree angle. The next hole was on the edge of the port side wall, just a few meters from where she crouched. She sucked in a ragged breath, pushing back against exhaustion and pain, and she crawled back toward the gash. She tried to slip around the high-pressure jet of incoming water, increasing in strength with every passing second and every meter *Pegasus* sank. She was almost in place, but her foot slipped on the wet metal of the wall, and she dropped down and hit hard…and then rolled over into the column of incoming water. The jet slammed into her and sent her flying across the bridge, almost to the ceiling on the far end of the wall. Her head slammed into the hard metal, and her vision went dark. She could hear the water coming in, the normally lifegiving resource that was now going to kill her. That was going to kill all her people.

She struggled to cling to consciousness, to continue the fight for survival, but she felt it all slipping away, until all that was left was darkness.

Chapter Sixteen

Rock Shelf
Just Outside Sector Nine Landing Craft Alpha
Olystra System
Year 302 AC

"Lieutenant, I think I found something."

Javais turned, and he moved toward the trooper who'd just spoken. Private Bescalon was on the far side of the formation, and it took some time to navigate his way there in the heavy underwater pressure suit and weighted books. He came up behind, and without ceremony, said simply, "Show me."

Bescalon gestured toward a gap between two shafts of rock. No, it wasn't a gap. It was a tunnel, a cave.

"Well done, Bensacon-2110. We'll move forward, but let's exert extreme caution." He gestured for the soldier to move in the opening, even as he pulled his own rifle from the back of his suit and prepared to follow.

Javais was Foudre Rouge, and that meant he'd been cloned to serve as a soldier, trained to obedience since childhood. He didn't usually spend much time considering the motivations of missions. He was there to aid in the search, and to provide security. But he was troubled by one thought. The imperial artifacts he'd heard of were sometimes buried under the ground, or even the sea. But that was usually the result of time, and of seismic activity.

But it was clear the facility laying before him—if there indeed *was* an imperial site beyond the cave—had been deliberately hidden. The surface was devoid of human life, but it hadn't been blasted into a radioactive nightmare, either. Whatever had happened to Aquellus, it had lacked the raw power to sink a facility two kilometers below the sea. The facility that awaited the expedition had been purpose built where it was, and that meant it had been intended to remain hidden.

He pushed the thoughts aside, a lifetime of conditioning assisting in the effort. It wasn't for him to worry about such things. But whatever was waiting inside, whatever threats might still be lurking in there, that *was* his problem.

"Calvais-2109 and Calvais-2110…report to me at once. The rest of the squad, continue searching for anything out of the ordinary."

"Did you find something, Lieutenant?" Caron stepped up behind he Foudre Rouge officer. The Sector Nine operative was having considerably more difficulty navigating in the massive underwater pressure than the soldiers. Foudre Rouge weren't trained specifically for underwater operations, but they were conditioned to endure combat conditions in space at high g forces. It wasn't the same thing, of course, but it wasn't *entirely* different.

Sector Nine operatives received some training for space maneuvers as well, but most of their indoctrination covered different specialties. And the deep sea operations suits were *damned* cumbersome.

"We don't know yet, sir. There seems to be a cave here, but we have no idea what is inside. We are just about to investigate." As he spoke, the two additional privates appeared. Javais was having difficulty adapting to the slow speed of movement underwater. When he called his soldiers, he expected them to jump, and he had to remind himself, the plodding, cumbersome gait his people were exhibiting *was* jumping, at least when operating two kilometers beneath the ocean.

"With your permission, Agent Caron, we will advance inside and scout the area. If all is clear, I will call for you."

Caron nodded, an almost pointless gesture in the massive underwater suit. Then he spoke into the small microphone just in front of his mouth. "Very well, Lieutenant. Be careful…we know we've lost some people from previous expeditions…though we don't know that they found this particular entrance, if that's what it is." A pause. "Did you find any signs of previous activity anywhere?"

"No, sir, but I do not believe that is a reliable data point. There is aggressive and fast-growing plant life all around, some of it apparently carnivorous, and strong water currents as well. Even if the previous expeditions had come this way, it is doubtful we would be able to track them."

"Yes, of course, Lieutenant. Let us move on."

"Yes, sir." The Foudre Rouge officer was aware of the arrogance of the Sector Nine agents, and perfectly knowledgeable about just how focused on the acquisition of power they truly were. It was a culture that had its advantages, he suspected, but also its weaknesses. The Foudre Rouge were different, conditioned for obedience, and Javais's opinions on the Sector Nine personnel were purely academic. He didn't think one way or another about it in terms of worthiness or anything of the sort. His was to obey, and that was all he had known, since the days he'd taken his first, halting steps.

He gestured toward his small group of soldiers, as well as he could in the suit. "Let's move out." He lumbered forward, just behind Bensacon-2110, but in front of the two Calvais privates. Standard organizational protocols generally avoided the assignment of crechemates or genetic identicals to the same squads, but the force pool assigned to Sector Nine operations in the Badlands was small, and it had proven to be unavoidable. There were schools of thought, Javais knew, two camps, arguing opposite sides of the question of whether having duplicates deployed in close quarters created problems, or streamlined operations. Javais suspected there were valid points to both arguments, but again, that determination existed for him in that strange theoretical domain apart from actual opinion. He'd have obeyed orders to separate DNA-matches without question, just as he would ones to organize them together in their own units. Obedience was the only salvation for Foudre Rouge.

The cave snaked into the rock wall, twisting and turning. Javais scanned every section, his eyes moving around over as much a range as his suit would allow. There were a few places that looked like they might have been carved by artificial means, but none where he could be sure. It could all have been natural, too.

Then, he turned the corner, and he saw a stretch of smooth rock. It was old, and deep sea mollusks and other life forms covered most of it. He stepped over and extended his arm, flipping a small switch that extended the blade stored in the suit's arm. He poked at the wall, and he scraped along the surface, pulling off a series of small shells and other debris. And below, he saw what he'd been looking for. A section of flat rock so smooth, it could only have been carved by a plasma torch or some other manmade implement.

"Agent Caron, I believe we have found a section of rock almost certainly carved out by power implements. We are continuing on, looking for some form of access."

"Very well, Lieutenant. Continue. And report anything you find immediately. Anything."

"Yes, sir." Javais gestured for Bescalon to continue, and he followed his subordinate closely. The section of carved rockface continued on for another ten meters.

Suddenly, Bescalon stopped. Javais almost admonished

the private, but then his own eyes focused on what had halted the Foudre Rouge. It was a door, a glimmering silvery metal showing in the light of the portable torches, one that showed no signs of rust, nor even of age.

Imperial alloy.

The door was a find, of course, almost incontrovertible evidence that they *had* found some kind of ancient facility. But that wasn't what gripped Javais's stomach, what overrode decades of antifear conditioning and left the veteran Foudre Rouge officer barely able to remain focused. It was nothing more than a small light that did that.

Imperial artifacts were sometimes the merest scraps, while others were more substantial ruins. But there was something on the door in front of him different from any find he'd ever heard of. It was a small indicator light, no more than two centimeters in diameter.

And it was *on*, glowing in a soft red color.

Whatever was behind the door in front of him, whatever remains from imperial times, it was still operational, at least on some level.

As dangerous as the mission had been, the hazard level had just increased tenfold. Javais stood in place, struggling to return to the shelter of his conditioning, to regain the iron-hard control expected of a Foudre Rouge officer. Then he tapped his comm unit again, activating the main line.

"Agent Caron, we found something. I think you need to see this, sir. Immediately."

* * *

This is amazing…

Caron stepped into the corridor. He was scared to death, but curiosity—and the realization of just how much power and advancement would be his if he was able to return to Montmirail with the artifacts that almost certainly lay inside the imperial facility—kept him going. He'd been stunned to see that the entrance from the cave had appeared almost as new, and even more shocked when he'd actually set eyes on the small status light. The Foudre Rouge had found more than a bit of well-preserved imperial alloy. They'd found a system that was still under active power.

And that meant the facility had some kind of energy generation, a reactor still functioning after centuries without human activity.

He'd considered trying to blast the door open, but he didn't dare deploy explosives powerful enough to destroy an armored door constructed of imperial alloy. He couldn't risk flooding the facility…or bringing the towering rock wall down on his people.

Then, he'd reached out and touched the door, and realized almost immediately that his hand had passed through some kind of sensor field. The door opened at once, triggering another duel between Caron's lust for power and his cold fear.

He'd gestured toward the first Foudre Rouge trooper, and followed it up with a direct command. "Go in, Private. See what is inside." To him, Foudre Rouge were almost manufactured resources, created to be used, and if necessary, expended.

The private hesitated for just an instant, an attestation to the fact that Foudre Rouge, while massively conditioned, were still human, and as such, not utterly without fear.

Caron watched the soldier step inside, and he peered in, his eyes picking up what they could as the trooper's helmet lamp lit up the murky blackness. It was a small compartment, no more than two meters square. An airlock, Caron realized. He wondered if it was still completely operational, and he decided it probably wasn't…right before an interior light flicked on.

Caron felt as though his heart skipped a beat, and he stood still for a moment, regaining control over his emotions. A functional imperial facility was a find that could change history, and lead not only to victory in the next war with the Confederation, but to total annihilation and conquest of the hated enemy, even dominance of the entire Rim. The rewards for those who made it possible were almost too immense to calculate, and once again, Caron's greed for position and power overcame the terror working around the edges of his mind.

"Let's go, Lieutenant." Caron had regained a grip on himself, enough not only to push the Foudre Rouge along, but to go with them. The realization of just what his people had possibly found drove him forward. Still, he was cautious, on edge. A working airlock and a few lights didn't mean there are imperial bots waiting in there, weapons charged.

But then, something happened to the other expeditions.

He waited until the lead private and Javais had stepped inside, and then he followed them, turning and watching as the last two troopers came up behind. He looked around, his eyes focusing as Javais said, "Here, sir. It looks like an airlock control to me."

Caron nodded, realizing it was mostly a gesture to himself. He took a deep breath, and then another, becoming a little lightheaded from the oxygen rich mixture in his suit. "See if it works." He fought back the fear, and the haunted feeling that seemed to descend all around the small party.

Javais poked at the controls, struggling for a few seconds with his large cumbersome gloves. Then, the outer door closed. There was a loud sound, like metal sliding across metal...and the water level in the tiny room began to drop. It took perhaps twenty seconds, and then the five men stood there silently.

Javais felt a little wobbly for a moment, until his suit adjusted to the relatively sudden pressure reduction. Then, perhaps ten seconds later, the door in front of them slid open, revealing a corridor beyond.

There were lights on the ceiling, or at least illumination

coming from some kind of panels there. The fixtures themselves looked like the rest of the metal roof, save for the light they emitted. It looked like about half of them were functional and half were dark, though that was hard to ascertain for sure when he could only see about eight or ten meters.

The entire group stood for a moment, looking out on the long hallway in front of them with varying degrees of astonishment. Then Javais gestured toward the nearest private and snapped out a command. The Foudre Rouge stepped out of the small compartment and into the corridor.

Caron could see from the seemingly damaged light panels, the facility wasn't *entirely* functional. But there was no doubt there was still active power generation, and that much of the structure appeared to remain functional and more or less intact.

"Check atmospherics, Lieutenant." Caron was doing that himself, but he wanted confirmation. A moment later, he had it.

"Human normal, within one point three percent, sir."

Caron's numbers were the same. The air in the facility was not only breathable, it was closer to human ideals than Montmirail's. He was still suspicious, though his bio detectors read negative across the board for harmful pathogens—for *any* pathogens. There was no trace of any gas, any fumes, any substance at all harmful to human life. But Caron still hesitated. It felt safer to stay in the suits...but the undersea survival gear was even more unwieldy in the dry corridors, and staying on bottled air would place a sharp time constraint on their exploration.

"Private, pop your suit." It was cold, arrogant, to expect the Foudre Rouge to test the air like some kind of scanner. But the soldier obeyed without question. And Caron would never have imagined he should hesitate to risk one of the clone soldiers before himself.

The trooper stepped out of his suit and breathed deeply,

looking entirely unscathed. Caron waited perhaps another minute, long enough to be sure the oxygen was real and to confirm the absence of any deadly gasses or the like. Then he popped his own suit.

He repeated the soldier's actions, confirming to himself the strange freshness of the air, so much cleaner and crisper than the recycled mix pumped through the Union's spaceships. He waited as the others stepped out of their own suits, and then he looked down the corridor.

It was time to explore. Time to see just what kind of wonder they had found.

Chapter Seventeen

Free Trader Pegasus
Somewhere in the Endless Sea
Planet Aquellus, Olystra III
Year 302 AC

"Andi!" Gregor swung again, his massive arms, one of them now mechanical and even more powerful than the enormous hunk of muscle remaining on the other side, hurled the massive prybar into the door. He'd been struggling to get onto *Pegasus*'s bridge, and his initial efforts to open the shorted out lock mechanism quickly gave way to a primal fury. Gregor tended to fall back on brute strength whenever anything else failed, most likely because that had usually worked for him.

But it wasn't working this time. The armored door protecting *Pegasus*'s bridge had been Captain Lorillard's doing, the response to an incident...what was it, five years ago now?...when rivals had almost managed to hijack the then-*Nightrunner*. It had been the kind of thing that seemed to make sense, but Gregor couldn't remember it ever being useful, and now it was actually threatening Andi and Barret, and maybe all of them.

He swung again, a blow so titanic it actually dented the reinforced chromium-alloy door, as well as letting out an almost-deafening clang. But the door held. It had been designed to resist forced entry, and any power a human being could exert against it, even a towering giant like Gregor.

"Let me up there, Gregor." Lex Righter was crawling over the wall turned temporarily into a floor. He almost stumbled on one of the antigrav handholds, but he caught himself and came right up behind *Pegasus*'s largest crew member. "You're never going to bash your way through there, not in the time we've got at least." Righter put his hand on Gregor's arm and pushed the giant aside, something he could only encourage and not force, he knew. If Gregor didn't want to move, nothing Righter did was going to move him.

Gregor turned and glared at the engineer for an instant. Righter realized what a tightly knit group *Pegasus*'s crew was, and also that he was the newest member...if he really was even a member.

But he also knew he was the one most likely to get into the bridge in time. To save all their lives.

The others had all listened to his instructions, with reluctance in some instances, but in the end, they'd been able to patch up the leaks in the engineering section and the lower deck. But unless they could get onto the bridge and finish the job...and activate the navigational auxiliary control circuits from there, they were all going to die. *Pegasus*'s systems were badly damaged by the water, and the bridge controls were the last hope.

He reached out, his fingers moving across the electronic locking system. He was risking a shock, perhaps a dangerous one, but he figured they had maybe four minutes to get the positioning jets firing to stabilize their depth. After that, it would be a very short time, perhaps only seconds, before the increasing depth and water pressure crushed the ship and they all died very unpleasant deaths. Cold realities like that made it far easier to prioritize concerns. And worrying about electrocution from soaking wet circuits was surprisingly low on that list just then.

He reached inside, his finger trying to reach a small cable. He could feel it at the end of his index finger, but he was having trouble pulling it in. He was making wild guesses, on what to do, how to get the door open as quickly as possible. If he could pull the small wire out, and reroute it the way he wanted to, it would short things out worse than the water had, but his gut told him it would also open the bridge door.

He was far from sure it would work, but he gave it two chances out of three, and considering the lack of other options, he'd gone all in on that one.

If he could pull the wire in. He looked around, even as he pushed his finger in farther. There were no tools nearby, nothing that would help. But he almost had it. He managed to pull it a few millimeters, and then his finger slipped off the wet casing.

Damn!

He reached in again. Gregor was still standing right behind him, but he didn't think the huge man had a chance of shoving his fingers into the small opening. And everybody else was finishing up the patching job, all of them doing the jobs he'd laid out for them, pushing aside any resentment they still held for a chance, however tenuous, of survival.

If anyone is going to get onto the bridge, it's you…

He pushed his fingers back in, jamming his hand painfully on the jagged metal around the opening. He could feel the sharp edges slicing into his flesh, his palms became slick as blood poured out into them. He ignored it all, the pain, the fear. He *had* to succeed. He had to do it for himself, because it was his only chance for survival. And he felt a driving need to save his new shipmates, though none of them seemed especially fond of him.

He had to save Andi, too…because he knew, however much he resented her more or less kidnapping him, or how she'd thrown him into the hold and beaten and threatened him, deep inside, he knew one thing with irresistible certainty.

Andi Lafarge had saved his life. And the sober, more or less functional Lex Righter paid his debts.

He stretched his fingers out, struggling to get a tenuous grip on the errant cable. It slipped from his grasp, once, twice…and then he managed to get ahold of it. He pulled, moving slowly and cautiously, despite the fact that he was almost out of time. If the thing slipped away one more time, it was over. He knew that with a certainty so heavy, it felt like a neutron star.

He felt the cable moving closer, and he managed to press it against the inside of the lock mechanism. He slid one finger from his other hand inside, grabbing hold, and pulling it through the small opening. He gripped it hard, not allowing himself to forget it could still slip back inside. He reached around, grabbing for the small clippers in his pocket, and he stripped the tiny cable, exposing the live metal below. A hundred ways to deal with the lock slipped through his mind, his vast pool of engineering knowledge mobilizing to face the problem at hand. But there was only one thing he could do quickly enough. Connect the two leads together and burn out the mechanism.

And hope that the door froze in the open position and not closed as it was then.

Also, that I don't fry myself…

He took a deep breath and moved the wires, closing his eyes at the last second as he pushed them together.

He fell backwards, a wave of pain, followed almost instantly by numbness, ripping up his arm. He landed on his back, on the wall about two meters from the lock. He was stunned, verging on the edge of unconsciousness for a few seconds. But something held him there, a realization that only he could save them all. His chest rose up, and he filled his lungs with air, ignoring the considerable pain that accompanied the act.

He started to get up, and he turned his head toward the door, almost afraid to check and see if he'd succeeded.

"You got it open!" The voice was Anna's, a startled shout as she stumbled up onto the small deck outside the bridge.

Righter was never sure if he'd seen the open hatch first, or if Anna's shout had informed him his gamble succeeded, but he quickly decided it didn't matter.

It was open. They still had a chance.

He dragged himself up to his feet and staggered to the hatch, realizing from the flow of water coming out that the bridge had probably taken more damage than the lower levels. "Gregor, you've got to get those leaks patched up. Anna, find Andi and Barret. I'll get the auxiliary control circuits activated." He hardly realized he was snapping out orders to them both, despite the fact that neither of them likely considered him a real comrade, much less a superior. But he knew what to do. Whatever chance *Pegasus* had, it was in his hands…and they seemed to understand that.

He tried to keep his focus on the controls he had to reach. A quick glance at the bridge told him the workstation he needed was going to be difficult to access. But, despite the urgency of the situation, he spared an instant to scan the bridge, to find out what had happened to Andi and Barret. He saw the patch job, ugly as hell, but still holding. Wherever Andi and Barret were, one of them at least had managed to do partial repairs.

Then he saw them, Andi lying on her back, clearly unconscious, her bodily reflexes fighting back against eh water lapping up around her, trying to fill her lungs.

Barret was about two meters from her, in much the same situation. Righter had to fight the urge to race over, to save the woman who'd saved him. But Anna was almost there already.

You have work to do. What's the point of saving her only to be crushed by the pressure?

He leapt up, trying to grab hold of the workstation chair, but he fell short and landed on the wall, splashing water all around. He jumped back to his feet, trying to forget about the new pain in his legs.

It can't be too bad…you can still stand…

He crouched down, ready to leap as hard as he could, when he felt a giant pair of hands under him, shoving hard, and practically throwing him up to the workstation. He reached out, grabbed the chair with both hands, and managed to force himself into a somewhat stable position. He muttered, an almost indistinguishable grunt intended as a thanks to Gregor. He hadn't actually seen who had helped him, but there was only one person on *Pegasus* who could throw him around like a rag doll.

He reached out, his hands moving over the workstation's controls. He'd been focused on getting there, but the realization suddenly set in that he was making a wild bet, that he was hoping against hope this piece of equipment, unlike the others he'd tried, would work. It was possible— much of *Pegasus* remained operational amid the scattered system failures—but all of a sudden, it seemed a very tenuous thing to be the arbiter of whether they all lived or died.

He hesitated a few seconds, the fear and uncertainty that often plagued him, that had contributed to his control issues, rising up inside, threatening to freeze him in place. He knew where it all came from, the disastrous failure—his failure. His comrades had all died that day, every one of them. And Lex Righter had spent the next five years reliving the nightmare, and drowning his guilt at failure, and at life's sick twist of making him the only survivor, in oceans of alcohol and endless flows of whatever hallucinogens he could lay his hands on. He'd even lied to Andi, told her he'd been depressed about a girl. He'd never managed to tell anyone the truth, to share his great shame and regret with another human being.

He couldn't do this. The doubt flooded in. He wasn't strong enough, capable enough. He couldn't handle the responsibility for all their lives...not again. At least this time, he too, would die. He wouldn't endured the guilt, the shame, of surviving those he'd failed.

And yet, something else rose up inside him, some vestige of what he had once been. A war raged inside his head, his tortured thoughts battling against each other, the urge to give up, to surrender to the peace of death warring with the need to survive. To save his new shipmates.

Despair came close to victory. Indeed, it would have had Righter's life been the only one at stake. But he couldn't fail his comrades again, couldn't endure the thought that they would all die.

Not again.

His fingers moved again over the console, typing in the access data. The station was responding, at least part of it was. The flickering of the screen sparked hope inside him, and a few seconds later, he hit the final button.

There was nothing at first, nothing save the continued descent. Righter could feel the despair strengthening again, every bit of self-loathing that lived inside him coming to the surface.

And then *Pegasus* lurched.

It was different than the movements the ocean currents had caused, and the ship vibrated as *Pegasus* shook hard again. The battered vessel's systems were struggling, fighting to activate, almost like a living being desperate to survive. For another few seconds, the ship rolled to its side, but continued its descent. Then it vibrated wildly, almost as though it would shake itself apart.

And it began to rise.

Righter checked the instruments, trying desperately to confirm what he already knew. The positioning jets, at least, were functional. And they had stopped the ship from dropping lower.

They were still in trouble, deep trouble.

But *Pegasus* was no longer sinking.

Chapter Eighteen

Free Trader Pegasus
Somewhere in the Endless Sea
Planet Aquellus, Olystra III
Year 302 AC

Andi could see the ceiling above her. She was groggy, still a little disoriented, but she realized almost immediately she was in the cot in *Pegasus*'s tiny infirmary. It took her a few seconds to get her thoughts together, to remember how she had gotten there, or at least the last thing she could recall.

Then it came to her. *Pegasus* had been sinking. Whatever had happened, it had to be better than any hopes she'd had when she lost consciousness, because she'd been beaten then, resigned to the loss of her ship and all her people.

She tried to lift her head, but the pounding pain, already almost unbearable, increased enormously, and forced her back. Something was wrong. For a few seconds, she thought her vision was damaged. She could see, but everything was dim, almost like a dusky evening. Had she damaged her eyes, or was the problem in her brain? A concussion? Some other kind of problem?

Then, she saw a series of lights on the med station about a meter to get side. They were as bright as ever, and she could see them all crisply. It wasn't her eyes that were damaged, it was *Pegasus.*

"I'm glad to see you're awake." Doc's voice, genuine joy at finding her conscious…but something else, too. Stress, fear…whatever had happened to save her ship, she knew they weren't out of the woods yet.

"You guys got me out of there…and you managed to patch the leaks. We'd all be dead if you hadn't."

"You can thank Gregor for most of the patches. I've never seen a force of nature match him when he's riled up. And, your new engineer saved the rest of the day…or at least got us this far."

"How far are we?" Andi gritted her teeth and pushed back against the pain as she tried again to raise her head up. She made it on the second effort, but she was far from sure it had been worth it. The pain was bad, and the payoff was a view out through the small doorway into the main lower deck. She'd known, on some level at least, that it *had* to be a mess, but actually seeing it was something else entirely. There was water everywhere, and piles of toppled equipment. Whatever was keeping *Pegasus* running, it had to be by the slimmest of margins. "The truth, Doc. There's no time for sugarcoating anything. Not now."

"Lex Righter has the reactor operating at thirty percent, but it's taking most of that to stabilize the ship. Best we could tell, we were almost three kilometers down. I don't want to think about how close to disaster we came, but it couldn't have been far."

No, it couldn't have…

Andi didn't know exactly how much depth *Pegasus* could endure, but she'd have bet three kilometers was beyond that point. She knew the ship's survival had come down to the alloys in the hull and the inner structure, physical properties definable by pure mathematics, but she couldn't help believing the vessel's spirit had played a role as well.

"Where are we now?"

"Holding   at   two   kilometers.   There   was a…discussion…about what to do while you were unconscious. We held a vote. Staying down here won against going up to the surface to really check the damage. It was close."

Andi imagined it had been close, but her people had managed to do what she would have ordered. As much as she wanted to address any needed repairs—and that would certainly be easier on the surface—she had no idea where the Sector Nine ship was, or if the enemy was still searching for *Pegasus*. Better to stay as hidden as possible, at least until she could figure out what to do.

"Help me up." She shifted her legs off the cot, and she shoved herself the rest of the way into a seated position, biting her lip as the pain hit her again. "And, my God, I know damned well we've got painkillers on this tub…how about getting me a handful?"

"I was afraid to medicate you too heavily until I had a better idea of your condition."

"My condition is fine…at least if my head doesn't explode."

"Okay, sit tight. I'll add something to your IV mix."

"Add a lot to it, Doc. I've got to be able to function, so let's jump right to something potent and save some time…and no warnings about addictiveness or the like. We've got bigger problems right about now."

"Understood." Doc sounded a little doubtful…he'd always been wary about the use of powerful narcotics. But he didn't argue.

Andi sat for a moment, sucking in a deep breath and trying to hold back the nausea beginning to take her. Part of that was from the pain, but whatever the cause, she knew exactly how she was going to handle it. She was going to ignore it. If she threw up all over the floor, that wouldn't even make their top ten list of problems.

She felt a wave moving across her head, pushing away the pain—most of it, at least—almost like a hose extinguishing a fire. The relief was more than welcome, and her thoughts came alive, her concentration increasing in intensity almost immediately. She took a deep breath and she slid off the cot onto her feet.

She wobbled a bit, enough that her hand swung instinctively behind her, grabbing onto the edge of the cot. She stood for a moment, waiting for her equilibrium to return.

"You really should get some rest, Andi. And you should let me check you out."

"Why? What would that serve? Do you think there is anything you will find that will change our situation?"

Doc was silent. *Pegasus*'s anointed medic tended to take his duties seriously, but he was one of the family in every way, a hardcore Badlands adventurer, and he knew as well as Andi did, they all needed her just then.

Pegasus needed her.

She stepped away from the cot, looking better, if still a little shaky. *Pegasus*'s deck wasn't exactly flat, and she found the six or eight degree slant wasn't helping her coordination any. She stumbled toward the wall, reaching out and gripping the handholds and other constructs along the way.

She opened the hatch leading to the engineering space, and she climbed down the small ladder leading to the cramped and tiny section. She stumbled down the last couple rungs, but she made it down, intact, more or less.

"Lex...I'm thinking I owe you a thanks."

Righter had been crouched down, half his body thrust inside an open access panel. He pulled himself out when Andi fell down the last section of the ladder, and he was sitting on the deck looking up at her. "We're all in this together, Andi, aren't we?" The engineer paused for a few seconds. "Besides, maybe I still have a few gripes about the hospitality on this ship, at least at first, but you saved my life, Andi...there's no arguing that. And believe it or not, I like to pay my debts."

Andi just nodded. She had come to understand more about how things like loyalty was born…but she still wasn't very comfortable with it all. By gross count, those who'd tried to injure her in her life vastly outnumbered those she'd been able to trust. "So," she finally said, "where are we at?"

"We're stable enough right now. Holding at two kilometers. We have enough power to surface, if that's what you want. The consensus while you were unconscious was to stay here…and hide."

"Hiding would have gotten my vote, too. But sooner or later, we're going to have to do *something*. We've got a mission to complete, and if this old ship can manage it, that's our next order of business. And if not…" She had no idea what to do if *Pegasus* was *really* in bad shape. The enemy ship was still out there somewhere, and it was more than a match for her vessel in top condition. A damaged *Pegasus* wouldn't stand a chance…in either a flight or a in a race to escape the system.

"Actually, we may have gotten lucky. It will take more time to really check everything out, but from what I've been able to see, *Pegasus* came through it all with only minor damage. We're going to need to do stress tests on the metallurgy, but that's going to have to wait until we get back to a shipyard. For now, the best we can do on that is hope for the best…and patch up whatever fails." A pause. "She looks awful, Andi, but this ship of yours is one tough hull."

That she is…

Andi nodded. The situation was less than ideal—hoping for the best wasn't on her list of 'go to' strategies—but it was the only choice. "How about the reactor and the engines?" A short pause. "And the weapons?"

"I haven't managed to run real diagnostics on all of it…hell, on most of it. I focused on the reactor first, at least once we managed to patch all the leaks. After Gregor managed to patch all the leaks. But from what I've managed to see, I think the engines are fine. Most of their main mechanisms are designed for vacuum conditions anyway. It's mostly electronics that took it hard, primarily from the leaks. And, of course, whatever damage the pressure did to the hull. Some of the scanner dishes and antennae took it hard, but those will be easy repairs once we get to the surface, or at least closer to it."

"I don't think it's going to be a surprise when I say, we need this ship fully operational…and as soon as possible. We've got enemies out there, either waiting at the surface, or at least in orbit or nearby space. And we've got to find the imperial installation we came for. Going back empty handed is almost as bad as not getting back at all." Durango had promised a hundred thousand credits even if Andi and her people failed in their effort, but she didn't think running at the first sign of trouble met his likely definition of effort.

Besides, she despised Sector Nine. If there was something under Aquellus's seas, artifacts of value, she'd be damned if she was going to let the Union have them.

"I knew you were going to say that." Righter sounded a little nervous, but he seemed mostly onboard with her way of thinking. "Give me an hour."

Andi was startled. She'd expected the engineer to ask for days, to prevaricate, to try to limit expectations. Anything but giving her a timeline so quickly. And one so short.

"An hour?"

"I'll have the engines ready to go by then, and the reactor up to at least seventy percent. Weapons will still be a guess, but like I said, they look okay to me now. We'll know for sure when we try to fire them."

Andi felt gratitude for Righter's honestly, and a little worry over how blithely he'd said they'd 'know when they tried to fire them.' Since that was likely to occur when someone else was shooting back, she hoped the engineer's instincts were on point.

"When we finally bust out of here, my first choice is to make a clean run for it, but if they're positioned someplace they can intercept us…we just might have to fight it out." A pause, and a bit or surprise that Righter hadn't argued, but had only nodded his agreement. "We're going to need the scanners fully operational, Lex…assuming the guns are working. If we find the imperial facility, is there any way you can repair them while some of the others and I head in and find the artifacts we're here for?"

"The underwater suits are bulky as hell, Andi, but that's not the biggest problem. I'll manage to get it done. The question is, can the scanner arrays take the pressure, even at his depth? It's pretty rough out there. I can replace the things—we've got spares in the hold—but if we're not careful as hell, we'll strip them right off again."

Andi stood still, silent for a moment. Then, she nodded. "That will have to do, Lex. You get started on that hour…" Andi still wasn't sure she really believed that. "…and I'm going to check what shape the bridge is in, and see if Vig and Barret and I can make something of the nav data Durango gave us."

She turned and grabbed one of the ladder's rungs, hesitating for an instant, and then realizing how much surer she felt on her feet than she had a few minutes before. She was ready…ready to do whatever she had to do.

And the most amazing, mystifying, wonderful thing of all…the pain in her head was almost completely gone.

Chapter Nineteen

Unidentified Imperial Ruin
Somewhere Under the Endless Sea
Planet Aquellus, Olystra III
Year 302 AC

Caron moved cautiously down the corridor, following closely behind the two Foudre Rouge up on point. He'd started out leaving more room between the soldiers and himself, but despite his cautious nature and his feeling the Foudre Rouge were expendable, he found his curiosity taking the lead. He'd never seen anything quite like the complex, in either vastness or condition. He'd come to think of the imperial artifacts he'd dealt in for the last five years as trinkets, bits and pieces of advance technology. Valuable certainly, but often less than impressive to the naked eye.

The complex stretching out before him was anything but unimpressive. It was vast, astonishing, and even his cold, focused mind was distracted with thoughts of who had built it and worked there centuries before.

Caron imagined what could be gleaned from the structure, what wonders and secrets could be uncovered through years of painstaking research. But it was not to be. The expedition's orders were clear. He was to find what he could, retrieve anything portable enough to store on *Phantasia*.

And then they were to destroy the facility.

It was a horrible waste, a crime against human history and science, and the thought of it made even his cold heart shiver a bit. But he understood the rationale, and he agreed with it entirely. The Union had a border with the Badlands, of a sort at least, but it was a circuitous route through barely inhabited frontier systems. The Confederation, on the other hand, had a vibrant and bustling border far closer to the heart of the Badlands. Sector Nine had taken advantage of the disorder endemic in the corrupt and disorganized republican government of its rival to garner many of the artifacts trading on Dannith's black market, but the Union had no real chance of maintaining an ongoing presence in the Badlands. Anything left on Aquellus, anything that couldn't be removed from the facility, would almost certainly fall into Confederation hands eventually.

And that was something Sector Nine and the Union could never allow. Their rival already had a small technological edge, and a far more vibrant economy. Matched up against the larger size of the Union that had resulted more or less in a stalemate, at least over the past fifty years. A major leap forward in Confederation tech levels would shatter that balance of power, and threaten the Union to its core.

"Sir…there is some kind of hatch up ahead. I suggest you remain here while we investigate."

Caron stopped abruptly. He didn't know if there were any active security systems or any kinds of traps that might pose a threat…but he *did* know that several teams had already vanished investigating the planet.

He also knew—at least to his perspective—it was better to risk the Foudre Rouge than himself.

"Yes, Sergeant, of course." He gestured forward, his signal for the two soldiers to proceed. Lieutenant Javais came rushing up from behind, snapping out a series of warnings and commands to the two Foudre Rouge.

"Lieutenant, you are the commander of the squad…best you remain back here for now as well." Caron wasn't sure the lieutenant had intended to go forward with his troopers, but he'd dealt with enough Foudre Rouge to suspect it was likely. And as uncomfortable as the clone soldiers made him, he preferred to keep the sole officer alive, if possible. Commission Foudre Rouge received more training, especially in interactions with those outside the corps. Dealing with Javais was unpleasant enough, but the thought of working directly with the enlisted solders made his stomach flop.

"Yes, sir." The tension in the officer's voice suggested he *had* been planning to move forward with the two soldiers. Instead, he stopped about one third of the way to the front and watched.

The troopers stopped at the door, and the sergeant stared at the small panel next to the entryway. Caron knew his people had explosives if they needed them, but he wasn't sure just how much power it would take to force open an imperial alloy door.

A few seconds later, he found out that answer wouldn't be forthcoming, at least not yet. "Lieutenant, Agent Caron…it appears that the mechanism on this door has been hacked. The lock has been disconnected, and we should be able to open it any time. Shall we proceed?"

The lieutenant turned and looked back at Caron. The Sector Nine agent paused for just a second, steeling up his nerve, pushing forward his curiosity, and his lust for the power success would feed so richly, and he nodded.

The lieutenant turned and gestured back to the two soldiers. Caron didn't know much of the Foudre Rouge's unspoken battle language, but he understood the gesture for 'proceed.'

He turned to the side, an instinctive move to lessen his

exposure to anything that came down the hall, and he watched as the sergeant poked once at the control panel…and the door slid open without incident.

The two Foudre Rouge turned and looked back toward Javais…and the lieutenant did the same to Caron. "Shall we move forward, sir?"

"Yes, by all means." Caron had half-expected some kind of imperial weaponry to open fire, and a wave of relief swept over him at lack of any sign of danger.

For a few seconds. Then he realized the door had likely been hacked by one of the previous teams, that they had almost certainly come the way his people were…and that they had never been heard from again. He could feel his heartbeat echoing in his ears, and sweat pooling up along his neck and back.

He continued on, pushing one leg forward after the other, making each step with considerable effort. His hand dropped to his side, to the pistol holstered from his belt. It was a powerful weapon, as handguns went, but against the visions of imperial might beginning to dance around his head, it felt like a pea shooter.

He looked around the instant he walked through the door. It was a fairly large room, perhaps ten meters square, with several workstations, and a series of storage lockers. The cabinets were empty, most of their doors open, and a few broken and laying on the floor. He wondered if there had been anything in them before the previous teams had come through, or it they'd taken whatever they'd found.

If they did, it's all probably inside somewhere, where they all…died.

He didn't *know* they were dead, of course. He'd wondered if they'd just found something and gone into hiding, trying to keep it for themselves. That might have been possible for one group, but he couldn't imagine three different teams digging up the courage to betray Sector Nine. The spy agency had spent almost two centuries building a reputation for ruthlessness, and it took a special kind of courage to challenge it to its worst.

The room looked like there had at least been some valuable electronics there, but the workstations had all been thoroughly picked over. That, too, was recent work, and again, almost without doubt, he decided that one or more of the previous teams had been through there.

The most interesting thing remaining in the room was a series of doors, two on the far wall, and one off to the right.

"Check the doors, Lieutenant. See if any—or all of them—have been tampered with."

"Yes, sir."

Caron walked over to the closest workstation, and looked down at the gaping hole where the electronics had been. The screen was still there, a razor-thin sheet of material—something like glass or plastic, but not exactly either. It had no visible power source, and Caron knew it was centuries old. Yet, it looked almost new, and he could have sworn there was a faint glow inside the thing.

"Agent Caron, the door on the right side is unlocked…again, apparently the result of recent hacking. One of the doors on the far wall as well. The one on the left appears still to be locked. We can connect the portable AI if you wish."

The portable system was designed for a high-tech version of lockpicking. It was almost certainly more sophisticated than whatever the previous teams had used. Of course, Caron had no idea if they simply hadn't gotten to the third door…or if they'd tried and failed to get through.

Or if they *had* gotten through and some active security system had relocked the door after they had passed. That last thought gave Caron a chill.

"See if the AI can work that lock on the third door." The words came out almost involuntarily. He didn't know the locked door held the most valuable artifacts behind it, but he intended to find out. And, if the others had not gone through that entry, if they'd gone through the two open ones…well, they didn't come back from wherever they went, so that made those doors look nearly as sinister. "Lieutenant, send two-man teams through each of the other doors. I want to know what happened to whoever went that way before.

Caron walked over toward the door, standing about a meter behind Javais and his two soldiers. The other Foudre Rouge had fanned out across the room, taking up what looked very much like defensive positions. For an instant, Caron was concerned they had heard or seen something. Then he realized it was just standard practice, their Foudre Rouge training and discipline on full display.

A few minutes went by, and then one of the teams came back from the far door on the side.

"Anything yet, Lieutenant?" Caron was edgy, almost on the verge of ordering his party through one of the other doors.

"I believe we have found at least one of the previous teams, sir. They appear to be dead. The scouts also found what appear to be the remains of an imperial bot of some kind, probably a security unit."

Caron wasn't exactly surprised that some or all of those who'd come before his expedition were dead. In fact, he'd have been surprised to discover anything else. But the certainty of it still hit him with a dull coldness. "How about the lock? Any progress?" He turned back toward the forward door, his eyes resting on the two troopers hunched over in front of it.

"Negative, sir. The lock is significantly more complex than the others. The encryption is 32,768 bit. I'm no expert on cryptography, sir, but the AI advises the lock is vastly more sophisticated than anything possessed by our own technology."

"The other locks aren't the same?"

"No, sir…the lock we came through was 4,096 bit. Still

extremely sophisticated, but on a level with our own most advanced systems."

Caron wanted to pull away from the door, to give up on it at once. To not even look in its direction again. But he knew that wasn't an option. Whatever the original imperial occupants of the facility had placed behind such sophisticated security, it seemed inconceivable to leave without investigating it. "Can you get in?"

"I'm sorry, sir, but I really don't know. The AI is doing all the work, and its reports..." Javais put his hand over the small earpiece connecting him to the device. "...are all vague and non-specific. A machine's way of saying maybe."

It was the closest thing to a joke he'd ever heard from one of the Foudre Rouge, and if he'd felt anything except fear and tension, he might even have laughed. Instead, he said simply, "Proceed." Then, a few seconds later: "Anything else from the other corridors...besides the bodies?"

"No sign of hostiles, sir, but as reported, there are remains of one or more imperial security bots of some kind. It appears that the parties were able to destroy or repel their attackers, but that they were all killed as well. Perhaps several survived with wounds, and were unable to escape."

"Very well, Lieutenant. Carry on."

Caron turned and looked back toward Bissel. His number two looked as nervous as he suspected he did...and she was trying just as hard, and unsuccessfully, to hide it. They'd both served in dangerous roles, and both had killed, and narrowly escaped death themselves. But the ancient imperial ruins were somehow...different.

Haunted.

He wasn't sure if it was the centuries they had lain dormant or the incredible sophistication of humanity's lost technology. Or just the realization of how little anyone on the Rim understood about their roots, about where humanity had come from. But something made the feeling of danger bite deeply, like a frigid sensation in his bones.

He was about to ask Javais for another status update—a waste of time, he knew, but he was going to do it again anyway.

Then, the door slid to the side with a scratching sound that spoke of centuries since it had last opened. And, a second later, the door his people had used to enter the room slammed shut, and the lights went out.

Caron reached down and pulled out his pistol, even as he heard the sounds of the Foudre Rouge sliding their rifles from their backs. A light appeared in the center of the room, and then one directly ahead…the soldiers lighting their portable lanterns.

Caron stared straight ahead, and down the corridor past the newly opened door, he could see something in the flickering fringes of Javais's lantern. Something moving.

Something heading toward his people.

Chapter Twenty

Free Trader Pegasus
Somewhere in the Endless Sea
Planet Aquellus, Olystra III
Year 302 AC

"We're picking something up, Andi." Barret was leaning forward at this station staring hard at the sporadic scanner data coming in. With half her scanning dishes and antennae stripped away, *Pegasus* was partially blind. But partially blind wasn't *blind*.

"I see it." She moved her hands over her own controls. She switched and cross-routed the data flow. "Let's see if we can get the AI programmed to estimate location based on water movement." Andi's experience captaining the ship—serving on it in any way, for that matter—had been limited almost entirely to operations in space. Ships moving through near vacuum didn't displace anything, but vessels moving through the water did.

And that difference might just save her people.

"Water displac..." Barret suddenly turned and nodded. "Yes, of course. We've got a good read on our depth, and the pressure levels and water movements just come down to mathematical formulas." Barret spun back around, and his hands moved like blurs. Andi was staring at her own screen, following what her shipmate was doing. It had been her idea, perhaps, but as an ex-naval gunner, Barret knew his way around the scanner suite better than she ever could. Andi believed in taking charge when it was called for...and stepping aside when that was the right call.

She diverted her attention toward what to do if Barret could track whatever was coming—and she had no doubt it was Sector Nine. For an instant, she was afraid the ship that had chased them down through the atmosphere had pursued them into the sea as well. But it didn't take long to confirm that the likely size and mass of whatever was back there wasn't close to large enough.

Which didn't mean it wasn't dangerous.

"Everybody...get in your suits, now." Just in case. Andi was hopeful she could deal with whatever threat had emerged, but she wanted everybody ready in case the hull was breached again, worse than it had been before.

And what will they do in their suits? Make it to the surface somehow, and float along on an endless sea with no hope of escape, no chance of rescue. Even assuming decompression sickness doesn't kill them before they can make it up to the sunlight?

It didn't matter. If Andi could keep her people alive for another hour, another minute, then she was damned well going to do it.

"And, Gregor...get down to the hold. Make sure everything is secured." A pause. "Except one of the torpedoes. Make sure one of them is loose, and as close to the hatch as you can get it."

"On it, Andi." It wasn't clear if the giant understood what she was planning or not...but then, she wasn't sure it mattered, as long as he did what she told him to do.

She turned toward Barret. "I don't imagine your gunnery skills extend to dumping a torpedo out of the hatch and into the path of...whatever that is out there. But that's just what we've got to do." It seemed desperate, but *Pegasus*'s lasers weren't going to get the job done, not with the scanner suite a mess of twisted junk. Andi would never get her ship close enough to target the enemy, not before the presumably fully-operational vessel on their tails opened fire and obliterated *Pegasus*. She couldn't even imagine what the ocean currents and the density of the water would do to the power and accuracy of a ship's lasers, but it wasn't an exchange she wanted to try without her scanners in top condition.

"We'll make it work, Andi." A pause. "The AI's tracking the vessel behind us. It's about three thousand tons…my guess is some kind of landing craft." A pause. "And it's not having any better a time in the water than we are. If it's armed, it's probably just a forward laser, which is useless down here, unless they get up *right* on our tail."

Andi shook her head. That was just what the ship was trying to do. But she wasn't going to let it happen. She'd ram the bastards before she allowed them to get the bead on *Pegasus* they needed to kill her ship.

"Increase thrust to thirty percent. Make it look like we're trying to evade…but don't try too hard. Let them think they can close enough to fire their laser. Then, we'll drop the torpedo on them."

Barret turned and stared back at Andi, and she understood the expression on his face. The torpedo was immensely powerful, a warhead designed for use in deep space. The problem wasn't calculating a drop point to catch the enemy ship within the kill zone.

The problem was getting *Pegasus* the hell *out* of the kill zone.

"It's our only option, Barret…unless you've got an idea I don't."

The gunner sat still for a moment, and then he shook his head. "No, I don't have any other ideas…but if Righter doesn't have the engine ready to blast at full—and I mean *full*—the second we let it go…" He didn't finish the sentence. It didn't need to be finished.

"Just get the drop point calculated. I'll make sure we're ready to get the hell out." She wasn't convinced she believed that entirely, but she was impressed with the certainty she'd managed to force into her voice.

* * *

"Enemy ship fourteen kilometers ahead, sir. They appear to be damaged, but they are still attempting evasive maneuvers."

"Continue on our present course. Adjust our thrust lines to match their moves." Francois Gabine sat next to the pilot's seat. The landing sled had been designed to bring an attack squad of Foudre Rouge down to the surface of a planet—and the dozen clone soldiers were back in their places, strapped in and waiting for orders. But the landing craft had a different mission at that moment, one born of necessity. To track down and destroy the unidentified ship...assuming it had somehow survived the crash into the sea, something he had seriously doubted, but now knew to be true.

"We've got more thrust than they do, sir...or at least what they've shown."

"If they had more, they'd be using it. Increase our output. We're going to have to get close—and I mean *close*—to take that thing out with our laser under the water."

"Increasing to maximum power, sir."

Gabine felt the ship shaking hard. Full thrust was well beyond recommended levels for operations in water, at least to the miniscule degree that usage underwater had ever been addressed. But he knew the importance of the mission, and the consequences of failure. A lifetime of service to Sector Nine left no doubt about how such things were typically handled.

The ship rocked and shook even harder, but Gabine could see that they were closing on the target. The enemy was making a run for it, but they weren't going to get away. He would make sure of that.

"Charge forward laser." He leaned over the controls as he snapped out the command to his comrade.

He could hear the whining sound as the already straining reactor fed power into the weapon circuits. If the ship hadn't been blasting its engines at full, the laser would have charged in twenty seconds or less. But unless he was going to slack off on the pursuit, it was looking more like two minutes.

"I'm working on a firing solution." His hands moved over the workstation. Mostly, actually, it was the AI crunching the targeting data, though Gabine was adding all he could to the process. He really didn't know just how well-programmed Union targeting computers were for underwater fire, and he was going to do everything he could to make damned sure the thing didn't miss.

He would do that not through prescient anticipation of enemy moves, nor detailed analysis of water currents and refraction. No, it would be far more simple and direct. He was going to bring his ship right up behind his target and open fire from so closely, missing was almost an impossibility.

He was damned near going to ram the thing.

* * *

"Andi, they're getting closer." Barret's voice betrayed his stress. His hands were fixed on the makeshift trigger mechanism, the controls that would—hopefully—open the cargo hold door and drop the torpedo out behind the ship. It was a deadly dangerous operation, one calling for all the intricacy and detailed planning possible…and having almost none. Gregor and Lex Righter had thrown the rugged apparatus in the hold together with whatever spare parts they could fine, and then the engineer had connected it to the launch control system on the bridge through the primitive and straightforward method of running a heavy black cable the entire way across the lower deck, up along the ladder, and onto the bridge itself.

Andi had just flooded the cargo hold, an initial success for Righter's machinations. When *Pegasus* had come out of the shipyard, she suspected the last thing anyone imagined the freighter would want or need to do was fill its hold with tons of water. But Righter had managed to rig the thing to do just that.

Hopefully without this saltwater eating away at half the mechanisms in there.

It was a desperate plan, one that Andi suspected would seem foolish, almost ridiculous, to an outside observer. She also knew it just might work. Assuming, of course, the pursuing vessel got caught in the warhead's destructive radius—likely enough—and that *Pegasus* somehow managed to escape from it.

Far less likely.

That was the problem. Righter had been neck deep in the solution for that as well, but neither he nor Andi had any idea if it would really work. *Pegasus*'s engine was powerful, far more so than the landing sled in pursuit. But a crash burn, underwater and a few meters from a thermonuclear warhead, was at best, a wild gamble. A hundred things could go wrong, but two of those possibilities were enough to worry about.

Would *Pegasus*'s massive thrust kick in soon enough to clear the blast zone, to get the ship away before the titanic explosion?

Even if the engines fired on time, would the fury of the exhaust, and the massive volume of steam it would produce, affect the torpedo, even destroy it...or perhaps worse, detonate it before its fuse had counted down?

Andi felt stress, fear...and exhilaration. There was some part of her that craved danger, that thrived on it. Her hands were gripping the armrests of her chair, and she leaned forward, a feral glint in her eye. She despised Sector Nine, and as much as she hated that her people were in such danger, part of her wouldn't have changed anything.

Part of her wanted to flip the controls and release the torpedo.

To kill the Union bastards who were trying to kill her.

* * *

"Laser fully charged, sir. Ready to fire as soon as lock is established."

Gabine sat, every muscle in his body tight, every nerve electric. He commanded the third team of Foudre Rouge, and that meant the others were likely to find any artifacts before his people even reached the imperial facility. They would get the credit. They would advance their careers.

Or, at least, they would get whatever rewards slipped past Aimee Boucher. In the Union, those at the top grabbed the lion's share of the glory. But on something as important as the current mission, even the crumbs were enough to vault one to high position and wealth.

"Not yet…just a little closer." Every fiber of his body was screaming to fire. But the water currents were too strong, the volume of water separating his ship from the target still too great. He was close, very close, but he had to cut the range even farther.

The target was about four kilometers ahead…and he going to close to less than one. At that range, the chance of the AI-assisted shot missing was less than two percent, despite the worst the wild ocean currents had to offer.

Ninety-eight percent were odds he could live with.

The ship shook hard again, four or five times in rapid succession. The data on Aquellus had been sparse, with no mention of significant volcanic activity. But he was almost certain by then that the undersea landscape was littered with them. The power and speed of the currents were two or three times the estimates, and Gabine couldn't think of another explanation.

"Three kilometers to target."

He checked his targeting sequence again, and then he ordered the AI to redo all of its calculations. He intended to update continuously until the instant he fired. He was going to catch any last second course changes or tricks. He didn't know if that ship was just some prospector's vessel...or it if was Confederation Intelligence, but one thing was certain. After he fired, and the thing sank below recoverable levels, he was damned sure going to report it as Confed spy ship. He wouldn't be able to prove it, but no one would be able to disprove it either...and, amid the celebration of a successful mission, there would likely be little scrutiny.

"Two kilometers."

Gabine clutched the control, his finger tightening on the firing stud. The AI would aim the shot, mostly at least. But he would actually fire the weapon. His eyes focused on the scanner, and on the increasingly erratic evasive maneuvers of the target. He didn't know what shape the vessel's scanners were in, but it seemed they were at least aware of his own ship's presence. They were frantically trying to escape.

No...there is no way out, not for any of you...

Gabine had been mostly concerned with success, with gaining the rewards a successful operation would bestow, and avoiding the terrible consequences of failure. But now there was something else. He imagined the crew of that ship, and the fear descending on them. No one dedicated themselves to a career in Sector Nine without a bit of a sadistic streak, and Gabine was no different. He relished the terror of his enemies, the growing realization in their minds that they were all about to die.

That he was going to kill them.

His hand tightened, even as the AI indicator light flicked

to green. The fire lock was set.

"One kilometer."

Gabine almost pulled the trigger, but he held back for another few seconds. Then, his eyes darted to the light.

Still green.

"Time to die," he muttered under his breath as his finger began to press down…

* * *

Now!

Andi's hands closed around the controls, and *Pegasus* shook hard as the rear bay doors swung open, and an instant later, the makeshift catapult sent the torpedo flying out into the water behind the ship. It had taken everything Andi had to place so much trust in her newest comrade, and a hundred disastrous possibilities had ripped through her mind in a matter of seconds. The slightest malfunction, the most minute failure of precise calibration, and the weapon could have slammed into the bay doors rather than floating out behind her fleeing vessel.

But everything went exactly as Righter had promised.

The scanner array, what little of it was working, confirmed the torpedo was away, trailing behind *Pegasus*…and right in the path of the pursuing vessel.

Now, only one thing remained…to see if *Pegasus*'s engines could fire immediately at full power…and clear the blast zone in the twenty seconds before the warhead detonated.

Andi had no idea how far that would have to be, how much distance *Pegasus* needed to survive the underwater detonation, and the nightmare of steam and currents and radiation that would come billowing after them as they ran.

She'd worked up an estimate though, a scientific term she like to call…a whole hell of a lot.

"Lex…go! Full power!" She shouted into the comm unit,

more her tension slipping out than any concern the engineer wouldn't hear her.

There was no response, at least nothing verbal. But an instant later, less than a second, really, *Pegasus* lurched hard, and the engines roared, every millimeter of the battered ship rattling as though it was falling to pieces.

And she was slammed back into her seat hard as the engines fired, turning the sea all around into a roiling cauldron of bubbling water and billowing steam pushing relentlessly toward the distant surface…and pushing *Pegasus* away from the doom it had just unleashed.

Chapter Twenty-One

Unidentified Imperial Ruin
Somewhere Under the Endless Sea
Planet Aquellus, Olystra III
Year 302 AC

Gunfire ripped down the corridor, flashes from the barrels of the Foudre Rouge rifles sparsely illuminating sections of the room that the portable lanterns didn't reach. The soldiers were firing from right in front of the corridor, and also from the far side of the room. Caron could almost feel the bullets ripping by, and he quickly realized the Foudre Rouge reputation for marksmanship was well-earned.

He could barely see the target they were firing at. He wouldn't have know what it was, or even that it was hostile…save for the fact that it too, was firing. He thought he heard one of the troopers behind him fall to the ground, without so much as a shout of pain or distress. For a second or two, he wondered if the soldier had even been wounded, or worse, but then he was distracted by another of the Foudre Rouge doubling over…and this time there was no doubt.

It was one of the troopers by the door, the private who'd been up front with Javais. Or what was left of him. A stream of projectiles—four, five, six, Caron couldn't tell—had struck the man, tearing off the right side of his head, and covering Caron himself with a shower of blood and chunks of brain and bone.

Caron gasped for air, and he sucked in a bit of bloody gray tissue with the breath. He gagged and spit it out, and then he felt his stomach heave. He vomited, but he quickly regained most of his control. He was in a life or death struggle, he knew that much, and even as the foamy bile from his gut dribbled out down the front of him, he had his pistol out, firing. He wasn't sure if the light weapon could hurt what he assumed was an imperial security bot—for that matter, he wasn't sure the Foudre Rouge assault rifles could either—but he kept firing nevertheless, even as he moved to the side, slipping down behind the central workstation. The electronics, the guts that had made that station do whatever it had done, were gone, but the metal structure remained. It didn't look like the same imperial alloy as on the doors and walls, but with any luck at all, it would provide some cover.

The approaching bot's fire was heavy, but as the thing closed, coming farther into the light, he could see three of the four weapons affixed to it were silent. The bot didn't particularly look damaged, but it clearly was, and in that realization, Caron's hopes flared up.

"It's only got one active gun...focus your fire there." He shouted out the command, realizing as he did that Javais had already said something very similar, and the Foudre Rouge were already targeting their shots on the only weapon firing back at them.

The bot itself appeared highly resistant to the fire, but the autocannon—at least it looked very much like a sleeker version of the Union weapon of that name—seemed to be taking at least some damage. Or the moorings attaching the gun to the bot if not the weapon itself.

The cannon was bent out to the side a bit, just a millimeter or two, but clearly enough to affect the targeting. Shots were still flying around the room, but the Foudre

Rouge had all taken what cover they could find, and the incoming fire was mostly ripping by them, slightly off what Caron suspected had been the uncannily accurate targeting of the AI running the thing.

Caron reached around and pulled another cartridge from the combat belt strapped around his waist. His eyes focused on Javais as he snapped it into place and extended his arm again. He held his fire, and an instant later, he ducked down.

He'd thought the lieutenant was throwing a grenade at first, but then his eyes caught sight of the thing. It was one of the satchel charges, explosives they'd brought to blast their way through imperial alloy doors. Caron was no expert, but he knew the thing had twenty or thirty times the power of a frag grenade.

And Javais was throwing it out into the corridor.

How far can he throw that thing? Caron couldn't imagine the lieutenant could hurl the heavy charge far enough not to blow them all to bits, but he was surprised as he watched the thing sailing down the corridor.

It went farther than he'd imagined it would, but he still wasn't sure it was far enough. He ducked as low as he could and threw his hands up in front of his face. As he did, he watched Javais diving to the side, and as the Foudre Rouge officer turned in front of him, he could see that the lieutenant had taken a round in the arm. A light spray of blood left a trail behind Javais, but then Caron hit the floor, and he lost his sight of his subordinate.

An instant later, the room shook, and a massive blast echoed off the walls. A gout of flame poured out of the corridor, coming within a meter of his position before it receded. He turned his head, trying to shake off the shock he felt, but by the time he managed to get back to his feet, the Foudre Rouge had all raced past. Half of them were lined up on the two sides of the door, and the other half had rushed down the corridor, spraying the remains of the bot with a steady stream of fire. The bot looked dead to Caron, at least once he managed to get enough of a look to see it, but it was clear the Foudre Rouge weren't going to take any chances. They kept it up for another five or six seconds, and then they obeyed Javais's order to cease fire.

The lieutenant was clearly wounded, and Caron knew it *had* to hurt, but Javais showed no signs of pain or distress. At least no more than a slight squinting of his right eye the agent caught for an instant.

So Foudre Rouge do feel pain...they just hide it...

He leapt up, as much as because he didn't want to look like a coward in front of the Foudre Rouge as anything else. He considered the soldiers expendable, second-class citizens all, but the thought of looking bad to them somehow bothered him anyway. It didn't make any sense, but that didn't make it any less true.

"Imperial bot?" he shouted as he ran toward the corridor.

"Looks like it, sir. I've never encountered one myself, but it looks like a Mark IV or Mark V from the descriptions and images I've seen." Javais was affixing a pressure bandage to his arm wound as he reported to Caron. He'd already sliced open his sleeve and pulled back the remnants. A few seconds later he was done, no sign remained, other than the bulky bandage—and the blood all over his arm and uniform—to suggest he'd been wounded.

Caron had studied up on known imperial security systems as well. Mark IVs were relatively light units, but reasonably state of the art at the time of the Cataclysm. Mark V's were a bit heavier, and even more modern in design. Both were moderately powerful units, designed for routine security duties. The general theory held that there were also military-grade units, but as far as Caron knew, only small scraps of those had been recovered, and their full capabilities, assuming with some certainty that they actually existed, remained a matter of conjecture.

"Two dead, Lieutenant. Two wounded but capable of

continuing, including yourself." One of the Foudre Rouge had stopped in front of Javais to report. Caron watched, but he wasn't sure which of the troopers it was. He'd be damned if he could tell the Foudre Rouge apart, despite the fact that all were from different genetic lines, save for the one pair of DNA-mates in his force. Javais was easy enough to pick out, both his insignia and the distinct look of the genetic specimens bred for officer's roles helping with that. But the others were one swirling jumble to him.

Part of it, he knew, was that he just didn't care. The Foudre Rouge were manufactured as far as he was concerned, as expendable, or nearly so, as the builders of the imperial bots had no doubt viewed their own creations.

"Okay then, let's press on." Caron wanted nothing more than to turn around and run back to the ship. But, of course, that route was blocked now, at least until his people had time to force it open. The AI might manage to reopen the door, it probably would—though now that the security systems had been alerted, escaping might be more difficult.

Caron's mind filled with concerns. Perhaps that's what had happened to the previous parties. Had they triggered alarms and been trapped somewhere in the bowels of the facility? The Foudre Rouge had enough firepower and explosives to have a chance, at least, of blasting their way out. But Badlands prospectors would likely have had to make do with far less powerful ordnance in any escape attempts.

Caron took a deep breath, and then he continued forward, deeper into the haunted and deadly halls of an empire long lost.

*   *   *

"We're picking up a signal from team two, Commander. They've popped a comm buoy and come close enough to the surface to transmits."

"On my line." There was nothing likely secretive about the report, but years as a Sector Nine operative had made Boucher stingy with information. She could always share something later, but there was only one way to correct an information leak...and she didn't have the crew to spare, not so far from any help.

"Commander Boucher...we have located landing sled one. It is positioned on a shelf approximately two kilometers below the surface. We are about to return to that position and debark and follow team one into the facility." A pause. "We have also detected something...unexplained...that I feel I must report. Significant water currents...so strong, we were barely able to navigate to our current location. The epicenter of the...disturbance...is approximately fifty kilometers from our current position, and I can offer no explanation."

Boucher inhaled deeply as she listened to the transmission. She cursed under her breath. Louis Moreau was the commander of team two, and he'd shown initiative in deploying to buoy to transmit his report to *Phantasia*.

But why the hell didn't the damned fool send the actual scanner data as well?

Phantasia's AI could crunch the numbers a thousand times faster and better than anything on the landing sleds. Boucher had been well-briefed for the mission, and that had included a fairly substantial dossier on the planet Aquellus. There was no particular evidence suggesting the world was particularly geologically or volcanically active. That didn't mean there couldn't have been some kind of sizable eruption or tremor. But it was more coincidence than she was ready to believe.

That ship? Could team three have found it intact...and destroyed it? Could that be what Moreau picked up?

She shook her head. It was possible, she supposed, but the only weapon on the landing ship was a laser, nothing with the power to cause such a massive tremor. *Unless the target's reactor went critical...*

Maybe.

She didn't buy it, though.

Could team three have been destroyed? She found it hard to believe the unidentified ship had even survived its hard landing into the sea, much less that it had been in any condition to attack her landing craft.

Was it possible, though? Could some Badlands scavenger's ship had carried some kind of weapon powerful enough to explain what the report described?

That would have to be a nuclear warhead...and a damned big one.

Just like the one that destroyed the bombers...

She felt her stomach tense. She'd told herself the explosion that had taken out her attack ships had been some kind of modified reactor, some old ship rigged to blow as a trap.

That *might* have described one such detonation. But not two.

If she was dealing with weapons, with nuclear warheads...they were damned big ones.

Where the hell would some old tech prospector get something like that?

She shifted in her seat, the tension growing with each passing second. The mission already had her stressed out, on the edge, and the strange haunted feeling so prevalent in Badlands space had done its work eroding her resolve. She'd at least allowed herself to believe the ship that had blundered in, that had employed a ruse to destroy her two attack ships, had itself been chased down to its destruction.

Now, she wasn't sure. It didn't make sense, didn't seem possible.

But it was eating at her gut, and a bad feeling was growing stronger with each thought.

"Scanners at full power, Drusus. We've got what, three scanner buoys left?"

"Yes, Commander."

"Launch them all. I want maximum coverage of the surface. If anything but one of our sleds comes up, I want to know…and long before it reaches orbit.

She wasn't going to take any chances. *Phantasia* was strong enough to take on anything that could be down there…as long as her people were ready.

There was just one question boring its way through her skull.

Who the hell is in that ship?

Chapter Twenty-Two

Free Trader Pegasus
Somewhere in the Endless Sea
Planet Aquellus, Olystra III
Year 302 AC

Pegasus lurched hard, toppling end over end as it tore through the wild seas. The detonation had caused a massive tsunami, and the ship was enduring its impact. The delayed fuse had given Andi and her people a bit of a head start, and Lex Righter had massaged the reactor to full power faster than she could have imagined. Still, they were caught up in the force of the disaster they had unleashed, and Andi clung to her seat for a tense few seconds, her harness holding her in place as she waited to see if *Pegasus*—if any of her people—would survive their own attack on their pursuers.

A stream of water flew across the bridge. The breach was smaller than the earlier ones, the flow intensity the result of the enormous pressure outside the vessel. She wasn't sure if it was a new hole in the hull, or if one of the patch jobs had given way. But she was pretty sure it was manageable, as long as it remained the only one.

She felt relief, or at least something vaguely like it, as she felt the ship's buffeting seeming to slow. "Lex...cut the engines." The thrusters had given all they could give, done all they could do to facilitate their escape. They'd either gotten *Pegasus* far enough from the detonation or they hadn't. There was little to be gained by pushing her tortured ship any harder, or adding a reactor breach to their list of problems.

"On it, Andi." The ship shook again a few second later, and she could feel the vibrations slowing as the engines shut down. A few seconds later, she felt another lurch as she tapped the positioning jets, and righted the ship.

"Gregor, as soon as the ship settles down, see what you can do about whatever leaks we've got again. Looks like just one up here on the bridge, but we need to check the whole ship."

"Yup." She could hear his boots pounding loudly on the deck through the comm, and she knew he'd followed his one-word answer by springing into action.

"Gregor, wait until…" She let the words trail off. Her comrade had already grabbed the patch kit, and she could hear him pushing through a blast of water toward what sounded like at least one leak on the lower deck.

She reached down to her comm unit, switching to the general channel. "Vig, is everything okay down there?" She hadn't realized just how worried she'd been until she heard his voice a few seconds later.

"Yeah, Andi. We're okay. We've got a couple small leaks, but Gregor's on them already. Anna and Jackal are heading up to the bridge with the second patch gun. We should be airtight in a few minutes."

Andi let out a soft sigh. She'd been worried about leaks on the lower level, too, but Vig's tone had told her, any problems down there were manageable.

She wanted to do down, see for herself, but she had other things to do. The Sector Nine ship was still waiting somewhere…and even if the torpedo had destroyed the lander that had been chasing *Pegasus*, there could be others out there.

And they still had to find the imperial facility, assuming the location data she had was even close to accurate. She felt the urge to make a run for it, to forget about artifacts, to trust in *Pegasus*'s engines to get her people out of the system. But she'd told Durango she would do her best. She'd given him her word. And for all her reputation as a scoundrel and an ill-tempered rogue, Andi Lafarge kept her promises.

"How's that looking over there?" Anna Fasarus had splashed through the bridge door and over to the leak. She was already spraying the breach, and the flow of water had slowed to a trickle. The job looked a little sloppy, maybe, but as Andi watched, the leak stopped entirely, so Anna's work also appeared to be effective.

"All set, Andi. It was one of the earlier leaks. I covered it up good this time."

Andi nodded. *Yes, you certainly did.* The giant glob of patching medium extended close to half a meter around the breach. Her mind couldn't help but guess at the cost of the stuff, but it didn't seem like the time to have a shipwide sit down to discuss economical use of supplies.

"That's good, Anna. Now, head to the lower deck, and make sure they've got things under control down there."

"I'm on it, Andi." Anna headed swiftly toward the hatch at the back of the bridge, and she disappeared into the hallway, the sounds of her feet clanging on the ladder reverberating through the bridge a few seconds later.

Andi turned toward Barret. "Let's see if we can figure out where we are in relation to these nav instructions I got from Durango. We shouldn't be too far from the facility." *I hope...*

If it even exists...

"It's not going to be easy to figure just how far we went since we hit the water. We can only guess how far we drifted when we were sinking, and that last run, courtesy of the torpedo, isn't going to be much easier. If we could go to the surface, get some star sightings, we might manage to…"

"No chance on that, Barret. When we get out of this ocean, it's going to be a dead race to the transit point. We can't risk surfacing and opening ourselves to detection, not until we're ready to go."

"That doesn't leave much in the way of navigation, Andi. It's more like…instinct."

"If instinct is what we need, then it's what we'll use." Andi had always had a strange combination of grim realism…strangely tempered with an amorphous belief her people could do what they had to do. It had never made much sense to her in pensive moments, but it was how she felt nevertheless.

"Let's start with the real data we've got. If we can figure out where we were when we first hit the water, that's the first step."

And the second will be taking a wild guess where these crazy ocean currents have taken us since…

* * *

"There's definitely something there, Andi. We're still pretty far out, at least with the scanners so beaten up, but I'd say that is *definitely* some kind of vessel."

Andi nodded, an unconscious expression of her agreement. Her eyes, and most of her focus, was on her own small screen, on the incoming data, searching almost frantically for any details, any images she could make out through the heavy interference. The scans were fuzzy, and as much as her gut agreed with Barret's assessment, she knew it was still mostly guesswork.

We'd have reliable scans by now, if we hadn't lost most of the dishes and antennae. We're going in almost blind, and that's asking for trouble. But what choice do we have?

The whole state of affairs was a stark reminder that

Pegasus had been roughly handled on the mission so far. Andi trusted her ship, knew the old vessel was tougher than she looked, but she also knew it could only take so much. And they already faced a deadly challenge once they emerged from the sea. A mad dash for the transit point at the very least, one that would take every bit of thrust *Pegasus*'s savaged engines could produce. But Andi didn't really believe the enemy would let their guard down enough to allow for such an escape. And that meant a fight, a desperate battle against a larger and stronger vessel. One that would be all the more hopeless if her people couldn't get *Pegasus*'s scanner suite a lot closer to normal operating levels before the ship surfaced and headed back into space.

She renewed her focus, pushing the vessel no doubt waiting in orbit out of her mind and staring at the screen as the image in front of *Pegasus* slowly sharpened. Suddenly, the indecipherable figure on her display became clear, at least in her mind. She realized two things, almost instantly. First, the initial contact *was* a ship, a landing sled just like the one they had destroyed with the torpedo.

And second, she wasn't looking at one contact. There were two of them, the second tucked in just behind the first.

"Barret…"

"I see them, Andi." A pause, as both of them stared at the steadily sharpening images. "They're disguised, made to look like old freight shuttles…but those are Union landers, I'd bet my pension on it." An empty gesture, Andi knew. Whatever sequence of events had led Barret from Confederation naval service to his place on *Pegasus*, had cost him his pension, and probably a lot more. But she took the point as he'd intended it.

"That makes sense. That ship that chased us down…it's too big to be a rival outfit's." She'd suspected Sector Nine since she'd first set eyes on the enemy ship. Now, she was sure. "We're up against Sector Nine again, Barret." She tried to keep the concern out of her voice…and she tried to tell herself it was only tension and not fear she felt. She wasn't sure either effort had been entirely successful.

"Looks that way." Her shipmate did an even worse job of hiding his fear. Sector Nine was ruthless, an organization that had spent almost two centuries building an image of coldblooded savagery. That was bad enough, but Andi's concern was more specific. If Sector Nine had deployed a vessel as large—and expensive—as the one *Pegasus* had encountered, her people were almost certainly outmatched as well as outnumbered.

There might even be combat-equipped Foudre Rouge in there…

"It doesn't matter who's in there. We're going in." Andi rode a surge of defiance, and she fought back almost immediately against the reflexive regret that followed. Part of her still wanted to run, to face the danger of escaping from the system, but not to seek out more.

But her integrity was all she had. Maybe if Durango hadn't paid her the ten thousand in advance, but he had done as he'd promised, and more. She couldn't do less.

They had to go in.

"Alright, Andi." Barret sounded a little shaky, but she knew he'd be ready for whatever happened.

"We've got to take out those two ships before we land." She had no idea how many of the Union personnel were in the ships and how many had gone inside the facility she was still only assuming was there. But she couldn't leave those landers. She couldn't give them a chance to launch and engage *Pegasus*.

"The lasers are fully operational, Andi, but the scanners are shit. Even at a range this close…"

"You can do it, Barret." It was a simple statement, devoid of any facts or evidence to back it up. But it was the kind of thing human beings needed sometimes, and it was all she had to give her gunner.

"We should come in closer, Andi. The water is going to attenuate the hell out of our laser blasts…and the lower the range, the more chance we've got to hit those things."

"We don't have time. We can see them, and that means they've almost certainly spotted us. We may have caught them by surprise, but that's not going to give us very long. If they get launched, we're going to be fighting moving targets, with their own lasers and intact scanners. We've *got* to hit them now, Barret. You *can* do this."

The gunner didn't answer. He just sighed softly and pulled down the targeting scope. He pressed his face against it, his hands reaching out, taking hold of the controls. Andi could feel the tension gripping her shipmate, even as her own ratcheted up as well. She was waiting for activity on the screen, for the instant the enemy ships began to move. She knew that was probably only seconds away, and even as Barret stared into the scope, she had to hold back the urge to try to push him along.

No…he knows the situation. Trust your people. That has never led you astray before…

She stared across the bridge, her eyes fixed on the rumpled mass of sandy brown hair on the back of Barret's head. It was half soaked in sweat, and she could see the grinding tension in his arms, in his hands, wrapped so tightly around the firing controls, his fingers were stark white.

She knew only a few seconds had passed, but it seemed like hours. *Pegasus* outgunned the landing ships, and assuming Barret could effectively target with the scanners little more than a pile of twisted wreckage, she knew her ship could blow the enemy out of the water.

Come on, Barret…

Andi's eyes were fixed on the screen, searching for any data *Pegasus*'s tortured dishes could provide. For a few more seconds, the two enemy ships remained still, no sign of any response to *Pegasus*'s approach.

Then, she saw an energy spike. The closest ship first, and then a second later, the other as well. The landers were lifting off. They were out of time.

Barret…

She could feel the sweat pooling up under her hairline, and she realized her hands had balled into tight fists. Barret was going to have a hard enough time dealing with *Pegasus*'s battered scanners and the swirling ocean currents shooting at stationary vessels. If those ship got off the ledge, he'd have to hit moving targets.

Andi held her breath as she saw the closest enemy ship begin to move slowly upward.

The next few seconds were almost a blur. She heard the familiar whine of *Pegasus*'s guns, and her eyes dropped again to the screen. The scanners were having as much trouble tracking the laser shot as they were the enemy ships, but there was no mistaking the movement of the first vessel, back down to its initial position…and an instant later, a billowing explosion, vast currents of water buffeting *Pegasus*, a torrent that could only have been caused by an explosion.

One down.

She felt a wave of excitement at what she knew in her heart was a kill, even as she instinctively reached out for *Pegasus*'s controls, activating the positioning jets, trying to stabilize the ship. The lasers fired again, but Andi didn't even have to look to know the second shot had missed. *Pegasus* wasn't wildly out of control as she had been earlier, but she *was* jerking around wildly in the onrushing currents, making targeting a virtual impossibility.

She shifted the controls, pulsing one of the jets, and then another, trying to stop the ship's movement, to give Barret a decent shot at the last enemy vessel.

It was a struggle. She'd never piloted a ship in the water before, and she fought hard to gain control, even with the navcom's help. Finally, she managed to right the ship, and the wild rocking stopped. Barret would have a shot now, a chance to take out the second enemy ship.

She turned her eyes back to the screen, to the fuzzy depiction of the rocky ledge. There was wreckage all around, debris that confirmed the first shot had, indeed, been a kill. There was just one problem.

The second ship was nowhere to be seen.

Chapter Twenty-Three

Unidentified Imperial Ruin
Somewhere Under the Endless Sea
Planet Aquellus, Olystra III
Year 302 AC

"Hold your positions." Nicolas Caron was crouched down behind a stack of metal crates. The room seemed to be some kind of supply facility, and he'd been about to order his people to search thoroughly for artifacts when the two Foudre Rouge he'd posted to guard their rear reported sounds approaching.

Caron's first reaction had been undisciplined, and the fear almost gripped him. They'd fought one partially operable security bot, and suffered four casualties, two of them dead. They'd lost another two dead when a second bot, also only partially operable, attacked them in another compartment. He'd known, of course, that imperial bots and other security mechanisms were deadly dangerous, but it was something different entirely to encounter them in reality, to feel their deadly projectiles ripping by over your head. Most imperial ruins were long dead, their protective features expended long ago, in the endemic fighting of the later Cataclysm. Caron had hoped the second bot would be the last, but he wasn't sure he believed that. As soon as the

Foudre Rouge gave the alert, he was sure they faced another attack.

But now he heard sounds, not those of an ancient warbot, but voices. For a few seconds, he couldn't make out what was being said, but then he recognized the distinct barking of Foudre Rouge battle language. The special form of communication used by the clone soldiers sounded like gibberish to him, but it was distinctly recognizable for what it was. He tapped his comm unit, switching to the general channel. "All Union forces…this is Nicolas Caron. You are approaching our position. All Union forces are to maintain maximum caution before engaging." Caron wasn't a soldier by trade, but he knew well enough how easily friendly fire casualties could result without strong communications. His people were certainly on edge, ready to blow away anything that showed itself down the corridor. And he couldn't imagine whoever was heading his way was any less tense.

"Nicolas…it's Louis. I've got the second team. We came past the remains of two imperial security bots. Your work?"

"Yes…costly work. We can hear you coming down the corridor, so you've got to be close. Make sure your people know we're up here. The last thing we need is to lose more people fighting each other." A pause. "And hurry up. We've found what looks like a cache of artifacts, but I'm at half strength now. We could use some more hands and eyes up here."

"On the way."

Caron turned and looked out across the room. He hit the comm again. "You all heard that, so stand down. We've got friendlies approaching, so hold all fire."

He stood up and walked toward the center of the room, coming out from behind the pile of boxes. A moment later, two Foudre Rouge walked in, followed by Louis Moreau.

"Louis, I'm damned glad it's you. Whatever this place is, it's far from completely dead. I don't know what else is prowling around, but I've got a feeling we can use all the firepower we can get."

"It looks like you've found something. Boxed up parts? Electronics, maybe? This could be a massive discoveries, maybe the biggest ever."

"Maybe. We just started looking through all of this. The crates are locked. We could blast them open, but that might damage the contents. We're working on hacking our way in. But getting another team working on them can only speed things up." A pause. "And we need to send out an exploration party. We've got to find the reactor core or some other system we can sabotage. We take everything we can get out of here…but our orders were clear. When we leave, we destroy this place, before the Confeds can get here. That directive came from the top, from Gaston Villieneuve himself."

"Understood." Moreau was technically at the same rank as Caron, but the leader of the first team was the senior operative, and the overall commander on site. "Any word from the third team? They've got the warhead."

Caron sighed. "No. I was about to ask you the same thing. They should have made contact with you shortly after you landed. If they don't show, we've got a problem. Without that warhead, we've *really* got to find the reactor and sabotage it. Maybe we're lucky in a way that this place *is* still somewhat operative. The power generation system has to be at least partially functional, and that's our best bet now. Nothing else we've got besides that warhead is powerful enough to take this whole place out…and I for one am not going back and telling Gaston Villieneuve we left the place intact and ran home."

Moreau just nodded. The expression on his face adequately communicated his complete agreement. Villieneuve was the head of Sector Nine, and if he was a bit less prone to random violence and cruelty than his immediate predecessors had been, his utter intolerance for failure was well known. The cells under Sector Nine headquarters were legendary. Caron had been there a number of times, on the side of the inquisitors. He had no desire to experience them from the other perspective.

"Okay...let's split your people up. Put together a team to find the reactor and report back here with its location. And send a pair of Foudre Rouge out to patrol, and supplement my pickets. If they encounter any security bots or other problems, they are to withdraw and report at once."

Moreau nodded again, clearly trying to hide his resentment at having to take Caron's orders. "Yes, sir." The tone almost hid Moreau's true thoughts.

Almost.

Caron understood his comrade's point of view, but he was still defensive of his seniority on the mission. Sector Nine's hierarchy was built almost entirely around the naked pursuit of power. Every operative was focused the those on the next rung, ready to move up, whatever that took. Whether it was the promotion of senior agent that opened a spot...or something darker...was generally of little concern. Outright mutiny was out of the question, of course. That was a good way to land in one of those cells. But Caron had no doubt Moreau would be less than heartbroken to see him become a casualty of the operation...and to return in the senior position to deliver the captured artifacts, along with news that the facility had been destroyed.

He had to direct the mission...but he also had to watch his back.

"Choose your teams, and order the rest of your people to join mine in searching these crates." Caron let a bit of his arrogance slip out, a brush back of sorts targeted toward the resentment he'd heard in his subordinate's voice. It was counterproductive, perhaps, at least in some ways, but he wasn't about to allow Moreau to start thinking they were partners in the mission.

"Yes, Nicolas. I'll see to it immediately." Moreau sounded slightly chastised...but still resentful. He turned and walked back across the room, shouting out commands to his people. Half a minute later, four Foudre Rouge moved toward the single door on the far side of the room. It had been opened, but the corridor beyond hadn't yet been scouted, at least not past twenty meters or so to confirm it was unoccupied. The best data the portable scanners had been able to gather in the imperial alloy clad rooms and hallways, suggested energy output in that direction.

A moment later, two more Foudre Rouge from the second team walked toward the original entry door, weapons at the ready. Caron wasn't sure if there were anymore threats behind them, but he'd left plenty of unexplored corridors, and he felt better with a second pair of Foudre Rouge covering the rear.

The entire place gave him the creeps, and he couldn't wait until his people were back on their ship, and headed toward *Phantasia*. He knew almost everything in the facility was priceless, one irreplaceable artifact after another. But he would be happy with enough stashed in the hold to call the mission a success. The sooner he was back in Union space, the better he would feel, and if that meant blowing a chunk of mankind's lost legacy to atoms, so be it.

* * *

"No word, Commander. Not from any of the landers. The scanner buoys haven't picked up any signals since the strange...detonation. Of course, at two kilometers depth, we wouldn't pick up normal operations, or even combat."

"Keep scanning. I want continuous updates." Boucher sat in her chair, telling herself for the tenth time, the enemy ship had been destroyed, that the detonation her scans had picked up had been the vessel's reactor losing containment. But she wasn't buying it, not even from herself. The energy profile wasn't quite right, the radiation patterns...off. It looked more like a warhead to her, a *big* one. *Where would some Badlands prospector have gotten two nukes like that?*

"Yes, Commander. All scanner buoys sending constant data streams. If anything happens down there, we'll know about it."

Boucher nodded. She didn't have any rational concerns. She'd sent three teams down, ten agents in total, plus thirty-one Foudre Rouge. It was more than enough to deal with any Badlands adventurers. Her people had numbers, and they had the advantage in armament, too. The lack of a report didn't mean anything, not yet, at least.

And, even if there *was* some kind of trouble she couldn't specify, if through some miracle that ship *had* survived, if its tiny crew somehow defeated five times their number of fully-armed Foudre Rouge and three landing craft...they wouldn't stand a chance against *Phantasia*. Her ship was nearly as large as a light frigate, and its armament vastly outclassed the popguns mounted on any prospector's ship. The Confeds had slipped past her, gotten lucky. But if they weren't dead already, she would finish them as soon as they tried to escape.

But the detonations still bothered her. She was even more convinced that could only have been a warhead of some kind...a military grade one. And that kept her on edge. Whatever she faced—perhaps was *still* facing—it was no normal adventurer's ship. It was something special, and it packed more power than she'd expected to face. Those warheads were of particular concern.

Especially if that ship has more of them...

She resisted the realization that *Phantasia* itself could be in danger, but it crept around the edge of her thoughts anyway, pushing and pushing with each hour that passed with no word from her people.

"I want all scanners checked every thirty minutes. Full diagnostics. I want them functioning at one hundred percent." She paused, staring at the main screen.

If that Confed ship is still down there, I want targeting on it before its hull dries off.

Chapter Twenty-Four

Free Trader Pegasus
Somewhere in the Endless Sea
Planet Aquellus, Olystra III
Year 302 AC

The flash on the screen had lasted only an instant, *Pegasus*'s damaged sensors showing little more than an undefined energy surge. But to Andi, it was confirmation of what she'd feared for the last half minute.

The second enemy ship *had* managed to lift off from the ledge, and now, it had fired at her vessel. Any thoughts of catching both Union landers idle was gone. *Pegasus* faced a *real* fight.

The shot had gone wide, by a considerable margin, though her vessel's battered sensor suite couldn't provide more than a wide and almost meaningless range of numbers. The enemy laser had accomplished little save to heat the normally frigid deep sea water to the vapor point, the heat intense enough to overcome even the immense pressure of more than two kilometers of depth to create a wild vortex of air bubbles rising steadily toward the surface.

It did one more thing. A billowing shafts of roiling steam traced the laser's path...and it showed the way back to the enemy ship.

"Barret...the steam." *Pegasus*'s scanners were still searching for the enemy ship, but that last shot had provided at least a line back to its approximate location. It was far from precise, but it was something, and to a skilled and experience gunner like Barret, perhaps something significant. Eyeballing a shot was almost impossible in space combat, where the distances involved where immense, but the current fight wasn't in the vast vacuum of space, it was deep under the oceans of Aquellus. Andi knew *Pegasus*'s enemy was no more than a kilometer or two away, ranges that seemed almost gibberish to her space honed sensibilities.

Pegasus's savaged scanners hadn't yet detected the target's location, but the effect of the vessel's laser shot, combined with its engine output on the surrounding ocean, were creating a rough roadmap to follow.

"I'm on it...but they're moving, too. I'm tracking their engine output, trying to get some kind of fix. But there's still a lot of guesswork in this, Andi." Barret was silent for a few seconds, then he added, "A *lot* of guesswork."

Andi moved her hand on her own controls, increasing the thrust slightly, bringing *Pegasus* around toward her best guess at the enemy's location. It was guesswork for her as well, but it was all she had. She glanced down at the AI, but she knew it would be of limited use in the current fight. Fighting underwater was too different from the space combat for which it had been programmed. She'd monitor the data, review the recommendations from the computer, but she knew in the end, this fight was going to be won on instinct, on raw focus and determination.

She tapped the controls again, her eyes moving from her own screen to the main display, looking for something, anything to give her a better idea where the enemy ship was...and where it was heading. There were some new readings, almost certainly the result of the enemy's maneuver, of the pilot in that thing doing just what she herself was, struggling to bring that ship to bear, to get a another shot at *Pegasus*. To destroy her ship before she could do the same to them.

Another laser blast ripped by, closer this time. Andi recoiled from the screen, surprised by the flash even as she'd expected it.

That was too damned close…

She pulled up all the scanners could give her, every reading, every partial stream of data. The line of the shot traced back again, a long column of boiling seawater, bubbling up, before the frigid temperatures all around condensed it and stopped the upward flow, more than a kilometer short of the surface.

But it was more than a lesson in underwater thermodynamics. It gave her another line on the enemy ship…and a chance to calculate the vessel's speed and vector. The kind of wild evasive maneuvers so crucial to space combat were impossible in the ocean depths, or nearly so. The warring vessels were cumbersome, their moves slow, predictable. Whichever ship could locate the other first would almost certainly win the battle.

Andi was determined that would be *Pegasus*. Her stubbornness had taken her far, from the misery of the gut to ownership of her own spaceship. She was relying on it again, on her outright refusal to lose.

"Barret…wait to fire until you feel you have a good shot…a *really* good shot." It was difficult, almost unbearable, to endure enemy fire without returning it, to sit there hoping against hope that the vessel attacking you didn't score a hit. But Andi had a gambler's mind, and she grasped the odds with practiced skill. Wild shots were a poor trade, a tiny chance of scoring a lucky hit, purchased at the price of giving the enemy real targeting data. It was worth forgoing three or four ten percent chances of success, in return for one sixty or seventy percent shot.

The fact that the enemy presumably had fully functional

scanners only made it more imperative not to give them any further advantages by giving them missed shots to track *Pegasus*, even as Andi and Barret were using their own to develop their attack.

"I'm working on a fix, Andi." A pause, then *Pegasus*'s gunner continued nervously, "One more shot from them, and I think I can get solid coordinates." Barret's voice was hoarse, the stress he was feeling evident in every word.

Andi understood the tension. She felt it herself. Sitting there, waiting for the enemy to shoot again, it went against every natural instinct she had. She had always been one to act, to seize the initiative.

But she knew waiting—gambling that the enemy missed again—was the right move. So did Barret.

That didn't make it any easier. She shifted around in her seat, pawing almost unconsciously at the harness holding her in place. Andi had faced danger her entire life, she'd fought her first battle to the death at an age when most children in the Confederation were still in school. She didn't back down from fights, no matter how strong, how tough the enemy.

Sitting there and doing nothing was harder for her than any combat, any struggle.

Pegasus's bridge was almost eerily quiet, the faint hum of the reactor in the distance almost inaudible next to the sound of her own breathing. She fought a war with herself, a desperate battle to hold back the order she longed to give, to command Barret to fire before the enemy had another chance to finish them. But she held firm. She knew what they had to do.

Her mind warred with itself anyway, and shouts flew back and force inside her head, grim warnings that her maneuvers had given the enemy targeting data they needed, that even holding fire was no guarantee the Union spacer at the gun controls out there couldn't score the deadly hit he sought. *Pegasus* was a tough ship, but she was damaged, too, and Andi had very little idea how the water pressure pouring in from a serious hull breach would compare to the vacuum of space. Gregor had managed to patch them all so far, but those were small gashes in the hull. A direct hit would be far more serious...and deadly. Space sucked out anything—and anyone—not secured, and it necessitated survival gear if the crew was to survive. But the water was a force on its own. It wouldn't just flood *Pegasus*, and short out every exposed electrical system. It would tear her ship apart from the inside. It was a massive force amplifier, and it made the first hit even more important than it was in space combat.

It very probably made the first direct hit the last hit as well. The killing shot.

She waited, concentrating on her breathing, trying to maintain a cold focus. It was far more difficult, often, to patiently pursue the right course. Wild, impulsive action at least gave the feeling of *doing something*...even if it was mostly illusory.

She nudged the controls again, tracking the enemy ship as well as she could, even as Barret was doing the same with the gunnery station. Her comrade was silent, the intensity of his concentration clear to see in the brittle tension gripping his body. Andi almost spoke three or four times, words of encouragement or suggestions on targeting, but she realized the best thing she could do for Barret was to leave him alone.

The time passed with agonizing slowness, and for an instant, Andi wondered if the enemy had fled instead of continuing the fight. That would be dangerous, too, and the idea of an enemy ship running around loose in the open sea was daunting. At the very least, it would make landing a deadly dangerous course of action, leaving *Pegasus* a sitting duck if the Union vessel returned.

Assuming, of course, she could land the ship on the now debris strewn platform.

She pushed the thought aside, discarded the notion that

the enemy had run. She reminded herself of Sector Nine's policies regarding failure, a legend about the spy agency she had found, in her own limited experience, to be entirely true. Andi was vengeful against her enemies, and merciless at times as well. But the idea of torturing and killing her own people for failing at a task…it was unthinkable to her.

She saw the utility in it, perhaps. Merciless brutality sometimes created a kind of pseudo courage, and she suspected the realization that the only other options were to face a horrible death at home, or to remain forever hiding in the haunted Badlands, made a heads up fight with *Pegasus* seem like a good choice.

From that perspective, it was. It was exactly what she would do in her enemy's place.

Her eyes caught the flash even before her thoughts processed it. Her first realization was, it had been *close*. The scanner report confirmed that a second later.

The beam had come within eighty meters of *Pegasus*.

Whoever is handling the gun on that thing knows his shit. Come on, Barret…this may be our last chance…

She turned and looked at her comrade, silent as her eyes bored into the back of his head. She could see his hands tight around the controls, moving slowly, deliberately, to adjust the shot she knew was coming, but seemed to be taking forever.

Her own hands balled up into fists again, and she struggled to maintain her deliberate breathing. She glanced back at her screen, checking *Pegasus*'s position, and confirming to herself there was nothing further she could do to help Barret. Her fate—the fate of everyone aboard the ship—was in the gunner's hands. The enemy had come close, too close, with that last shot, and if Barret missed, if they gave the enemy the additional location data the laser pulse would provide, she had no doubt the next attack would be a hit.

And under two kilometers of water, any significant

damage to the hull would likely finish *Pegasus*…and all her people.

Her eyes darted to Barret's hand, drawn by the slightest visible motion. Her mind processed the data her eyes provided, and came to its conclusion an instant later. Barret was about to fire.

She lost track of her controlled breathing, and she held the last gulp of air, watching, waiting. The near silence on the bridge assaulted her ears, deafening in its own way, and she stared at Barret. The next second or two would likely determine if they lived or died. She wondered what was worse, to be in Barret's position, knowing the lives of his friends and comrades rested on his actions in the next few seconds…or on the rest of *Pegasus*'s crew, facing the same likelihood of death, but doing so helpless to intervene, to assist in any way.

She never got an answer.

The familiar whine echoed off the walls and deck of the bridge, and her tension ramped up even more, as she realized Barret had fired. The laser beam itself moved at lightspeed, and she knew whatever had resulted from the shot had happened already. But it would take a few seconds for the water currents and the battered scanners to give a clear view of what had happened.

If Barret had destroyed the enemy ship…or if her people were staring into the cold eyes of their own likely deaths.

Then, the wave of water crashed into *Pegasus*, upending the ship again. Andi felt a sharp pain in her chest as her body lurched forward, and the harness caught her and held her in place. She reached out, grabbing the controls, but despite the wild rolling of her ship, and amid her desperate efforts to regain control, she let out a laugh, and almost maniacal sounding cackle.

The wild torrent of water meant only one thing to her, and before Barret reported, before the scanners displayed the results, she knew exactly what had happened.

Barret had scored a hit. He had destroyed the enemy vessel.

The Union ship had exploded, and the waves of the tsunami engulfing *Pegasus,* and sending the ship careening again through the tortured water were the spoils of victory.

Chapter Twenty-Five

Free Trader Pegasus
Somewhere in the Endless Sea
Planet Aquellus, Olystra III
Year 302 AC

Andi moved the controls to the port, so lightly, she couldn't even see the movement. *Pegasus* lurched gently as the positioning jets on the starboard side fired at five percent power. It was a delicate move, a slight adjustment...but it was a critical one.

The landing approach felt strange to her, utterly different than the wild maneuvers she'd executed to pull *Pegasus* out of the wild roll that resulted from the destruction of the enemy ship. She'd given herself a few seconds after that to ponder on the unlikelihood of her people surviving so far into the mission. They'd destroyed three Sector Nine landing ships, and they'd endured a crash into the ocean, near destruction from the enormous warhead they'd detonated themselves, and a duel against that third enemy vessel.

Now, they were landing. The fact that the enemy ships had been there was something short of absolute proof there was, indeed, an imperial ruin there...but there wasn't any doubt left in Andi's mind.

The space on the rock shelf was large enough to accommodate *Pegasus*. Just. It was littered with small bits of debris, but they would all fit under her ship's landing struts, unlike the large chunks surrounding the safe haven on every side. Barret had hit the last enemy ship dead on, and even as she struggled to land amid the scattered field of wreckage that remained from the two vessels, she couldn't help but feel pride once again in her people. They were a band of misfits, most of them with checkered pasts, but they knew their stuff. Together, they became something very special, most definitely more than the sum of their parts.

Still, proud or not, she was nervous about their adversaries. She was confident her people could handle their counterparts, and she'd put them up against any Badlands prospecting crew out there. But Sector Nine was out of their league, and she couldn't help but worry about just how high on the spy agency's list of enemies she and her people had risen. That was the kind of problem that would follow her comrades wherever they went, and for all her normal confidence, it felt a little like an open-ended death sentence.

Andi could see—mostly *feel*—Barret watching her, the gunner extending her the same courtesy she had him, remaining silent while she did her job. She tapped the controls again, trying to right the ship after a strong current pushed it forward twenty or thirty meters too far.

She'd decided one thing, without the slightest doubt in her mind. She hated piloting her ship underwater, and if she managed to get her people out of this, she resolved to laugh in the face of the next Spacer's District hustler who tried to send her to some water world. Space's vacuum was deadly and dangerous, but it was a familiar threat. Two kilometers of water overhead was something entirely different, a danger she found far more difficult to deal with, at least in some ways.

Her people had taken out three Union landers, all they'd found so far. Her analysis of the enemy ship, its mass and dimensions, suggested that three was likely the full complement, especially since the vessel had launched two bombers as well. Anna's own calculations reached the same conclusion. But it was still more of a guess than she liked. She'd gained the edge by catching her enemy sitting on the rock shelf, and she didn't much like the idea of getting caught in the same situation if there was another enemy lander out there somewhere.

But it was the only way. She *had* to go in, and any thought of *Pegasus* dropping off a landing party and taking off again was quickly disqualified by the need to allow Lex a chance to repair at least *some* of the damage. If *Pegasus* launched with her scanners in their current condition, any battle with the enemy's main ship would be over in a matter of minutes. She was counting on the ability of her kidnapped engineer, relying partially on what she'd already seen of his abilities, and partially on Durango's assurances Righter was one of the best.

Best, worst, or something in between, he was all they had.

She tapped the controls again, more lightly even than the first time. *Pegasus* shifted slightly. Maneuvering underwater seemed like something between operations in space, where a ship would travel along a vector indefinitely, at least until a counter force was exerted, and flying in atmosphere, where friction from the air would quickly slow lateral velocity and gravity would pull a powerless vessel relentlessly to the ground. There was no effective influence of gravity in the sea, though she knew that was a tremendous oversimplification of the force patterns at work. All that really mattered to her just then was the fact that she found it difficult and frustrating, especially when she was trying to land with less than three meters to spare in any direction.

She checked the readings. Six meters above the rocky landing pad. She nudged down the vertical thrust, allowing *Pegasus* to float lower.

Five meters.

She tapped the lateral jets again, pushing the ship slightly to starboard.

Four meters.

A hard landing in water wouldn't be *as* dangerous as one in open atmosphere, but it wouldn't be good. If she came down on a large chunk of debris, she could damage one or more of the landing struts. Or worse.

Three meters.

Pegasus was rocking back and forth. Even with the minimal thrust, the jets were stirring up the water all around, creating a difficult environment to control touchdown. Andi was a perfectionist by nature, but she was ready to accept any landing that didn't further damage her ship. Even if it wasn't particularly comfortable for her crew.

Two meters.

She took a deep breath, and she tapped the lateral jets one last time, before she cut the vertical push completely. *Pegasus* dropped through the water, sliding slightly to port before coming to an abrupt halt. Andi had missed her target point, but not by much, and a few seconds of frantic staring at the display told her she'd come close enough. *Pegasus* was down, and less than six degrees from level. All the landing struts were on solid ground, and as far as she could tell, no area of the hull had been damaged by any impacts.

It wasn't an award-winning landing, not by any measure. But it would serve.

That left just two things to do.

First, she had to *really* check the ship, and make certain there was no additional damage. Then she could turn things over to Lex...and see what her engineer was really made of.

The second task gave her stomach a flop or two, but she knew what she had to do. Even then, her mind was racing, picking out the people she was going to take with her...into the depths of the imperial facility she knew was out there, somewhere very close.

*   *   *

"Remember…there are almost certainly hostiles in here, and by that I don't mean some crew of loudmouthed prospectors looking to get into a brawl over swag. I mean Union personnel, Sector Nine operatives…even Foudre Rouge. We're probably outnumbered, and we're almost certainly outgunned, so I need all of you at your best. No, better than your best."

Andi almost laughed at her own choice of words. *All of you…that's a pretty grandiose term for five people. Including yourself.*

She'd left Lex back at *Pegasus*, of course. He was the only one who could get the ship ready for what awaited it back out in the space around Aquellus.

She'd ordered Barret to stay as well. She still held some hope *Pegasus* would make a successful run for the transit point, but in her heart, she knew they had a fight ahead of them. She had no idea how much progress Lex Righter would make, but she knew whatever chance they had to prevail in a battle, it was higher with Barret on the guns. She didn't like to think about her people being killed or wounded, but she just couldn't risk losing Barret in some gunfight in the ruin. After Righter and his engineering skills, there was no one more vital to her people's chances of surviving the mission. And no one more qualified to assist the engineer in getting *Pegasus* ready for whatever awaited them out there.

She'd left Doc, too, though he'd argued almost as emphatically as Barret had that he should come. She could absolutely see the need for a medic. She was too experienced an adventurer not to imagine the chance-probability?—that her people would take casualties, but as fond as she was him, he just wasn't as fit as the others, nor as skilled in combat. She was counting on moving in and out as quickly as possible, and she imagined any fights would be sharp and quick. Doc could be of help to any of her people who were wounded, but she knew if she brought him, he would likely be the first casualty.

"This is definitely it, Andi." Vig's voice was higher pitched over the comm unit than it was in person. "Someone's been here, too, and recently. I don't think there's much doubt about that." He gestured toward the rocky ground around his feet. The sandy grit on top of the stone had been disturbed, even where her own people had not yet tread. She knew the sea would quickly cover up any such signs, and that meant whoever was inside hadn't been there long.

But will they be expecting us? From what she'd seen of imperial facilities, they often interfered with communications. It was possible the Foudre Rouge, or whoever was waiting inside, knew she and her people were coming, even that *Pegasus* had destroyed their landing ships. But her gambler's instincts kicked in again, and she bet herself the Union forces inside were cut off, that however outnumbered her people were, they just might have some element of surprise.

"See if you can get it open." She stood still for a moment, waiting to see if Vig managed to activate the airlock mechanism. Her newest and youngest crew member had a considerable talent for picking locks. She'd teased him a bit about that, but she wasn't about to become judgmental about anyone's past. Vig might have learned to steal at a young age, but Andi had learned to kill.

"I think it's filling with water, Andi. With any luck, we'll be inside in a minute." Vig's tone was a strange mix of cockiness and trepidation. Those two things seemed contradictory, but she understood it completely.

"Stay on it, Vig. If there's some kind of alert or security, we need to know as soon as possible." She reached for the waterproof rifle attached to her suit. The undersea suits Durango had given her people were leading edge, and they allowed almost effortless movement, even at the tremendous pressure two kilometers under the surface, at least if that movement was nothing more than straight forward or turning slowly. The suits were also well equipped for battle, with specialized assault rifles, though Durango had warned her that even the custom-designed weapons had extremely restricted ranges underwater.

She took a deep breath, too deep for the oxygen rich mixture in her tanks, and she felt lightheaded for a few seconds. She caught herself, and she slowed her respiration rate. She'd known better, at least Durango's people had given her some quick instruction with the suits, but she was edgy, tense. She felt edgy under the water, claustrophobic, and it was starting to get to her.

She stood still, staring at Vig, watching as he struggled to work the controls in his own bulky suit. The gloves were the thinnest part of the apparatus, designed to facilitate close work. But they still had to protect against the massive pressure, so they were pretty thick, if less so than the rest of the suit.

Andi was about to ask Vig for s status report when the door slid open, revealing a fully-flooded interior compartment, several meters square. Vig stepped inside almost immediately. Andi opened her mouth to warn him off, to tell him to hold back until she got a closer look, but he was already in, and she remained silent. She made a mental note to speak with her brash young crew member, almost forgetting, as she always did, that she was barely older herself.

Vig turned and looked back. "Come on…it's clear."

Andi almost responded, but there was no point. She just nodded, for whatever that gesture was worth in the suit, and she said to the others, "Let's go."

She walked in next, followed by the rest of the small party. "Okay, Vig, so far so good. Can you get us in now?"

"You bet. This thing's not so complicated." Andi was

usually good at shifting through bullshit, but she couldn't get a solid fix on how much of Vig's confidence was based on fact, and how much on youthful cockiness.

I guess we'll find out…

She watched as he worked the controls, taking longer than his brash statement would have suggested. Finally, Andi heard a creaking sound, and the outer door slid shut. A few seconds later, the water bubbled all around as it drained out of the room. Half a minute later, she was standing on the ground, suddenly feeling the oppressive weight of the suit.

Vig continued his efforts, and the inner door opened, revealing a large chamber inside. Andi's eyes darted around, scanning the room for threats. It didn't take her long to find them, at least signs of them.

There were a dozen suits laying against the walls. No, more than a dozen. Twenty-three in total. For a few seconds, some part of her tried to believe they were artifacts, ancient imperial equipment, laying there for centuries. But it only took a second to realize half of them were still wet.

"She looked down at her portable scanner, confirming that the air was breathable. There were no pathogens, at least none the small device could detect. And the risk of some unknown disease seemed less ominous than that of the enemy coming into the room fully armed, and catching her people almost helpless in their undersea gear.

She reached down and pulled the release, popping open her suit. She was the leader, and to her that meant she went first, confirming the scanner reports with her own lungs. She took a deep breath. It was musty, and the scent had a feeling of…oldness…to it. But it seemed perfectly breathable.

"Okay, pop your suits. It looks like we've got company, and we don't want to get caught in these things." She waited for perhaps a minute, while her people opened their suits, and climbed out with varying degrees of grace. Or clumsiness.

"I want everybody ready for anything that happens." Even as she spoke, she pulled her assault rifle from the waterproof sack she'd carried. She didn't even reach for the underwater weapon laying on the floor next to her discarded suit. Her own guns were far handier in a fight than the single shot underwater jobs Durango had given her. She checked to make sure the clip was firmly in place, and she reached down and grabbed a utility belt covered in small grenades. She draped it over her shoulder, and she looked around, waiting impatiently as the others armed themselves. She pulled a shiny blade from a scabbard, staring at the razor sharp edge for a second, before she slid it back and attached the whole thing to her belt. Then, she looked all around, at the room, at the possible exit doors, and at her people.

"It looks like there's only one way to go, so shall we?" She gestured toward the single door on the far side of the room. It was closed, but Vig was already at the control panel, and he turned toward her. "It looks unlocked, Andi." He paused for a moment, and then he took her lack of an immediate response as approval to press on. He moved his finger against one side of the glass panel, and the door slid open.

Andi peered down the corridor ahead. She hesitated for a few seconds, checking and double checking the long, straight hallway beyond the door. Then, she turned toward Vig. "You're with me. The rest of you stay back a couple meters. We don't need to make it easy for them to take us all out." It was an ominous thing to say, but she knew they were going into danger, probably desperate danger. And sugar-coating things wouldn't be a favor to her people.

She needed them at their best. And fear would sharpen their senses, improve their response times.

It was sharpening hers.

Chapter Twenty-Six

Unidentified Imperial Ruin
Somewhere Under the Endless Sea
Planet Aquellus, Olystra III
Year 302 AC

Andi stared at the two corpses, and the pools of semi-congealed blood around them on the floor. There had been a serious fight in the room, but it wasn't until she glanced down the corridor that her stomach really tightened. There was debris everywhere. The battle had been no struggle between rival prospecting crews, nor even Sector Nine thugs fighting such a group.

The Union party had run into something far, far deadlier. An imperial security bot.

Andi moved toward the corridor, knowing it was a bit reckless, but doing it anyway. She knelt down and picked up a chunk of metal, knowing immediately what it was.

Imperial alloy.

The strange metal found in so many artifacts and imperial ruins was remarkable in a number of ways. Strength, durability...but Andi had always considered the most amazing thing to be the way the material defied aging. No rust, no tarnishing, nothing at all to suggest that it hadn't just rolled out of the foundry, freshly polished. Even the piece she held was more or less intact, a section of the bot's outer casing, she guessed, detached from its mounting, but otherwise undamaged. She wiped her hand across it, and the blackened soot from the explosion that had destroyed the bot came away, revealing a shiny silver surface. It was so smooth, she could see her reflection in it.

"It took more than a frag grenade to take this thing out." Her words were grim, but she didn't voice her true concern. She didn't know for sure what they were facing, and she wasn't going to jump to conclusion. Sector Nine operatives were brutal enough, but she'd put her crew up against them in anything close to an even fight.

Foudre Rouge were a different matter entirely. The clone soldiers were deadly fighters, but the real difference would be the ordnance they carried. She had an assault rifle and a belt full of light grenades, no light armament. But Foudre Rouge were combat soldiers. If there were any of them loose in the facility, they'd be armed to the teeth. Sector Nine operatives could be there to explore, to research imperial artifacts, just as her people were. But if the feared Union regulars were present, they were there for only one purpose.

"I want everybody alert, ready for anything." It was a stupid thing to say, she realized immediately. They were prowling around an imperial ruin after fighting off three enemy ships. Anyone who wasn't wide awake and alert was probably already dead.

"So, what are you worried about, Andi? More imperial bots? Or Foudre Rouge?" Vig hadn't hesitated to speak the name she had kept to herself. His question was the one she knew was on everyone's mind, and there was only one reply, single word to answer them both.

"Yes."

They were both deadly threats...but there was some advantage, she supposed, to having the Union personnel ahead of her people. They would flush out the imperial defenses, as they clearly had the bot she was staring at even then. If she followed them, maybe her people could avoid running into any imperial defenses themselves.

And, if we're really lucky, the bots will take out some more of these Union bastards…

She imagined finding the last Sector Nine operative, lying wounded on the ground as she relieved him of a large sack of imperial artifacts…and put a bullet between his eyes. It was an unlikely occurrence, she knew, but a pleasant thought, nevertheless.

Andi had a strong sense of fair play, and in most cases, she wasn't the sort to murder a wounded man. But as far as she was concerned, anyone at Sector Nine was fair game. They all deserved to die, at least in her book.

"Okay, there are a number of doors leading off from here, but it looks like…whoever…was here went this way. I'm all for someone flushing out any residual imperial defenses for us, so let's follow." That was one of her reasons for choosing to follow the apparent course of the Union personnel. The other was just as tactical. She'd rather run into her enemy head on than push forward along a different route and risk having them come around behind her. Most of her missions had involved snooping around, and even dealing with the occasional imperial security response or a rival expedition. But she'd never seen a ruin so well-preserved as the one she stood in then. The thought of what Union forces she might run into paled in comparison to nightmare of what fully operational imperial bots could do.

Not even Foudre Rouge could move the needle on that comparison.

"Okay, let's not jump to any conclusions…but let's be ready for whatever we find. We're here to grab some imperial artifacts, and from the look of this place, there should be some to be had. We'll press on and see what we can find." The mission was going to be a score, that much was clear. Assuming, of course, her people somehow managed to get out...and make it past the Union ship waiting for them.

The half million Durango had offered her seemed paltry as she looked around, imagining the value of the electronics and other components to be had. She fully intended to keep her word...but she was still tempted to grab a few pieces for her own people's account.

Who would miss a box or two of the swag most likely tucked away in this place?

"I left the others explicit instructions to stay with the ship. That leaves the five of us, and we're all here. So, anything we see or hear, even the slightest draft we feel, is an enemy. Imperial bot, Sector Nine killer, Foudre Rouge soldier..." She finally acknowledged what they were all thinking, and what she'd already come to believe...that there *were* Union clone soldiers loose in the facility. "...it doesn't matter. Anything is an enemy. We kill them before they kill us. Understood?"

She looked back as her people responded with a series of grunts and nods. Then, she turned back toward the corridor and moved out, her rifle in front of her, and her eyes darting around, almost wildly, looking for threats.

Looking for anything.

*   *   *

"Corporal Palloux-7364 calling Lieutenant Javais. Please acknowledge." The Foudre Rouge shook his head as he listened on his headset, hearing nothing but static. He'd been briefed on the jamming effect of the imperial materials in the facility's structure, but he was agitated by his absolute inability to reach the lieutenant. He'd been ordered to report in every half hour, and obedience was hardwired into his psyche. He'd been bred for his role, his DNA cultivated and engineered to produce the perfect soldier, as it had been for all his comrades, and he'd been conditioned almost since birth. He felt something very much like frustration at the deviation from normal procedure.

"I cannot reach the lieutenant. One of us will have to go back on foot to report if we find anything of importance." He turned toward the other Foudre Rouge present. Ellian-3041 had been his squad mate since he'd begun active service at age nineteen six years before. Foudre Rouge policy was to keep units together as long as possible, though casualties and other factors often made that difficult. "We will proceed for now." He turned and continued down the corridor. He was alert, watchful, and his weapon was at the ready. He wasn't sure he expected to find anything, but he was certain that didn't matter. Procedure called for maximum readiness in any potential combat situation. It wasn't for him to analyze the chances of encountering hostiles. His duty was to be ready for any he found.

He moved down the hallway, stopping every ten meters to listen. *Utilize all senses in combat situations.* He could still hear the words echoing in his mind, doctrine that had been driven into the very neurons of his brain. Many people thought Foudre Rouge were almost robots, automatons devoid of emotion, soulless creatures not quite human. That wasn't true. The reality was far more complex. Palloux-7364 was a slave to his programming, to a great extent at least. That *was* true. But he was a man as well. He felt fear at danger, anger at the loss of a comrade. Jealousy as well, at times, an envy of those free to choose their own paths...though he didn't entirely understand what such free will was like. He was also unable to imagine any purpose in life beyond soldiering.

He was about to resume his movement when his body froze, his instincts reacting faster than his conscious mind. He'd heard something.

He held his breath, extending his arm in a signal to his companion to remain still and silent. His hearing was excellent, as were his vision, reflexes, stamina. The Foudre Rouge genetic lines had long since had physical weaknesses bred out and strengths enhanced.

There was silence, and he almost decided he'd just convinced himself he'd heard something. But Foudre Rouge weren't subject to such distractions. He *had* heard something, and he remained in place, his head turned to direct his ear in the relevant direction.

Then he heard it again, clearer, more recognizable. A boot on the deck. He was confident, almost certain that was what he'd heard. Then, again, closer.

He turned his head and looked at his comrade, mouthing a warning without speaking. Foudre Rouge combat language was a vocal form of communication, but it also had its silent forms. He saw the private's arms tense, his hands tighten around his rifle, and he knew his message had been received.

He glanced around, analyzing every bit of data his eyes could collect, confirming what he already knew. There was no cover, not really, nothing close enough to reach before whoever was approaching turned the corner and came into view. He crouched down, pushing into a small indent along the wall, the best protection he could find, and he extended his rifle, and taking aim, waiting for someone to move into his field of view.

He only had to wait a few seconds. A figure moved cautiously around the corner, looking down the corridor. A woman. She spotted him almost immediately, and she started to pull back, ducking quickly as she slipped around the corner. But there was someone else, a larger, shadowy figure. A massive man, two meters tall and built like a house. He was less careful than the woman, slower to look down the corridor, to spot the threat.

And slower to respond.

The Foudre Rouge acted on instinct, firing one shot at the woman, realizing as he did, he was too late. He fired again, at the man. And again, even as his comrade opened up as well.

The target was moving back, as the woman had, but he was slower, more cumbersome...and the spray of red mist he left behind as he vanished from view told Palloux he had scored a hit.

Chapter Twenty-Seven

Unidentified Imperial Ruin
Somewhere Under the Endless Sea
Planet Aquellus, Olystra III
Year 302 AC

Andi dove back, in a move that started as an elegant combat roll and ended rather more clumsily, as she fell hard to her knees, wincing at the pain of impact. Her mind raced, combat instincts racing through her mind and body, evaluating any damage that would interfere with her ability to fight. She hadn't broken anything, she was pretty sure of that, and she didn't seem to have any sprains or major pulls. Just some hard bruises on her legs...and confirmation that there *were* indeed Union personnel loose in the facility.

She jumped back to her feet, bringing her weapon back around, even as the view she'd had down the corridor replayed in her mind. Two...there were two of them. And they were in the open. The tactical situation was a mixed one. The enemy troopers didn't have any real cover. They were caught in an open hallway, while her people had the corner for cover. But any attempt to take a reasonable shot at the Union soldiers would require exposing some part of herself...and from what she'd seen, the two were crack shots.

They'd appeared to be dressed in civilian garb, looking very much like a prospecting crew. But even the brief second's glance she'd gotten had exposed their tells. Posture, aiming, discipline.

They were Foudre Rouge. She'd have bet on it.

She was trying to decide how to come around, how to best get off a shot with the least risk to herself, when she heard Gregor's breathing. Heavy—heavier than his usual grunting. Then she saw the blood.

"Gregor…you're hit. Where?"

He looked at her and waved his arm, a wordless answer that it was nothing.

But Andi could see it was much more than nothing. He'd taken a hit somewhere between the shoulder and the chest. She couldn't place exactly where, but the rattling sound accompanying his breaths suggested the bullet had at least clipped a lung.

"Jackal, Vig…cover the corner. There are two of them, about twenty meters down. In the open, or close to it, but be careful. They're crack shots." That last part was mostly supposition, but Andi felt sure enough about it.

She knelt down next to Gregor, cursing under her breath at her decision to leave Doc on the ship. Her hand slipped into the first aid kit slung across her back, and she pulled out a pressure bandage, laying it on the deck next to Gregor. She pulled the combat knife from the sheath. The blade was a nasty-looking thing, long and razor sharp, with a series of notches cut along the back. It seemed out of place as a medical implement, but she had neither time to worry about it, nor more suitable tools. She sliced through Gregor's shirt, exposing the wound. It was an ugly puncture, irregularly shaped and spurting out blood with each of the big man's heartbeats. She glanced around his back, looking for blood. None. No exit wound. The bullet was still inside. Ideally, she'd have removed it, but that was beyond her meager medical skill and better left to Doc. She'd as likely do more damage trying to get the thing out than leaving it would causes.

She grabbed the pressure bandage, wincing as she heard the continuing fire. Most of it was close, Vig's rifle, the tone of the shots told her. A second later, she heard Jackal's too.

Return fire as well, but unless her perception was off, only one weapon. Had Vig or Jackal taken out one of the Union troops?

She pressed hard on the bandage, pushing the adhesive sides onto Gregor's exposed skin, and then activating the tiny mechanism that tightened the dressing. The giant liked to think he had a high tolerance for pain, but Andi could hear him wincing and struggling to hold back a series of grunts. "Sit tight, old friend. There's only two of them..." *Maybe one now.* "...we can handle them. Give that pressure bandage a chance to stop the bleeding."

Gregor started to shake his head, but Andi stared at him fiercely, practically daring him to defy her. He wasn't the type to sit out a fight, especially when his friends were threatened...but for all his herculean strength and unstoppable drive, he'd never quite had what it took to stand up to Andi Lafarge.

She leapt up to her feet. Vig and Jackal were at the corner, exchanging fire with the enemy. She was almost sure now there was only one trooper returning fire. Anna was standing behind them, her rifle in her hands. There was no place for her to engage, not without leaping out into the open space of the corridor.

There was nowhere for Andi to go, either. She shifted back and forth on her feet, edgy, tense at standing around and just watching the fight. Jackal was lying on his stomach, his rifle extended around the corner, firing repeated three-round bursts. Vig was standing, leaning over his comrade and jerking out around the corner every few seconds to fire fully automatic blasts. It was a good amount of fire, especially since the enemy had poor cover, and she knew it was tactically correct. What she didn't know was how many Foudre Rouge were crawling around the facility…or how long it would be before enemy reinforcements heard the gunfire and responded.

She told herself to be patient, to wait, to allow her side's superior position and cover to prevail. The enemy trooper had no escape. If he tried to run, he'd be a sitting duck. If he remained where he was, Vig and Jackal would eventually take him down.

Then she ignored all of that, and she lunged out into the corridor, executing a perfect combat roll and coming up prone, her rifle aimed toward the target, firing on full auto. It was audacious—stupid, perhaps, or at least reckless—but it caught her enemy completely by surprise. She had a far better vantage point on the Foudre Rouge than her two comrades did, and her fire ripped into his body, six or seven shots taking him before he could react, almost tearing him apart.

She knew it had been a gamble. If the Foudre Rouge had reacted just a bit faster, her own body would have been riddled with bullets as well. But Andi had always had a good sense of when to roll the dice, and she stared down the corridor, watching as her victim lay motionless, right next to his comrade.

She could hear the chatter behind her, all manner of admonishment and complaint from her four companions. She didn't listen, not really. She just put her hand up, silencing them all. Then she said, "There was no choice. We don't have time to waste. We don't know how many Foudre Rouge are loose in this place, but it's a fair bet someone heard all this gunfire. Now, let's get moving." She slung the rifle over her shoulder, and she turned back to help Gregor up. But Anna Fasarus had already assisted the giant back to his feet. He looked wobbly, but he was staying up on his own power.

"I'm good to go, Andi."

"I'd never doubt that, not for a minute. You're too big a hunk of meat for one shot to take you down." Still, Andi found herself surprised at the giant's amazing constitution. The wound wasn't desperately critical, but it *was* bad. The rasping sound in his breath told her the bullet *had* hit his lung. By all rights, he should have been headed back to Doc's infirmary, not pushing forward, looking very much like he was spoiling for a fight.

But he was who he was, and Andi needed him. So, she brushed aside the guilt, the sense that she really *should* send him back, and she reached out and put her hand gently on his arm. "Just be careful. You're pretty close, I know, but you're not *actually* indestructible."

Gregor nodded and smiled, wincing a little at the pain he was so clearly trying to hide. "I'll get the job done, Andi. You can count on me."

"There are few things I know better than that, old friend." She turned toward the others. "Alright, let's get going. The sooner we can find what we're here for, the faster we can get the hell out of this dump."

And into space…into the battle that's waiting for us up there.

* * *

"Lieutenant, we have reports of gunfire from one of the corridors." The Foudre Rouge was clearly tired and out of breath. Javais knew the soldier had run back with the report. It seemed almost absurd for a modern fighting force like the Foudre Rouge to rely on runners, but the imperial alloy walls of the facility interfered tremendously with comm signals. The effect was somewhat variable, the intensity of the interference varying on different occasions for reasons no one could adequately explain, but at that moment, Javais and his troopers were having trouble getting a signal more than twenty or thirty meters, leaving no real way to communicate except running back and forth from place to place.

"Very well, Private. You may return to you post." He turned. "Milland, Suvion...you will accompany Private Tienne, and reinforce the position in our rear." Milland-1902 and Suvion-9364 spun around and snapped to attention. "Yes, Lieutenant," they responded almost simultaneously, as they rushed to line up behind Tienne.

Javais watched as the three troopers jogged down the corridor, and then he walked toward Caron, who was already approaching him. "Reports of enemy activity, sir. I have dispatched reinforcements to the main position behind us. They appear to be following our route through the complex. I am uncertain if we have suffered any additional casualties, or if any of the enemy have been eliminated."

Caron took a deep breath and sighed. "I had hoped we could get in and out of here without any outside interference." He turned and looked back at the shelves, and the various boxes that had been forced open. They were full of electronics, all or almost all of it seemingly intact. It was a tremendous find, the kind of thing that would almost guarantee Union superiority in computing and artificial intelligence for a generation or more.

It was also enough to assure Caron and the others on the mission the great rewards that accompanied success in the Union. Javais and his Foudre Rouge weren't focused on the accumulation of personal power the way the Sector Nine agents were, but he understood the military importance of the find, and the advantages it would give his people the next time they went up against the hated Confederation Marines.

"Send a runner, Lieutenant. I want a status report on the team sent to find the reactor. We can't leave here until we've rigged the place for destruction, but if we can set the reactor to blow, I think the materials we've found here are sufficiently valuable. It's time to start getting this stuff back to the ship, I think. At least if we can confirm we've found the reactor."

"Yes, sir. Of course." Javais agreed, at least to the extent he had an opinion. Like all Foudre Rouge, he was far more comfortable just following orders than he was analyzing them or developing his own viewpoints. "I suggest we secure the boxes we intend to take with us, and take them back to the ship in one group. That will provide maximum protection against any enemy forces we encounter."

"Yes, Lieutenant, very good. Instruct your people to begin repacking the opened crates…and preparing as many as we can carry for transit. I want to be ready to go as soon as we receive word that the reactor has been prepped."

"Yes, sir." Javais stepped back and saluted, and then he walked forward, shouting out commands to the Foudre Rouge working on the crates. He'd been born and bred for combat, trained and conditioned from birth to ignore fear, pain, hardship.

But Javais-0194 would still be glad to leave the haunted imperial ruin behind.

Chapter Twenty-Eight

Unidentified Imperial Ruin
Somewhere Under the Endless Sea
Planet Aquellus, Olystra III
Year 302 AC

"You sure you're okay?" Andi was walking next to Gregor, not the easiest feat with the narrowness of the corridor and the bulk of her friend. He'd looked well enough, most of the time, but she'd caught a few winces and one or two deep, struggled breaths. She knew he was in pain, and she was far from sure just how bad the damage from his wound truly was. "I'm pretty sure it's all clear behind us. Maybe you should go back…"

"No chance, Andi. I'm not leaving you." Gregor's voice was harsh, at least for the first few words. Then, his tone softened. "If you want to bail on this expedition and head out of here right now, I'm all for it. This place gives me the creeps, and as far as I'm concerned, Durango can eat shit. But if you're staying, I'm staying." Andi turned and looked right at her friend. She had known Gregor long enough to understand she wasn't going to change his mind. The big man was good-natured and generally cooperative, but when he set his mind to something, he was as immovable as a mountain.

"Just be careful. You're a big target, and I don't care how invincible you think you are, that wound you've got is slowing you down. If it gets worse, you let me know right away, okay?"

Gregor snorted derisively, the closest thing to a response Andi was going to get.

She shook her head slightly, simultaneously annoyed with Gregor's obstinance, and impressed by it. Then, she pulled out the small portable scanner she'd hung from her belt. She'd tried half a dozen times already, but she did it again anyway. It was just as useless as it had been every other time. She hadn't really expected anything different. She'd seen what the materials in shattered imperial ruins did to scanner beams and communications. And she was in the middle of the largest ancient construct she'd ever seen, one that seemed nearly intact.

She turned back toward her comrade, belatedly answering his comment about leaving. "I'd like to go, Gregor, I really would. But we gave our word." A lie, one of a sort, at least. Some part of her *did* want to go, of course. The place was terrifying, and the fact that there were Foudre Rouge on the loose only made it that much worse. But Andi was driven by more than her promise to Durango. There was something about old imperial relics, about humanity's lost and amazing past, that always drew her in. She'd never spoken to anyone about it, not even her closest friends on the crew, but she'd felt it nevertheless, even from her first expedition under Captain Lorillard.

Andi Lafarge had come from one of the foulest pits mankind had ever created, and yet she'd come to see wonders the Confederation's vast and mostly prosperous billions could hardly imagine in their wildest dreams. She was driven by duty, certainly, and by stubbornness. But, also by curiosity, by the need to know more about a past that seemed almost a fantasy against the grim realities that had surrounded her most of her life.

"Well as long as you're here, I'm with you." Gregor's voice was full of defiance, but he couldn't quite keep the pain out of it. Andi winced, feeling a pang of guilt for her insistence on continuing. She could press on through her own suffering without hesitation, but watching any of her people enduring misery cut at her deeply.

"Well then, we'll…" She stopped abruptly. She'd heard something from up ahead. Her mind snapped into action, her eyes focusing, trying to make out the motion she could see accompanying the brief noise. Her rifle was out and in place, and her finger was tightening on the trigger before her mind was consciously aware of the threat. "Down!" she shouted to her people, almost by reflex, and then she dove forward, firing even as she sailed through the air and down to the deck.

She wasn't sure if her own fire had started first, or if the incoming shooting had beat her by half a second. But in an instant, the corridor was alive with intense fire crisscrossing back and forth in a wild storm of deadly force.

She stayed low, pressing her body down onto the cool metal floor, trying to present as small a target as she could, even as she aimed and fired again and again. She twisted her head, quickly confirming that her people were down, and that they were firing. They'd been caught in the open this time, the two sides meeting in a long hallway with nothing but distance—perhaps sixty meters—and shadowy stretch, courtesy of a series of apparently broken lighting fixtures, to offer protection.

At least it was even. The Foudre Rouge were as out in the open just as her people were.

She flipped her rifle to full auto. The enemy soldiers—she knew in her gut they were Foudre Rouge—were down also, doing all they could to evade her fire. The lying positions reduced the aim of all the combatants, and the withering fired ripped back and forth over the heads of those engaged.

Andi could feel her heart pounding, and she struggled to stay firm, to keep her arms and hands steady, and her aim true. Her mind was racing, trying to come up with an idea, some tactic or trick—anything—to get her people out of the firing line. But there was nothing.

Andi had been in fights before, brutal and deadly ones, but the haunted immensity of the imperial complex, the fact that she was fighting Union regulars and not Badlands toughs, and the looming threat of the enemy ship up there somewhere, just waiting for *Pegasus*, were all rapidly becoming too much, even for one of her grim and stony resolve. Hope was a fragile thing, and even Andi Lafarge relied on some expectation of escape to sustain herself…and that kind of expectation that was rapidly fading.

She wanted to run, to flee from the complex, to go back to *Pegasus* and get the hell away from Aquellus. But that wasn't an option. The instant any of her people got up, or even cut their own fire to crawl away, they were finished. They were in a fight to the death, with no other option but to continue. Even surrender—something she couldn't imagine—was off the table. She didn't believe the Union forces would take prisoners…and if they did, she knew it would lead to a worse fate that dying right there in the corridor.

She looked down the hall, trying to decide if she'd hit one of the Foudre Rouge. She wasn't sure, not until she could see another one from behind, crawling over the forward shape, shoving it to the side.

She locked her eyes on the soldier coming to the front. He was low, tucked in close to the deck, but he popped up a bit, five or six centimeters, as he shoved his fallen comrade aside.

It wasn't much…but it was enough. Andi's finger tightened, and three shots ripped down the corridor. The soldier's head disappeared in a wild spray of blood and bits of gray mush.

That's two, at least.

"Three," she muttered to herself, as she saw another Foudre Rouge hit. *Gregor's shot, she guessed.*

The giant was still in the fight, however badly hurt he was, however much pain his wound was causing him.

The enemy fire lessened in intensity. For an instant, she thought it was a trap, some lure to get her people to rush the enemy position. But then she saw movement.

The Foudre Rouge were pulling back.

She stayed where she was, resisting the urge to pursue. She knew she would encounter any survivors again, most likely with reinforcements, and almost certainly in a stronger position. But she still wasn't sure it wasn't a trap. She maintained fire, fairly sure that only one of the enemy was still shooting back. She tried to get a read on how many had escaped. Three? Maybe four?

Definitely only one left.

She didn't know if the remaining Foudre Rouge was a sacrificial rearguard, but it certainly looked that way. However much she despised the Union soldiers, she couldn't help but admire the self-sacrificial bravery she was witnessing.

That only went so far, though. She wasn't going to let him get away.

She maintained her fire, reaching around for another clip, reminding herself the entire time not to get careless, to stay tightly pressed on the deck. It slowed her reload a little. *A fair trade for not getting my head blown off.*

She was still shoving the new clip into her rifle when the Foudre Rouge made his escape attempt. He stayed low, exhibiting a level of discipline Andi had to respect, however much she hated the Union and its soldiers. She felt her hand shaking as she tried to hurry the reload, but before she could bring the weapon to bear, the enemy soldier rolled over on his side, clearly hit. Then, another round came in, and another. The figure stopped moving, and he lay there looking very much like he was dead.

She wasn't sure which of her people had scored the hits, but it didn't matter. They were a team.

A damned good team.

She stayed where she was for perhaps twenty seconds, her eyes locked on the bodies, and then on the corridor beyond. Carelessness got people killed, and she had no intention of leaping up and walking into some wounded soldier's fire. But the three motionless forms were pretty messy, and she discounted the likelihood that any of them could still be alive. One more glance down the corridor, and she decided the rest of the Foudre Rouge were gone.

She stood up, still slow and cautious, and she turned toward Gregor. "You okay?" she was staring at his shoulder, at the wound, looking for signs of renewed bleeding. But everything seemed fine.

"Yes, Mother...I'm fine."

"You won't be for long if you call me that again." She managed a smile, for a second or two. Then she turned toward her other shipmates. "How about you, Vig? You okay?"

"I'm good, Andi...but I've had enough of these Foudre Rouge, I'll tell you that much."

"Yeah, you and me both." A pause. "But I doubt we've seen the last of them." She turned her head. "Anna?"

"I'm okay, Andi." She was holding a rag, which Andi realized had been cut from her jacket, against her upper thigh. "I caught one, just a flesh wound. Bullet didn't even go in, it just grazed my leg." The amount of bleeding evident seemed like more than a graze to Andi, but she nodded anyway. Anna seemed fine.

"Hey," she said, looking at Jackal. He was still on the deck, looking back up at her.

At least his open eyes were looking up at hers. But he wasn't moving.

"Jackal?" Andi felt her insides tighten, and she reached down toward her friend. "This isn't funny, you know." Jackal was the closest thing *Pegasus* had to a trickster, and for a few seconds, Andi grasped at the hope that he was playing a practical joke on them all. But reality set in with a deathly coldness.

She knelt down, dropping her rifle to the deck as she reached out and grabbed Jackal's shirt, shaking him, pulling him upward. She could feel it immediately, even before she saw the widening pool of blood coming out from underneath him.

Her face was less than ten centimeters away, her eyes staring into his.

Into his empty, lifeless eyes.

Jackal was dead.

Chapter Twenty-Nine

Unidentified Imperial Ruin
Somewhere Under the Endless Sea
Planet Aquellus, Olystra III
Year 302 AC

"Take it…take it all, the ammo, the grenades. The knife, too." Every word sliced into her like a hot blade, but she said them anyway, instructing her people in excruciating detail to strip Jackal's body of anything that might be useful. She tried to tell herself it made sense, even that Jackal would have wanted his friends to make use of his equipment. It was the absolute truth, but it still tore her guts out.

But that didn't stop her.

"Let's go…we'll have to leave him here." Another blade this time, just as imaginary—and just as painful—as the others. Andi didn't really believe Jackal's corpse had any real meaning. She'd seen enough bodies left to rot in the Gut, that of her oldest friend, the Marine, among them. But it still felt somehow…wrong.

But necessary. There was no way they could carry him, not and maintain readiness for the fight she was sure was coming. Gregor had already tried to pick him up, but she'd ordered him not too. The giant was badly wounded, and the last thing he needed was a hundred kilos thrown over his shoulder as he pushed forward, almost certainly toward another fight.

"Jackal wouldn't want any of you to die here, not if his ammo or his weapons could make the difference. So, let's do what we have to do and then get the hell out of here." Andi's normal curiosity was gone, her fascination with the ancient imperial facility lost in a sea of regret and grief. But she was even more determined to complete the mission. Breaking and running earlier would have been bad enough, but if her people turned and skulked away now, Jackal had died for nothing.

That, she couldn't endure.

She reached down herself, scooping up several clips from the small pile of Jackal's possessions her somber and silent comrades had made in the corridor. Her rifle wasn't exactly the same as his, but they both took the same ammunition. She slammed one into place, and she looked down the corridor, her eyes frozen with malice. She'd fought the Foudre Rouge, killed them, because they were the enemy, because they were attacking her.

Now it was personal.

"Alright, we don't have any more time to waste. We move in, find what we came for…and anybody who gets in our way gets greased. Got it?"

She turned and began down the corridor, as the rest of her people replied with a series of grunts and acknowledgements, and then followed her.

She continued for ten minutes, then fifteen, stopping often to listen, and to look for any signs of the enemy. She was astonished at the apparent size of the facility, and somewhere between her focus on the mission and the roiling rage at Jackal's death, she wondered what it had been used for. It had clearly been intended to be hidden, which suggested some kind of secrecy to its purpose. Perhaps it had been a base of whatever intelligence agency the old empire had operated, or some secret research institute. If the latter, she could hardly imagine the value of some of the contents. Old imperial equipment was far more advanced than anything known on the Rim, so much so, some of it seemed almost magical. What kinds of wonders were imperial scientists working on when the end came?

She stopped at an intersection, looking carefully both ways before stepping out into the perpendicular corridor. There were small trails, tiny clumps of dust and debris left behind by boots. From what she could see, there had been traffic in both directions. That meant, whichever way her people went, they risked leaving enemies behind them. It was a disturbing thought, but one that would be lessened in no way by pointless delay. She flipped a coin in her head, and she turned to the right.

"Anna, Vig...keep an eye behind us. We don't need any surprises."

"Got it, Andi." Even Vig Merrick's usual exuberance was gone, driven off by Jackal's death and the fear and exhaustion running them all down.

Andi continued down the corridor for several minutes, and then she stopped and pulled out her portable scanner. She didn't expect to see anything useful. The imperial alloy had pretty much blocked the device every time she'd checked. But, to her surprise, there *was* something. Radiation. Not dangerous levels, at least not yet, but definitely something detectable, in spite of the dampening effect of the walls.

Weapons? Some kind of research lab?

She felt her stomach tighten. If the base had been some kind of scientific facility, there could be all sorts of exotic—and dangerous—materials present. And three centuries was a long enough time even for imperial storage units to fail.

She continued on, perhaps another two hundred meters. They passed six or eight doors, but they were all locked, and she didn't have the time to waste trying to access what were most likely secondary rooms. She had a hunch the corridor led somewhere important, something she became even more certain about when they began passing notices etched into the wall. The signs were written in Old Imperial. Andi hadn't known a word of the language when she'd first arrived on Dannith, but she'd picked up a fair bit in several years of prospecting. And she'd seen this particular word before.

It meant something between 'caution' and 'danger.'

She continued forward, slowing her pace and trying to remain as quiet as possible. It was a pointless effort, at least against any potential imperial defense mechanisms, but if there were Foudre Rouge wherever her people were going, she'd take any edge she could get. Half a second could be the difference between victory and defeat.

Part of her wanted to slip in, grab the swag they'd come for, and slip out again...but the other half *wanted* to find Foudre Rouge waiting. She owed them something, revenge for her friend, and that was the kind of debt Andi Lafarge always repaid.

She stopped. There was noise ahead. For an instant, her combat reflexes sprung into action, but then she realized it wasn't Foudre Rouge. It wasn't any kind of security bot either, just a soft humming sound, very regular, and coming from farther down the corridor. There was some kind of machine up ahead, very likely of imperial make.

And it was still operating.

She gripped her rifle tightly, and she pushed ahead, trying to ignore the rivulets of sweat sliding down her neck. She could hear her own breathing, every inhale and exhale echoing in her ears as she moved ahead. The hum increased in volume, and twenty meters farther forward, the corridor ended at a door. It was armored, some kind of secured accessway, but it had been blown out of its housing. The imperial alloy was slightly twisted out of shape at one end, but mostly, the door was intact. The side that had been connected to the wall was covered in a strange black residue.

She reached down, moving her finger across the sooty substance and bringing it to her nose. It was fresh, the remains of a recent explosion, she guessed. She put her hand on the alloy door. It was still a little warm.

Her body tensed from head to toe, and she pulled a grenade from her shoulder strap, her thumb resting on the arming button. *Someone* had blasted that door open, and recently. Likely Foudre Rouge. And if they were still in there, Andi was going to kill them all.

She gestured to the others to stay back, remain silent, and she edged forward, moving as quietly as she could. She'd heard Foudre Rouge had acutely developed senses, one benefit of the genetic program that created the clone soldiers, but she'd never been sure how many of those rumors she believed.

She listened herself, but there was nothing. Only the hum, fairly loud now, and definitely coming from the room.

She leaned forward, ready to throw the grenade and duck out. The room was huge, several hundred meters across at least, and eighty or more high. The door led onto a platform, something like a wide catwalk, overlooking the vast room out and below. There were no Foudre Rouge, no Sector Nine agents. No one.

This must be the reactor…

Andi was no expert on nuclear physics, and even less so on the antimatter she knew had so often been used in imperial ships and bases. But the rows of large tanks, and the intricate series of connecting conduits and transmission lines leading off in multiple directions left little doubt. Her eyes darted down to the scanner again, checking the rad levels. Up a little from the last scan, but still within tolerable parameters.

"I think we found the main power station. I don't know if this is a fusion plant…or an antimatter one." She shivered slightly at the thought of the latter. Andi knew fusion reactors could be incredibly dangerous, but the thought of antimatter really shook her. The substance was so volatile, so incredibly dangerous, all it had to do was leak out of its containment to cause a catastrophic explosion. A few kilograms of the stuff had a hundred megatons or more of explosive power, and Andi shuddered to imagine how much of the precious substance the facility might contain, and just how fragile containment facilities could be after three centuries without repair or maintenance.

"It looks like both to me, Andi." Anna stepped up, moving to the rail that ran around the edge of the platform. I'm no engineer, but I've seen power plants before, and that's a fusion core, if I've ever seen one." She gestured toward a large cylindrical structure. "But those tanks…" She pointed to a row of ten large canisters, each one ten meters tall and made of glittering imperial alloy. "…they're nothing to do with a fusion plant. That's *got* to be antimatter storage." She paused, and when she continued, her voice was hollow, almost awe-struck. "If those are full, Andi, that has to be *tons* of antimatter."

Andi stood stone still, her mind assaulted by cycling waves of fear, greed, and pure awestruck amazement. Tons of antimatter. The substance was so incredibly valuable, a single ton of it was worth more than everything else in the Confederation *combined*.

The poverty of Andi's childhood, the deprivation of the Gut, a thousand images of the lost and starving souls around her, all poured through her mind, and she imagined what just a kilogram of the rare and wondrous substance could buy for her and her people. The security, the comfort, the staggering wealth. Everything she'd dreamed of since those terrible days, since she'd left the Marine's body behind and resolved that she would *not* die there in the misery of the Gut as so many others had.

But realism quickly washed away those thoughts. She had no way to transport antimatter, nor any idea how to even begin to remove it from the containment tanks. But if Anna was right, if those cylinders were filled with antimatter...how could she risk allowing it to fall into Union hands?

"Andi..." Anna again, and Andi could tell immediately something was wrong.

She turned toward her friend. Anna was standing at the rail, looking down at something below.

"What is it?"

Andi walked over and stood next to Anna. She leaned over the rail and looked down. "I don't see..."

There *was* something. It was different, something sloppy and crude, amid the graceful elegance of the imperial tech. It took a few seconds for Andi to process it, but then she understood.

A bomb.

The Union operatives had no doubt come to the same conclusion she had. They couldn't risk their enemy—the Confederation—gaining control of the precious resource, any more than she'd have been able to risk Sector Nine securing it.

But the Foudre Rouge got here first...

And they had sabotaged the reactor.

Andi felt as though her heart skipped a beat. Her first instinct was to run for the exit, to get her people out of the facility, and off Aquellus, as quickly as possible. But rationality took hold. The Union expedition had come for the same reason she had, to secure whatever old tech they could transport off the planet. And they were still in the facility.

"That thing's got to have a timer of some kind. We have to try to disarm it...or at least figure out how long we have before it blows." She leaned over farther, her eyes moving about, looking for some kind of visible clock.

She couldn't see anything, and a few seconds later, she threw her legs, one after the other, over the railing. Gregor reacted first, rushing forward, grunting in pain as he reached out and grabbed ahold of her. "Andi, what the hell are you doing?"

"Somebody's got to climb down there and check that bomb, try to disarm it."

"And that's you?"

"Who else? You'll never get down there, not with that wound…and you know it. You might make an argument for Lex, if he was here. He'd have a better chance of dealing with that thing. But he's back on *Pegasus*."

"I could run back and get him." Anna started to turn toward the door, limping on her wounded leg over even those few steps.

"Anna, no. First, it's too dangerous for one of us—any one of us—to go wandering around with Foudre Rouge on the loose. Second, we need Lex on *Pegasus*. We're already counting on him having the ship ready for…whatever she needs to do…when we take off. Even if he's finished his work…" A doubtful proposition, she knew. "…we'll need him in the engine room. What if you run into Foudre Rouge on the way back, and he is…" She didn't finish. She didn't have to. Anna just nodded her acquiescence.

"You can't go down there, Andi." Vig hopped over the railing, holding himself up a meter and a half from her.

"Vig…"

"No…you're the only one who's absolutely not expendable. You've got to lead the crew out of here…and deal with that damned ship waiting up there. If we lose you, we'll never get out. You know it, you just don't want to admit it."

Andi looked back over at the crew's youngest member. She wanted to argue, but she knew he was right. She had co-piloted the ship with Captain Lorillard. She was the best-equipped to get them out of the system. If it had been any other member of the crew who met that qualification, she would have readily acknowledged it, but she struggled with it regarding herself.

The captain left me in charge...and a leader should lead...

But what was leading? Mindless courage...or unbroken focus on what it would take to get her people home?

Vig slid down, easing himself lower until he was hanging in the open, his hands gripped around the bottom of the rail. Andi turned, and she almost ordered him to climb back up.

But she knew he was right.

She also knew he wasn't going to listen to her anyway. That made it easier for her.

"Be careful, Vig. If you fall and break something, I'm not going to be able to carry you back up." *And Sy will never forgive me if I get you killed.* Sylene Merrick was Vig's older sister, and the closest thing Andi had to a best friend. She'd been the crew's computer expert, but the deaths of Captain Lorillard and the others had been too much for her. She'd retired to a quiet life, and Andi still missed her every day.

Vig had filled some of that role, she realized with sudden clarity. She still thought of him as the 'new guy,' or 'Sy's little brother,' at least in some ways. But he was rapidly filling his sister's role as her confidante and close friend.

"I'm always careful."

Andi almost snorted. She couldn't recall hearing a more blatant lie.

Then she stood and watched him make his way down.

Chapter Thirty

Free Trader Pegasus
Rocky Shelf Under the Endless Sea
Planet Aquellus, Olystra III
Year 302 AC

"I've got it on full, Lex. Looks like the power lines are operating at max capacity, or something close to it." Barret was standing on *Pegasus's* lower deck, shouting from the workstation through the open hatch to the engineering section.

"Close, I think...not max. Don't forget the size of that ship up there. We're going to need every watt of power we can get." A pause. "Give me two minutes. I think I can find the leakage and get it patched up."

"You got it, Lex." Barret leaned back on the workstation and let out a long exhale. He'd been upset when Andi had insisted he remain with the ship, but he'd since accepted that her decision had been the correct one. Lex needed help to get the ship back to full functionality, and that meant someone had to stay, and preferably two of the crew. Doc had been the easy choice.

But Barret knew he was the next on that list. As the only member of the crew with real Confederation naval experience, there was no argument he was most valuable on the ship…and there wasn't much question they were going to have to make one hell of a run for it when they left. Or fight there way out. Either way, his place was on *Pegasus*, helping to get the ship ready for whatever she needed to do.

"Try it again." Lex's voice echoed up from the cramped engineering space. Barret turned and reached down for the controls, turning the flow rate to maximum.

He watched for ten seconds, waiting for the readings to stabilize. "I'll be damned," he muttered to himself, as the reading continued past the previous level, and continued to rise almost ten percent higher. "Whatever you did down there," he shouted toward the hatch, "it gave us a nice boost. Looks like nine point five, maybe nine point six."

"I *knew* there was a leak. That extra power will come in handy in…if we need it."

Assuming we ever get out of this Godforsaken ocean…

Lex Righter came out of the engineering hatch and stooped down to clear the hundred twenty centimeter height of the door. His clothes were rumpled and torn in a couple places, and he was covered in a coating of dried sweat and dirt from the engine room.

Barret had questioned Andi's tactics in acquiring a new engineer for the ship, or the wisdom of relying on a clearly troubled alcoholic and addict to fill such a vital role, but he'd come to really like Righter, and he couldn't argue with the engineer's skills or his astonishing work ethic.

"There's more work to do, but we should be able to lift off now with full power, at least. I want to run a full diagnostic on the systems, but first, we need to get some better patches on those hull breaches. Gregor did a great job in an emergency, but I want to make sure they all hold…whatever we run into on our way out of here."

Barret nodded, and he opened his mouth to add his own viewpoint. But before he could say a word, his head spun around toward the ladder to the bridge.

"Barret!" It was Doc's voice, coming from the upper

level, and there was no question at all that something was very wrong.

"What is it, Doc?" Barret felt his insides tighten, and he turned and raced toward the ladder, leaping up and grabbing the highest rung he could reach. He grunted as he climbed up, and then he jumped onto the deck just outside the bridge, even as Doc's answer echoed in his ears.

"We've got company outside…and it's not Andi and the others…"

*   *   *

"Go, Private…now! Report to the lieutenant at once. Advise him our ships are both gone…no, not gone, destroyed." The Foudre Rouge sergeant stood along the sheer rock wall rising above the large shelf, the platform where both landers had been. The field of debris all around left little hope the landers had escaped.

The flat area now occupied by a single ship…unidentified, but definitely not one of theirs.

"Yes, Sergeant." The soldier spun around—or as close to 'spinning as was possible in the bulky underwater suit—and he moved into the airlock. The door slid shut, and Sergeant Samois-0079 turned back toward the ship sitting in front of him.

The ramifications of the discovery were staggering, and only his Foudre Rouge conditioning allowed him to quickly put them in their place, and coolly analyze the situation. The debris on the shelf, was enough to determine that one of the landers, at least, had been destroyed right there…and very likely both of them.

He was in command on the scene, at least until the private got word to Lieutenant Javais, and some higher authority arrived. He realized almost immediately what he had to do. He didn't know what the remaining ship was, or who might be inside of it, but it was very likely the only way out of the ocean depths, and off Aquellus.

He had to take control of that ship.

There was just one problem. He only had one other trooper with him after dispatching Private Regia to report to the lieutenant. Should he attack immediately, strike hard and hope surprise proved to be enough to prevail?

That ship may even be empty...

There were intruders in the facility. There was no doubt about that. It was possible everyone who'd come on that ship had debarked.

But attacking immediately risked losing strength. If the two of them were killed or wounded—and killed seemed the likely option fighting two kilometers under the water—whatever force the lieutenant sent would be that much weaker when it arrived. Two attacks with two soldiers each would be far weaker than one with four.

He tried to fall back on his training, but the situation defied easy choices.

He turned back toward the private, frustrated at the sluggishness of his movement. The suits were a significant disadvantage. If there were defenders on that ship, they'd be a lot more flexible and mobile. The answer to that would normally be to compromise the ship's hull, to kill its occupants or force them into their own suits.

But he needed the ship intact.

He struggled to reach around, to pull his underwater rifle from his side mount, and he watched at the private followed suit.

He still wasn't sure how hard to press an attack, but he knew he had to at least confirm whether the ship was occupied.

And there was only one way to do that...

* * *

Barret raced over to one of the open workstations. The

screen displayed a view of the rear camera feeds. There was nothing when he first looked, but then he saw a bulky figure lumber slowly past.

"Did you activate any tracking systems?" Barret held his gaze on the screen as he snapped out the question to Doc.

"No...they just walked across the fixed field. It's a good thing we had one of the screens set to display the feeds."

"They?" Barret had only seen one figure.

"Yeah, there were two. At least two."

Barret stared at the screen. He wished Andi was there, or even Vig. The crew's youngest member had rapidly become one of the ship's go to leaders in a crisis. "Lex...do me a favor. Run down to the armory and break us out three rifles, plus ammo belts." The last thing Barret wanted to do was start shooting inside *Pegasus*, inflicting incalculable damage on the just-repaired ship. But the alternative was suiting up and going out, and fighting out there. He'd hoped for the first few seconds the two figures had been part of the crew, perhaps returned with some comm failure. But that thought only lasted for an instant. The suits were different.

Whoever was out there, they were enemies.

"On the way, Barret."

"Doc, I know you're not normally part of our muscle, but..."

"Don't worry, Barret. I'm handier in a fight than you think."

"Here you go." Lex crawled up the ladder and leaned into the bridge, pulling the rifles from his back and handing one to each of his two shipmates. "These will do the job in here, but if we're going out, we'll need the underwater ones."

Barret frowned. Durango had provided them with all the undersea gear, and the fact that a full suite of weaponry had accompanied each suit told him their mysterious benefactor and taskmaster had likely expected them to run into a fight.

Barret had never liked the shipyard manager, and he

found himself hoping Andi rethought her opinion of the man…maybe even dealt with him the way she usually did with those who stabbed her in the back.

"We'd better take this outside. If they forced their way in, we may lose pressurization…and any fighting inside will tear the ship apart." A pause. "But if we leave them out there, it won't take much for them to cause some real problems. I don't know if they want to take the ship or not, but if they're just looking to disable us, we've got to hit them soon or they won't have any trouble doing it."

"I agree. We should suit up." Barret could hear the nervousness in Righter's voice. As far as he knew, none of the three of them had ever worn undersea gear. A fight to the death was a rough initiation for underwater operations, but it didn't look like they had any choice.

Or did they…

Barret turned and looked back at his station. "How long would it take to get the reactor powered up?"

Righter looked across the cramped bridge. "Powered up? To what level?"

"Enough to fire the topside laser." Barret gestured toward the gunnery station as he answered.

"You want to fire that thing? At this range? What if you hit the entrance to the station? You could flood the facility, kill everybody inside. Hell, you could bring down half that rock wall on top of us."

"I can handle it. Don't you worry about that." Because I'm worried enough for both of us. "It's a better bet than waddling out there in those suits and fighting it out, don't you think? Those are Foudre Rouge, most likely, and we've got a ship's gunner, a medic, and an engineer to throw at them. You think that's a guaranteed win for us? What if Andi and the others get back to find the ship in the hands of the Foudre Rouge, or just gone?" A pause. "Besides, I don't have to fire at anything like full power to take out a couple of Foudre Rouge a few meters away. The problem's likely to be getting a shot. I'm not sure how low an angle I can manage."

Righter looked like he still wanted to debate, but a few seconds later, he let out a deep breath and just nodded. "Right. Bad choice...but all the others are worse." He had already turned, and he was climbing down the ladder. "Get your targeting ready...I'm going to crash start the reactor. I'll have you power in a minute, ninety seconds, tops." A pause. "At least those guys out there don't start shooting at the ship...and if the reactor can handle the stress."

He didn't say anything else.

Barret just stared at the empty space where the engineer had just been.

There hadn't been anything else to say.

Chapter Thirty-One

Unidentified Imperial Ruin
Somewhere Under the Endless Sea
Planet Aquellus, Olystra III
Year 302 AC

Vig reached out, grabbing onto a support bar, and easing down another half meter. He was tall, and his feet were about a meter from the flat top of a section of machinery below. Perhaps a bit more than a meter. It was a feasible drop, but not one without risks, not when a broken ankle would likely strand him there beyond reach of the others, and leave him to his death.

He let go and let himself fall, repeating to himself silently as he did to let his legs give as he hit the metal below, to reduce the shock of impact as much as possible. He felt his heels land, and then his knees bent, and he rolled forward, landing in a prone position...about five centimeters from the edge of the platform.

He felt some jarring pain, but he realized almost immediately, he'd come down with no serious injury. He stared down for a few seconds, trying not to imagine what would have happened if his momentum had taken him over the edge and down the ten or fifteen meter drop looming before his eyes.

He pulled back cautiously, rising to his feet and gently putting weight on each leg. He was sore, and a little banged up, but he confirmed again to himself that everything seemed to be in working order. He took a deep breath and looked around. He was on top of a large structure, some component of the reactor, he supposed. He looked around, relocating the bomb. There was a small ladder built into the side of the structure, and he climbed down to the floor below. He looked up. He was about ten meters below the catwalk where he'd started, and the bomb was above him, at the top of a large cylinder.

He walked around the structure, towering about six meters above him. He looked all over, searching for some way to climb the thing. There has to be some way up. *Someone planted that bomb up there.*

But there was nothing, no ladder, no way to climb to the top of the smooth cylinder. He looked again, running his hands over the cool imperial alloy, looking for some kind of switch or other mechanism that might expose a way up.

Nothing.

Then his eyes looked beyond the cylinder. There was another structure, on the other side, close to his target.

Close enough?

He scrambled over toward the rectangular bank of equipment. There was some irregularity to it, places he could plant his hands and feet and just maybe climb up to the top. It looked like a dicey proposition, but it was all he could see…until he walked around to the other side. There was a ladder of sorts there, or at least a series of hand and footholds stretching up to the top. It was still a tricky climb, but he was sure he could manage it.

He looked up. Andi was leaning over the rail, staring down at him. He couldn't make out her expression, but he could *feel* her tension. He reached up, slipping his hands into one of the small openings, and then bring his feet up as well. He climbed, methodically but quickly. He might have preferred to go a bit slower, but he had no idea how much time they had. He didn't like the idea of risking a fall, but he preferred it to being caught in a titanic antimatter explosion. It wasn't even a close call.

He scrambled up and over the top, and he stood up, looking across, back at the cylinder. He could see the bomb now, at least part of it protruding from the place where it was set. There was a gap between the structure he was on and the cylinder, close to two meters, he guessed. He could jump it...but he'd have to do it just right. Too soft, and he'd fall short. Too hard a jump, and he might lose balance and tumble right off the other edge of the cylinder.

He could feel his heart beating, pounding in his chest like repeated claps of thunder. He walked to the far side of the structure, and he took a series of deep breaths. Then he crouched down, and he took off, racing for the edge, trying with all his self-control not to think too much about what he was doing. He saw the edge coming up, and he lunged across the gap.

He came down hard on top of the cylinder, stumbling across, out of control for a few seconds before he managed to grab onto a protruding conduit and steady himself. He looked up, his attention drawn to the concerned gasps of his shipmates. All but Andi. He could see her, but she wasn't looking any more. She was crouched down, doing something he couldn't quite see.

He turned and walked over to the branch of smooth metal pipes. The bomb was set just under them. He looked all around, trying to get an idea of the thing's makeup. He didn't touch it—he didn't dare. He had no idea how sophisticated a device it was, or how well booby-trapped. But he needed to figure all that out. He had to determine if he had a chance to disarm the thing, and if he didn't, how long they had before it detonated.

He leaned over the conduits, bringing his face closer...and then he saw it. A cable protruding from the bomb into a small hole drilled into the metal of the piping. For an instant, he considered cutting it, but even as the thought entered his mind, he could feel his head shaking. There was no way. Whoever had placed that thing had connected it somehow to the mechanism. Lex Righter *might* have had a chance to disarm the thing, but Vig didn't dare touch it.

He looked all around, almost frantically. Then he saw the timer, tucked almost under the main body of the bomb. He twisted and turned and tried to squeeze as deeply into the nest of pipes as he could. He squinted, trying to make out the time on the tiny screen. Just as he'd almost despaired of reading it, his eyes teared up, and the extra moisture sharpened his view just enough.

Fifty-three minutes.

He pulled back, looking up and waving his arms to the others, even as he fought to keep the contents of his stomach in place. "Fifty-three minutes…and there's no way we're going to disconnect the thing, not without taking a real chance at detonating it now. This place is done for."

He turned and ran hard, jumping back to the other structure before he had time to think about it. He landed hard again, letting out a yell as his knees hit the hard metal, and pain radiated up and down his legs. For an instant, he thought he'd really hurt himself, but a quick lunge to his feet confirmed that everything was still working.

He made his way down the makeshift ladder, and back to the original bank of machinery. He could get back to the top, but he had no idea how he was going to make it to the catwalk above. Dropping down had been one thing, but he couldn't leap high enough to grab hold of the edge of the floor above.

But he'd have to try, at least if he didn't want a front row seat to an explosion that would make the term gigaton look like a flickering candle.

He scrambled up, struggling to hold back the panic. *You*

can do it, he told himself, not believing it at all. He walked to the center of the structure, and he looked up, trying to get a fix on the right place to jump…and he saw something in front of him, dangling down.

He saw Andi, stripped down to the light shirt she wore under her jacket. Then he realized what was hanging down. She had cut the coat into long strips and tied them together. A makeshift rope, long enough to reach him.

And the other end was gripped firmly by Gregor. The big man was clearly in pain, but the expression on his face was the personification of determination.

"Come on, Vig…get the hell back up here now!" Andi was waving her arm as she leaned over.

Vig stood there for just a few seconds, coming to terms with his amazement at the whole state of affairs. Then he reached up and grabbed the cloth rope and started pulling himself up, counting down with each pull.

His mental clock was at forty-nine minutes when Gregor and Andi hauled him up over the rail.

* * *

"Okay, Lieutenant, it's time to pull your people off search detail. We've found enough imperial artifacts to make this the most successful Badlands mission on record. Whatever we haven't found will have to stay. We're down to fifty minutes. It's time to haul this stuff back to the ships and get the hell out of here. Get the materials crated up and ready for transport. We're heading back in five minutes." Caron couldn't help but feel destroying the place so soon was a terrible waste, and he certainly wished he'd had more time to complete the withdrawal of his people, but his instructions had been utterly clear. Get in and out quickly, and leave nothing behind. *Nothing.* The time limits had been set on a fixed schedule, and the fact that an unidentified ship had been found in the system and hostiles engaged in the facility itself mandated the fastest set of timetables.

He understood the rationale for all of it, even the destruction of so much precious technology. If the materials in the facility fell into Confederation hands, it would give the Union's enemy dominance on the Rim for generations. At least obliterating it all would ensure the crates of imperial electronics his people were hauling out would do much the same, if to a lesser degree, for the Union. It might take a few years to truly research and exploit the ancient materials, but he had no doubt they would ensure victory when war came again.

And they would certainly guarantee him considerable wealth and advancement, even after Aimee Boucher claimed most of the credit for herself. Sharing spoils wasn't part of the Union creed, but in this case, Caron had to admit, there was very likely enough to go around.

Waste of precious technology or not, it didn't matter anymore. That die had been cast. The bomb was in place, and booby-trapped against any attempts to disarm it. If Gaston Villieneuve himself walked through the door and ordered the station preserved, there was nothing Caron could do.

His thoughts now were on getting out with as many artifacts as possible. He had to have his people on the ships in twenty minutes, twenty-five at most. His mind raced, calculating the size of the likely explosion in the vaguest terms. He had no idea how full the antimatter containment tanks were, and he lacked the knowledge of physics to accurately calculate the energy of the explosion. But the numbers didn't matter. If would be big. Big enough to obliterate the entire facility, and probably the undersea mountain in which it was built.

Maybe even big enough to tear away a good portion of the planet's atmosphere. He wasn't sure what to expect, but he intended to be in orbit by the time the bomb blew.

"Let's go, all of you. We're out of here in three minutes.

All Foudre Rouge are to carry a single crate." He'd have preferred to have his soldiers out in front, ready for battle, but he had to get the cargo back somehow. He reached around and pulled the rifle from his back, looking across the room toward the other two agents present. They followed suit, clearly understanding his intention.

He looked around again, watching as the soldiers finished resealing the crates and began to pick them up. The boxes were cumbersome, and reasonably heavy, but the Foudre Rouge maintained themselves in constant combat condition, and the clone soldiers carried the burdens with a fair amount of ease. A moment later, they were all ready to move out, a good ninety seconds ahead of schedule.

Which was just fine with Caron. The sooner he and his people were out of the haunted and doomed ruin, the better. He nodded, and he walked toward the door, looking out into the corridor before he set out, turning his head back only once, to confirm his small column had followed his lead.

Chapter Thirty-Two

Free Trader Pegasus
Rocky Shelf Under the Endless Sea
Planet Aquellus, Olystra III
Year 302 AC

"Unidentified ship, this is your last chance. Surrender at once and open your airlock, or we will open fire."

Barret stared at the comm unit, listening to the harsh tone blaring from the speaker. *So, is that what a Foudre Rouge soldier sounds like?* The gunner had served in the navy, but only in peacetime, or what passed for that state between declared wars. He'd never seen a Union clone soldier, but he'd known Marines who had fought them. The leathernecks had always held their own against their principal enemies, and he'd never run into one who'd admitted fear at the sight of one. But, without exception, they were always deadly serious when they spoke about the Foudre Rouge, and overtly admitted or not, Barret knew that was a kind of respect.

He hadn't answered, not yet. For an instant, he'd hoped they might leave if they thought *Pegasus* was unoccupied. But then he remembered the Union ships were all destroyed. The Foudre Rouge in the facility, if that's what they were, had no way out.

No way except capturing *Pegasus*.

He looked down at the control panel. He trusted Lex, a surprising realization considering the engineer's personal issues, and the short time of their acquaintance. He knew enough about reactor operations to realize what Righter was about to attempt was no easy feat.

And no sure thing, no matter how skilled he was.

Righter needed all the time he could get. And Barret had to get it for him.

He reached out and tapped the comm. "identify yourself," he snapped, with all the apparent confidence and self-assurance he could muster.

"Surrender at once," the voice on the comm repeated. Barret was listening for signs of tension or fear, any indication he could bluff his opponent. *Not if they're Foudre Rouge*, he guessed. At least not from what he knew of the clone soldiers.

Come on, Lex…we don't have much time…

"I will not discuss any kind of terms until you identify yourself." If they were Foudre Rouge, he might have one advantage. Badlands thugs, and even Confed Marines sometimes, could be goaded into rash action. But the Foudre Rouge were conditioned from ear to ear to act rationally and methodically. That didn't mean whoever was out there wouldn't open fire, but they likely wouldn't do it in a fit of rage at his goading.

"You have thirty seconds to surrender." The voice was cold, almost unemotional.

Barret's eyes dropped to the screen. He sighed softly as saw the indicators were still where they had been. No sign of energy generation, not yet. He turned away, and then his eyes darted back. He'd seen something, just before he'd turned his head, and a few seconds later, he heard a dull whine, and *Pegasus* began to vibrate.

Way to go, Lex…

His hands moved over the gunnery controls, bringing up

the targeting scope. He looked at the images from outside, getting a fix on the soldiers with the newly repaired scanner suite. He cycled from one dish to the next, doing all he could to keep movement to a minimum. But the soldier saw it anyway.

"Surrender!" The tone was harsher, more demanding, and Barret could finally detect some level of stress in it. He was still trying to get an idea how many soldiers were positioned around the ship. He'd seen two, but he had no idea how many more there might be.

And the two he'd found were too far apart to target with one shot. At least too far to guarantee taking them both out.

He glanced down, watching the laser's power reading rise. His hands were on the firing controls, but even as he honed his targeting solution, he felt his insides tense. *Pegasus*'s lasers were designed for combat in space, at ranges measured in the thousands of kilometers. He'd set the weapons for one-tenth strength, but he still had no idea what they might do to the rocky shelf holding up the ship, or the sheer cliff wall rising above. There were just too many variables, and firing lasers underwater was one thing his years of naval training and experience had never covered.

He tapped the controls slightly bringing the targeting sight around...and then he heard a loud sound. And then another.

The soldiers were firing at *Pegasus*.

He was out of time. The gunfire was dangerous enough, but he had no idea what other weapons the Foudre Rouge had. He watched the power up sequence continue, the last two seconds or so feeling very much like an eternity. Then he tightened his finger, and he fired *Pegasus*'s topside laser.

* * *

Samois-0079 dove to the side, half swimming, half pulling himself along the rocky shelf back toward the airlock. The ship had fired its laser, a wild and reckless act, one that threatened to destroy the rock shelf, and even the ship itself.

Samois called for the private on the comm, but he didn't expect a reply. He was almost sure the laser blast had hit the soldier dead on. He doubted there was anything remaining of his comrade, and that left him as the sole member of the expedition aware of the situation, who understood that the only way off the planet was to take that ship...before the insane person or people onboard destroyed it in an effort to kill him.

The water was frothing about wildly, boiling violently in spots closer to the laser pulse, sending huge streams of bubbles toward the surface. The sergeant was no naval expert, but he'd been shocked at what he'd just seen. The vessel had seemed almost entirely powered down, at least according to his scans. He understood energy systems enough to guess that it should have taken five minutes more, at least, and more likely, ten, before that vessel should have been able to get its reactor back online with sufficient output to power the guns.

His best guess was, he had two minutes more before the ship could fire again, but he'd been wrong the first time, and he wasn't going to rely on his limited knowledge. He considered opening up at full auto, targeting fragile looking sections of the hull. But that was a fool's game. He was alone, and he didn't have the firepower he needed.

And he was injured. His leg hurt like fire. He followed his training, focused on the area, trying to determine what had been damaged. His knee.

He doubted he could walk if he went back inside, or even wriggle his way out of his suit. He had no choice. He had to wait until help arrived. And the best way to survive that long was to get back to the airlock, into the recessed area that led to the facility's entry point.

He made it back to the broad tunnel, and he worked the airlock controls as quickly as he could in the cumbersome suit. The door slid open and he lunged inside, reaching out and closing the door behind him.

He'd made it, for the moment.

At least unless whoever was on that ship decided to start shooting at the facility itself.

*   *   *

"Go…now. Lieutenant…send six of your troopers forward now. They are to leave their crates just inside the airlock and get into their suits. I want that ship taken, and in operable condition. It's our only way off this rock." Our only way to escape what we set in motion here."

"Yes, Commander." Javais turned and shouted out crisp orders in the Foudre Rouge battle tongue. Half a dozen of the soldiers moved forward, quickly accelerating to a fast jog, about as close to a dead run as they could manage with the heavy crates in their arms.

"Let's pick up the pace here, too. We've got to get moving." The news that both landing sleds had apparently been destroyed had come as a terrible surprise to Caron. He was still trying to get his bearings. He'd sent the Foudre Rouge to seize the enemy vessel, but he still wanted to get up there himself as quickly as possible.

My God…there's no way to disarm that warhead…

He felt the fear begin to take him, like a cold hand gripping him inside. He increased his pace, walking right after the troopers he'd sent forward. His people had enough artifacts to guarantee that everyone—Gaston Villieneuve included—would call the mission a great success.

But they had to get out first. In less than an hour, the facility, and a good chunk of the planet's surface, probably, would be engulfed in an immense explosion.

Caron had left enough time to get away, to reach the ships, load up, and launch. But was there enough time to fight for control of the only vessel remaining that offered hope of escape?

He shook his head as he walked forward, and increased the speed of his gait again, almost to a jog. "Come on, all of you. We have to get out of here."

*   *   *

"Everybody okay?" Andi knew they weren't, even as she asked. Jackal was dead, and that hung over them all like a thick fog, a dense gloom that weighed down every step. *Pegasus*'s crew was a family, and they had lost one of their own. The true pain would come later, Andi knew, in the somber darkness, but even as they raced to get back to the ship, she could almost feel her lost comrade, as though he was looking at her, watching every move.

Besides the loss of Jackal, Anna and Gregor were wounded. So was she, for that matter. Vig was battered, no doubt in as much pain as any of them, but probably in the best shape of them all.

Gregor was the worst off. There was no doubt in her mind about that. Her giant comrade had been coughing, doing his best to hide it from her, and especially the blood coming up with each spasm. He was slowing down, too, though Andi knew he was doing his best to keep pushing hard. She'd been a little intimidated by Gregor when she'd first joined *Nightrunner*'s crew, but she'd come to love her hulking shipmate like a brother.

"We're fine, Andi." Gregor answered first, the struggle in his tone suggesting anything but what his words said. The others followed, all trying to sound like they were better than they actually were.

"Alright. Well, we've got to get moving again." They'd stopped for a brief rest, just a few minutes. Andi would have pushed on right through, but she knew her people were hurt, worn.

The break had provided another benefit. The room

they'd ducked into was dark, all but one of the small ceiling lights out, but when her people had pulled out their portable lanterns, they'd discovered boxes of imperial artifacts. She'd opened one of them, and she'd been shocked at what she'd seen. Electronics, circuit boards and all sorts of bizarre looking chips...in the best shape she'd ever seen ancient swag. The things looked almost new, and Andi's natural mental reflexes started estimating the value of it all.

She'd been resolved to return empty-handed. The booby-trapped antimatter stores left her no choice. There was no time to search the facility, much less deal with the Foudre Rouge. But her people had just stumbled on this horde of artifacts.

"Take what you can manage." She grabbed a box, and she panned her eyes around the room, sharing a brief glance with each of them. "I know this stuff is valuable, but remember, we've got to get back to the ship...and we may have some fighting to do." She looked down at the box in her arms. It seemed watertight, though whether it was sturdy enough to stand up to the pressure two kilometers under the surface, she couldn't even guess.

She turned, but then she saw something else, and she paused. It was a smaller box. No, not a box, some kind of folio. It had writing on the front, but it was a variant of Old Imperial she couldn't read. She opened it and looked inside. There were data chips, twenty of them. It wasn't the kind of treasure the circuit boards were, but she found it intriguing, and she slipped it into the bag on her back.

"Alright, let's get the hell back to the ship."

Everyone in the room grabbed a box, except Gregor. He grabbed two, and he looked like he was going to try to manage a third one when Andi stopped him with a stare. She turned and walked back out into the corridor, her comrades following her in a rough single file. They walked for two minutes, maybe three.

Then Andi stopped suddenly, her hand flying up,

signaling to the others to halt. There were sounds up ahead…boots on the metal floor, moving quickly. Running.

She stayed where she was, listening, trying to count. Five, maybe six. It was a guess, but she knew she was close.

She kept her hand up, holding back the others, until the sounds died down. Her stomach felt like it had shrunken to a quarter its normal size. The sounds were moving back toward the entrance.

Toward *Pegasus*.

"Okay, let's go. Whoever that was, they're heading toward the ship." She moved forward again, her rifle out, ready. They were Foudre Rouge, she was sure of it. She had no proof, but she knew it for certain. And there was no way she was letting them get to her ship.

No way in hell.

* * *

"Are we clear?" Barret could hear Lex's voice on the comm. The engineer sounded tense, but under control. Righter's cool in dangerous situations continued to surprise him.

"Nobody is shooting at us, not right now. That's about all I can tell you." Barret was moving his scope, scanning all around the ship, looking for movement, for any sign of the enemy. "I'm almost charged up again, and I'm going to keep the laser ready, just in case."

"I think that's a good idea." A pause. "We've got the scanners back close to normal, and the reactor looks good. I've checked all the power lines, especially to the weapons, and they look fine, too. I'd love to have time to replace some of the transmission network, but I doubt we have time, and I couldn't anyway without shutting the reactor down."

"We'll just have to rely on what we've got. *Pegasus* is a good ship, Lex. She won't let us down. And neither will Andi."

"She's something, isn't she?"

"Andi? You bet. Captain Lorillard was our skipper for a long time, but...he was killed on a mission. He left *Pegasus*—and the rest of us—to Andi. Best thing he could have done. He was watching out for us right up to the end."

"I've never met anyone quite like her."

"I don't think there *are* many like her, Lex. I know she was hard on you, but..."

"But she saved my life." A pause. "I wasn't sure I wanted it saved...but I think I owe her."

"She doesn't want you to owe her, Lex. She wants your loyalty...and as long as you're part of her crew, she'll do whatever she has to do to look out for you, just like she does with us."

"She's pretty young for so much responsibility, isn't she?"

"You don't know where she came from, Lex. Andi crawled out of one of the worst pits in the Confederation. Normal ages don't apply to her. She's..." Barret paused, and when he continued, his voice was stern, serious. "We've got something outside, Lex. Looks like more Foudre Rouge coming out of the tunnel."

Chapter Thirty-Three

Free Trader Pegasus
Rocky Shelf Under the Endless Sea
Planet Aquellus, Olystra III
Year 302 AC

"Good shot, Barret, but you better be careful. Any closer to that rock face and you'll bring the whole thing down…and trap Andi and the others." Lex was speaking just like one of the crew, his concern for his shipmates of so short a tenure sounding heartfelt and sincere. "You'll be powered up again in forty seconds."

Righter looked at the tiny display down in the engineering section. The screen had been designed for schematics and scrolls of numerical data. But just then, the engineer was watching the outer feeds, the AI moving from one exterior camera to another, trying to track the activity outside.

The Foudre Rouge had scattered, clearly aware of the destructive capability of *Pegasus*'s laser. Barret had gotten three in one shot, just as they were coming out of the facility. That was the pulse that had prompted Righter's warning. Barret was a good shot, but he was guessing at what effect the laser would have on the cliff wall at a range so insanely short. Even the best placement was far from a guarantee against fracturing a small fault line…and bringing tons of rock down on the exit from the facility, or even burying *Pegasus* under a crushing avalanche.

His eyes were focused on the edge of the screen, as the power reading clicked back to full. He tensed, expecting to hear Barret's next shot. But there was only silence.

Maybe he's checking his aim…

But still, nothing.

He waited, not wanting to distract the gunner. Finally, he tapped the comm unit. "Everything okay up there?"

"Yeah…I just can't get a shot. They're all tucked back in the tunnel. If I fire there, I'll collapse the entrance to the complex. Andi and the others will be trapped."

Righter heard a series of clangs, reverberating through the engineering section. His head darted around to check the instruments, but then he realized what was happening.

They're firing on us.

The Foudre Rouge had clearly guessed that *Pegasus* wouldn't risk closing off the imperial ruin…and they'd taken cover there, just outside the entrance.

Where they had an open field of fire on the back of the ship.

Righter didn't know *Pegasus* all that well yet, but he was willing to bet the engine cone was vulnerable to enemy fire. A few shots in the right place just might take out a vital connection.

And if *Pegasus* lost its thrust capability, they were all finished.

* * *

"Okay, they were heading back toward the ship. We've got to get down there and take them out before…" Andi didn't finish.

Gregor knew her mind was swirling with images of *Pegasus* under attack, of Foudre Rouge forcing their way aboard, taking control of her ship. But his tone got her attention immediately. "We've got more coming, Andi." Gregor pointed not toward the ship, but back in the direction the first group had come from. Andi listened, and he could see she heard it, too.

"Damn!"

"Andi, we can't let them get behind us. We've got to take out this group first." Anna had stepped up from behind, and she had her rifle in hand. She was limping, but she was just as clearly ignoring it.

"But what about the ship? We've got to…"

She never finished. A series of dark figures appeared at the far end of the corridor, and they opened fire. One of the first shots hit Andi. She dropped hard, and her head slammed into the intensely hard imperial alloy.

"Andi!" All three of her companions shouted as one, as Anna and Gregor opened fire down the corridor.

One of the approaching troops dropped, just a few seconds after Andi. Gregor was holding his autocannon, hosing the corridor down with deadly fire. It looked like more Foudre Rouge approaching, but for all the skill and weaponry of the Union soldiers, they couldn't match the firepower of the immense weapon *Pegasus*'s giant wielded with the practiced ease with which they handled their rifles.

"Go! Get Andi out of here. I'll hold them back." Gregor's shout was like that of some titan from mythology, and it seemed to shake the very walls.

Anna looked up at him, uncertain, even as Vig shook his head vigorously. "We can't leave you here, Gregor, not alone." Pegasus's youngest crew member shouted piteously, clearly realizing even as he argued, that there was no choice. If they wanted to get Andi out, they'd have to leave Gregor. He'd have to hold back the enemy, buy some time.

"Go," he growled, even as the continued deep crack of his autocannon echoed off the walls. "Go now…get her out of here. I'll handle this." Even as he spoke, he threw the autocannon over to his right side, and somehow wielded the massive weapon one handed. His left hand reached around his back, pulling around a regular assault rifle, and he aimed that down the corridor and opened fire.

Aim was a strong word, perhaps. Both weapons were shaking in his overburdened arms, even his massive strength struggling to hold them in place. But hold them he did, and he swept the corridor with withering fire. Three of the Foudre Rouge were down, and the rest had pulled back to whatever cover they could find.

"Go!" Gregor shouted again, even as Vig and Anna were struggling to grab Andi, to carry her down the corridor. They'd gone perhaps four meters when a shot slammed into Gregor.

He felt the projectile hit him. Somewhere in the gut, he guessed, but though there was pain, he couldn't quite pinpoint it. He was focused entirely on maintaining his deadly fire. He had to hold the enemy back, buy Anna and Vig time to get Andi into her suit. He couldn't fail her.

He *wouldn't* fail her.

He saw another Foudre Rouge drop…and then his arm erupted in pain, and blood sprayed all around. The assault rifle went skittering across the floor, and he swung the stricken arm around toward the autocannon, adding what little support if offered to his grip. He could feel his strength slipping away, but he managed to hold the heavy weapon, and he continued to fire.

He coughed hard, and a blob of semi-congealed blood spit out from his mouth. He gasped for air, struggled to keep his weapon up and firing.

Then, another round slammed into his leg, and he dropped forward, wobbling for a second on his knees. He reached down, deep inside, pushing away the pain, the fear, clawing for every scrap of strength that remained to him. He was a killing machine, and he would hold that corridors. He would never stop.

Not until he'd bought enough time for Andi to escape. His comrade and captain was his friend too, and he knew she thought of him as a brother. But he'd never told her of his own thoughts, of the feelings he'd kept hidden for so long.

Gregor loved Andi, like he'd never loved anyone. He knew as he knelt in that corridor that he could never be with her, that she would never even know what he'd been too timid to tell her. Gregor was a warrior, a monster, a fighter, who'd faced all kinds of fearsome enemies in battle without the slightest hesitation. But he'd been too afraid to tell Andi the truth, to profess his love to her.

Now he was in his last fight. He knew that. And never in his life had he battled for something more important to him. He *had* to hold the corridor, for just a bit longer. He couldn't let the enemy get past, to reach the others before they got through the airlock.

He heard a loud clang, the autocannon dropping to the floor as his arms finally gave out, and his strength waned. He looked down the corridor, and his face twisted into a fearsome growl. He reached to his side, trying to ignore the pain of his wounds, and he pulled his pistol and his blade from his belt.

He gritted his teeth, grinding them so powerfully, it felt as though he'd crush them to powder, and he forced himself back up to his feet.

The pain was everywhere, agony, intense, relentless. But his mind was focused on one thing, on Andi Lafarge. On his shipmates carrying her to safety. He pushed forward, stumbling into the enemy fire, even as another round took him in the side.

He could see the enemy, watch the surprised looks on their faces. The fire slackened for a few seconds, as the Foudre Rouge looked on in stunned shock. Gregor continued down the corridor, closing on the Union soldiers. He extended his arm and fired his pistol, but the shot went well wide of any targets.

The enemy recovered from their shock, and they opened fire again. Round after round slammed into Gregor's body, but still, he pushed forward. He was on his knees by then, crawling, pulling himself toward the enemy with inhuman endurance.

The corridor was soaked with his blood, and he dropped his pistol and his knife. But still, he pressed on, until another wave of shots finally took him down. He lay on the floor, his strength gone, the last of his lifeblood draining away, and yet, there was one last bit of strength he could expend for Andi.

He heard the Foudre Rouge coming forward, and he could see his knife on the ground about ten centimeters away. He waited, spitting gouts of blood from his mouth with one coughing spasm after another.

But he waited.

Then, he saw the shadow, one of the enemy standing just in front of him.

He reached down inside him, gathered all that remained of his strength, of his life. He lunged forward, his hand stretching out, grabbing the knife, even as the enemy reacted to his move.

He could hear the fire, feel the rounds ripping into him, but still he lunged forward one last time, and he screamed, "Andi," as he plunged his blade upward, into the thigh of one of the Foudre Rouge.

Then he fell to the ground and lay motionless, his body riddled with bullets.

Gregor, the giant of *Pegasus*, and of *Nightrunner* before, Andi Lafarge's trusted friend, and the scourge of a dozen District taverns, was dead.

Chapter Thirty-Four

Unidentified Imperial Ruin
Somewhere Under the Endless Sea
Planet Aquellus, Olystra III
Year 302 AC

"She's all set. Now get in your suit, too, and take her out."
Vig Merrick stood next to Andi's still motionless form, but
he was looking back the way they had come. The sounds of
fighting had died down, and now he could hear someone
approaching. He gripped his rifle and he repeated, "Get
your damned suit on, and get Andi out of here!"

"Vig…he's not coming. He's gone." The pain in Anna's
words cut like the sharpest blade. Vig knew she was right,
but he couldn't accept that. How could they leave Gregor
behind?

Anna was climbing in her suit. "I can't handle her alone.
You have to come. Gregor sacrificed himself to save us…to
save Andi. Don't make his death meaningless."

Vig hesitated just a few seconds more, but the sounds
coming from down the corridor were clearly from more
than one set of boots. It was difficult to accept the loss of
his shipmate—*Pegasus*'s second fatality on the mission—
especially without seeing Gregor's body for himself. But he
knew it was true.

And he knew Anna was right. Any more of them who died only took away from what he'd done, lessened the impact of his final act.

He reached out and grabbed the suit, climbing into the cumbersome thing. Anna was already zipped up, and a few seconds later, he was too. There was fire coming down the corridor, even as they dragged Andi into the airlock, and he slammed his gloved hand against the controls, bringing down the armored door. He could see the water bubbling all around, filling up the small room, and he could feel his suit pressed against him, its billowy nature disappearing as the pressure in the airlock equalized with that outside. A few seconds later, the doors opened, and he could see the ocean beyond, and the tunnel leading back to *Pegasus*.

And three Foudre Rouge standing less than ten meters away, prone and firing out at something.

At *Pegasus!*

He felt a wave of fury take him, an uncontrollable tsunami of hatred. In that moment, he despised the Union soldiers with a passion he knew he'd never be able to describe to anyone. He didn't care if he escaped or if he died in those few seconds…as long as he got to kill his enemy.

He reached around for the underwater assault rifle, bringing it to bear and opening fire as he ran forward. He was screaming, a great, primal howl that only he could hear in the confines of the suit, and he felt the pure satisfaction of a predator as one of the Foudre Rouge lurched back and then floated motionless in front of him.

His shot had breached the soldier's suit, and the pressure had crushed the man in an instant. Vig was elated by the kill, but his mind was already on the Foudre Rouge just to the right of his first victim.

He fired again and again, and the second trooper suffered a fate much like the first. But the third was bringing his weapon around just as Vig reached him. Their bodies slammed into each other, and they tumbled out from the tunnel onto the rocky ledge.

Vig let the rifle go, and he grabbed the heavy knife strapped to his suit. It was cumbersome in the heavy gloves, and he almost dropped it. But somehow, he kept his grip. He struggled to bring it around, to slice into his enemy's suit, even as the Foudre Rouge tried desperately to bring his rifle to a firing position.

The two battled for seconds, for a minute. Then two.

Vig could see Anna moving behind, somehow pulling Andi with her as she did. The Foudre Rouge would kill them both if he lost the fight. That realization gave him renewed strength, and he brought the blade closer to his enemy, the point pressed up against the soldier's suit. He pushed, as hard as he could, but the suit's material was thick and tough, and it resisted.

He bit his lip as he struggled to put every bit of his strength into the effort, but to no avail. He couldn't push it through. His enemy was bringing his rifle around, getting the barrel closer. Vig had one final chance, one last grasp for victory.

He pulled the blade across his enemy's suit as quickly as he could, slicing rather than trying to drive the point in. He saw the knife moving along, ineffectually…and then it struck one of the seams along the top of the right leg. He wasn't sure at first that it had cut through, but then he saw his enemy convulse and drop his rifle, as the water forced its way into the tiny gash Vig had cut into his suit. The pressure rushed in, expanding the hole and finishing the job.

The Foudre Rouge floated away, motionless.

Vig turned, gasping for oxygen, even as he clawed his way toward *Pegasus*. Anna and Andi were already in, and the attackers were all down. There were more coming, but he knew it would take them some time to get into their suits and come through the airlock. He wasn't sure how long he had, but he suspected it wasn't long.

He pushed himself, marshaling his strength, struggling

toward *Pegasus*'s airlock…toward escape.

Escape at least, from the sea, from the doomed planet…and to the deadly fight that awaited them in space.

* * *

"Faster! We've got to get that ship!" Caron was losing control, and it showed. Most of the Foudre Rouge were down, including the lieutenant, killed in the fight with that gargantuan monster in the corridor. He'd watched with horror and frustration as the giant of a man had simply *refused to die*. He'd held them back, allowed his comrades to make good their escape.

Cost Caron and his people time they didn't have.

And if Caron and his survivors couldn't get out there in time to take that ship, he'd killed them all.

He climbed into the suit, as quickly as he could, checking the countdown timer. Twenty-four minutes. He turned and looked out at his people. There were six of them left, and four were suited up and ready to go. He waved his arm for them to follow him, and he stumbled into the airlock. He turned and fumbled clumsily at the controls, finally bringing down the door…just as the room shook hard.

He rushed to the other end, pressing his mask up against the tiny window on the airlock door. The outside was a swirling mass of bubbling water and roiling steam. He tried to fight off the realization, but it was stark and cold and inarguable.

The enemy ship had taken off. They were gone.

His people were trapped.

He turned, pressing the controls again, rushing back inside and clawing at his suit, pulling it off as quickly as he could.

"We're trapped here. We've got to get to the bomb, disarm it before…"

"It can't be disarmed, Commander. It will detonate if any

attempt is made. Those were your orders."

"I know that, you damned fool, but it's our only chance."
His voice was shrill, his panic taking control, turning him
into a hysterical wreck.

He ran down the hallway, shrieking wildly as he
surrendered his mind to madness.

* * *

Andi looked up, still for just a few seconds before she leapt
off the cot. She turned and stumbled through the doorway
from the tiny infirmary, and out onto the lower deck, before
the realization took hold. *Pegasus* was moving, shaking all
around. It wasn't the strange rolling sensation of maneuver
in the water.

We're out of the sea. In the atmosphere.

"Andi…"

"Doc, what the hell is…" She stopped suddenly. She
remembered. Enemy troops, fire. She reached down, feeling
a bandage where she remembered pain.

"I got you patched up, but you're going to rip it all open
if you…"

"Forget that now, Doc…I have to get to the bridge."
She staggered across the deck, grabbing the ladder and
hauling herself up painfully, amid a series of deep grunts.
She pulled herself up just outside the bridge, and then she
stepped through the access door.

"Andi!" It was Vig, in her chair.

Piloting the ship. The only problem was, Vig wasn't a
pilot.

"What the hell…how?"

"I've watched you before, Andi. I figured I could
manage. And there wasn't much choice. We need Barret on
the guns."

"He's a natural, Andi…he got us this far." *Pegasus*'s
gunner looked across the bridge.

Vig slid out of the chair, making way for Andi. She slipped into her place, and she reached out, grabbing the controls, as Vig moved over to the third station.

"Okay, we're moving into the upper atmosphere." Andi turned toward Barret. "How did you guys do on the repairs?" She could see that the scanners were operational, but she hadn't put them through their paces yet. "I want those guns ready, Barret. We don't know where that enemy ship is, but if it's anywhere close, we're going to have to fight our way out."

"All ready, Andi. The scanners are close to one hundred percent, and we've got full power to the guns."

"Good." She angled the thrust vector, adjusting the course slightly. She turned toward Barret, but before she could speak, the scanners went crazy. A few seconds later, *Pegasus* was hit by...something. The ship careened out of control, Andi leaning forward, her hands gripped tightly on the controls. For an instant, she thought they'd been attacked, that the enemy ship had somehow snuck up on them. But then, she realized.

The explosive...

She pulled the throttle back, steepening the angle as she fought to regain some kind of control. The energy levels on her scanners were beyond categorization. Beyond imagination. Every monitor was maxed out.

The temperature outside was rising dramatically, and *Pegasus* was engulfed in massive clouds of steam, as trillions of gallons of seawater vaporized almost instantly. It wasn't the bomb the Union forces had planted, of course. It was the antimatter.

Those tanks had contained an unknown quantity of the almost priceless fuel...and in a fraction of a second, it had all annihilated.

She stared down at her screen, and then she looked up at the main display. *Pegasus* rocked hard despite her best efforts to control the ascent, but she managed to keep the ship pushing toward orbit. The atmospheric pressure outside the hull was twice what it should be, and she rechecked her altitude readings.

Then she realized the immensity of the explosion, the almost incalculable force that had been released. The imperial facility was gone, she knew, reduced to little but pure energy and hard radiation, as was much of the planet's surface for a thousand kilometers in every direction. And the wave driving *Pegasus*, almost ripping her ship from her control, was a vast section of the planet's atmosphere being torn away, blasted out into space.

She slowly regained control as *Pegasus* moved around toward the other side of the planet, away from the worst effects of the explosion. She adjusted her course and steepened the ascent angle again, hoping to reach orbit before she came back around into the affected zone.

The wave of tension and fear that had gripped her receded, just a bit, as the forces battering *Pegasus* subsided slightly. The Union ship still lay ahead, or at least a desperate race to escape from its grasp, but Andi had learned to appreciate every step toward success. Toward survival.

"Is everybody okay?" Barret and Vig both nodded. "We're ready, Andi." There was a somberness in Vig's tone, one that seemed out of place for the normally cocky and aggressive youngest crew member of her crew.

"How about down below? All good?" She was speaking into the comm unit.

"We're okay, Andi." Anna replied, and the sadness in her voice was unmistakable.

"Okay," Andi said, both to her companions on the bridge, and into the comm, "let's stay focused. As soon as we get a read on the Union ship, we can decide what to do. Lex, I want you in engineering. You know what to do down there. Barret..." She turned toward the gunner. "...I want you working on targeting the instant we get a look at that ship."

"I'm on it, Andi."

She leaned toward the comm. "Gregor, I need you on the patching gun. We don't know how battered the hull is, and we…" She could feel Barret's and Vig's eyes burning into her, and the silence from the others was almost deafening. "What?" She looked toward Barret and Vig, but the two said nothing. Then she heard something on the comm, soft, distant sobs. Anna.

"What the hell is going on?"

"Andi…" Vig spoke first. He stood up, walked the meter and a half to Andi's chair. "It's Gregor…he didn't make it."

The words hit Andi like an avalanche. She remembered going down in the corridor, pain from the wound, and then her head hitting hard. Then darkness. Gregor had been wounded…but still on his feet, driven on by his incredible constitution.

You never even thought to check if everyone was back. You just assumed…

Guilt gripped her hard, and grief, and she could feel tears welling up in her eyes, streaming down her cheeks. "Gregor?" She struggled to hold back the emotion, but it broke free of her control. Her face was a mask of tears, and images of *Pegasus*'s giant, of her friend as well as her shipmate, floated in her mind. She couldn't even count how many times Gregor had saved her life, how many times he'd stood by her, resolute, unbreakable…and she had left him behind.

"How?" She barely managed to croak out the word.

"In the battle at the intersection. He saved us all, Andi. None of us would have made it without him."

Andi sat still, brokenhearted, inconsolable as the tears poured off her cheeks. She was drifting, lost, her concentration broken.

And then she heard Barret's voice.

"Andi…we've got the Union ship on the scans. She's in orbit, just coming around into our field."

The words grabbed her, pulling her back. The meaning was only too clear, though she struggled with it for a few seconds before understanding solidified. The enemy ship was close, far too close. Any chance of running was gone.

If *Pegasus* was to survive, if the rest of her people were going to make it out of the cursed system, they would have to fight their way out.

She struggled to drive away the grief. That had seemed impossible just seconds before, but now something new rose up inside her, something as strong as her sadness and guilt. Stronger.

Rage.

Fiery hot anger. An unquenchable thirst for vengeance. Andi wanted her friends back, she wanted to undo so what had happened. But all of that was impossible.

All that remained was to make the enemy pay. The Foudre Rouge and Sector Nine agents she'd left behind were already dead, far too quickly and mercifully in her estimation, but at least they were dead. The only Union personnel remaining in the system were in that ship.

She stared at the screen, her eyes frozen manifestations of death. The white hot fury slipped away, replaced by something far darker and more terrible. A frozen void, unstoppable, utterly without fear. She was going to kill everyone on that Union ship, whatever it took, whatever it cost…and in that moment, she realized that even if running had been an option, she would have stayed.

It was time to fight. Time to kill.

Chapter Thirty-Five

Free Trader Pegasus
60,000 Meters from Planet Aquellus
Olystra System
Year 302 AC

"Push up the thrust, Lex. Another ten percent." *Pegasus* was running, trying to escape from the vastly larger Union ship, struggling to squeeze power from its damaged and depleted engines.

At least that's what Andi Lafarge wanted her pursuers to think.

"Ten percent...coming through now." Lex Righter still sounded a little confused. That was fine with her, as long as he did what she told him to do. Righter was a fine engineer, one of the best she'd ever seen...but he was clearly no tactician. *Pegasus* was the weaker combatant in the fight. For all the pure, unrestrained fury driving Andi just then, she realized she couldn't win a head on confrontation. Being outgunned was a weakness, certainly, but maybe she could make it a strength, too. All it would take was a little bit of deceit, some delicate maneuvering, and her unstoppable determination to repay the enemy in blood for the deaths of her friends.

That, and a hold full of five hundred gigaton torpedoes.

She fed in the increased engine power slowly, haltingly, even backing off a bit before pushing up again. Just how a battered ship struggling to escape with barely functioning engines would do.

"They're on us, Andi. Distance eighty thousand kilometers. I'm guessing that's in range of their main gun, at least." Barret was *Pegasus*'s gunner, but on the small ship with its tiny crew, he was also the scanner chief.

"I see them." Andi's voice was stone cold, her eyes fixed on the contact, unmoving. She had her evasive maneuvers ready, both the vast library of randomized routines she'd stored in the AI, and a few new ones she was going to throw in the mix. But that kind of maneuverability would send up a red flare, tell the enemy *Pegasus* wasn't as helpless as Andi was struggling to make it appear. She had her plan, a way to destroy her much more powerful adversary. But to do it, she would have to take some risks, including offering her vessel up as a juicy target, at least for a while longer.

"They're not going to fire at long range. They figure they've got us. They'll come in closer and look to finish us quickly." Andi's tone was surprisingly firm as she recited what she knew very well was little more than a guess.

She tapped the controls again, feeding most of the extra power into the engines. *Pegasus* was blasting away at thirty percent power, and telegraphing in every way Andi could devise that even maintaining that level was a struggle.

"Lex...get ready to release on my command." She had something else for the enemy, just the kind of thing that might push a cautious captain to the arrogance she was hoping for.

"Seventy thousand kilometers, Andi. Still no fire." The last part of Barret's report was pretty pointless. Andi was focused, obsessed with her quest to destroy the enemy...but she doubted she'd fail to notice when the pursuing ship opened fire.

"Ready for release, Andi." A pause, then Lex added,

"They're getting close, aren't they?"

Andi didn't respond, she just frowned and stared at her screen. *They're going to get a lot closer...*

"Sixty thousand." A few seconds later: "I'm picking up energy readings. Andi, I think they're charging their guns."

"Understood." It wasn't the answer Barret was looking for, she knew that. *It's better they don't know how close I'm going to cut this.*

Her eyes were fixed on the pursuing ship's thrust. They were accelerating hard, seeking to close the distance, to finish *Pegasus*.

Just what she wanted.

"Fifty thousand."

Andi stared at the small symbol on the screen, the approaching Union vessel. She leaned forward slowly, and spoke into the comm, her voice soft, her tone frozen. "Release."

She pushed the controls, cutting the thrust dramatically, even as she heard Vig's acknowledgement, and an instant later saw the dim cloud appearing behind Pegasus. It was a combination of partially burned fuel and radiation, exactly what might leak from a ship with significant engine damage.

A ship whose engines were sputtering and beginning to fail entirely.

Or that appeared to be.

* * *

"We're picking up engine residue, Commander. Partially-spent fuel, super-heated gasses...and considerable radiation." An instant later: "They're losing thrust as well. Down fifty percent from previous levels. No, sixty. Looks like we were right. The ship is badly damaged."

Boucher had been about to order *Phantasia*'s guns to open fire. But now she saw that her prey was badly hurt, worse even than she'd expected. It was time to finish them, to crush them with a single attack.

"Maintain engine output and course. It's time. All lasers online." Boucher felt an instant's hesitation, a wave of mistrust. Was it possible the ship in front of hers was trying to deceive her in some way? She was suspicious by nature, but then she put the thoughts aside. The enemy ship was allowing her to close, to bring her superior weapons to bear, and they were exposing their vulnerable rear section. If it was some kind of ploy, it was a deadly dangerous one.

And one that is going to get that ship destroyed.

"Prepare to open fire at thirty thousand kilometers." That would be close enough to almost guarantee destruction, especially of a cripple with no real ability to evade. "And increase acceleration another ten percent. It's time to finish this."

"Yes, Commander…increasing thrust now."

Boucher felt the strange sensation as the engine output rose. It wasn't pressure, not exactly. *Phantasia*'s dampeners were absorbing that. But there was a definite sensation.

She looked at the display, watching as the range ticked down to forty thousand. *Phantasia*'s velocity was over a thousand kilometers per second and increasing. They would be at the firing point in seconds.

Boucher was trying not to think about the disaster the mission had become, or the near certainty that all of her landing parties, and any artifacts they'd found, had been lost in the cataclysmic explosion her scanners had detected. She dreaded reporting what had happened, and she figured she had maybe even money of coming out of it alive. But she would worry about that, and decide what to do, after she'd repaid whoever was in that ship.

Whoever had caused her so much trouble.

"Prepare to fire…"

* * *

"Thirty thousand kilometers, Andi."

Barret's tense report was accompanied almost immediately by a bright flash on the display. Andi hadn't been looking at the screen, but her eyes darted back immediately. The AI could have replayed the image for her, but there was no need. She knew what it had been.

The enemy had opened fire.

"That shot came within sixty kilometers, Andi."

She just nodded, but she didn't reply. That was closer than she'd hoped for the first shot. *Pegasus* was conducting some evasive maneuvering, disguises ad random bursts and materials releases affecting the ship's vector, but if that's all she did, Andi was begging the enemy to score a hit.

And if she did more, if she fired up the engines, and initiated *real* evasive maneuvering, the enemy would know *Pegasus* was fully functional.

Worse, they would know Andi had been suckering them.

And it was still too soon. She needed another ten thousand kilometers…maybe fifteen seconds.

"Lex, be ready down there."

"We're all set, Andi. Vig's suited up and in place. The hold's evacuated. We're as ready as we can be."

She nodded, a pointless enough gesture since Lex couldn't see her. She flipped her comm channel, and brought Vig onto the line. "You ready for this, Vig?"

"I'm good, Andi. Everything's set."

Andi struggled to accept the dangers of her plan, to *Pegasus* and all its crew, but especially to Vig Merrick. Vig was Sy's brother, and she had to push away images of herself telling her friend she'd gotten her brother killed.

She had managed to push aside images of Gregor and Jackal, and focus on the battle at hand. But she knew her friends would be there, when she closed her eyes, in quiet moments, when she was alone, when the ghosts could approach her.

"Twenty-five thousand."

Andi felt the urge to give the order, to set her plan in motion immediately, before the enemy could fire again. It *could* work at twenty-five. There was a good chance that was close enough. But she'd already decided on twenty, and there was no point in revisiting that. If she jumped the gun, if she moved too early and the enemy managed to evade her trap, *Pegasus* was as good as finished. She valued her ship, and the vessel and its crew were all that mattered to her in the universe. But *Pegasus* was no match for the Union ship, not in a straight up fight.

No, her plan either worked…or they all died.

That meant gutting it out, sticking to what she'd decided. She winced as another shot ripped by…and then a second later, she felt her hope slip away as *Pegasus* shook hard, and a whole series of relays on the far side of the bridge erupted into a shower of sparks.

One of the enemy lasers had hit.

Her hands were on the comm immediately, but Lex Righter spoke even before she could.

"It's not as bad as it looks, Andi. I'm still checking systems, but we've got at least ninety percent on the reactor, and the lasers are intact.

"Do what you can, Lex." She turned and looked over at the display. Twenty-two thousand kilometers. That would have to do. She couldn't wait any longer. The enemy had honed their targeting. One more shot, one hit, and it would be over.

"Vig…now! Let 'em go."

Andi braced for the series of vibrations she expected. But there was nothing.

"Vig…"

"I'm working on it, Andi. The bay door won't open. I think it's jammed shut."

Vig's words hit Andi hard. She could understand a reactor shutdown or a blasted laser turret. But the idea that her people were going to die because the cargo bay door was jammed was too much to bear.

"Do what you have to, Vig. Just get that thing open!" It was probably the least helpful thing she'd ever said. But she didn't know what else to do.

"I'm on my way, Vig." It was Lex Righter.

"No." Vig's voice was hard, decisive. "We need you in engineering. I'll get this done."

Andi felt a coldness when she heard his words. "Vig, what are you…" She saw the pressure gauge begin to move. Vig was repressurizing the hold.

She was confused for a moment…and then she realized what he was going to do. "Vig…no. It's too dangerous."

"There's no other way, Andi. I'm suited up, and there's a good chance it will work, especially if I over-pressurize."

"Over-pressurize? Vig, it will be suicide. We can blast the engines, engage the evasive maneuvers. You don't have to…"

"Yes, Andi…I do." The comm line went dead.

Andi tapped at it again. "Vig…Vig?" No response.

She knew what he was about to do. She couldn't stop him, not in time, at least not directly. She looked down at the controls. But she could fire up the thrusters to full, blast away from the Union ship's approach. That would warn the enemy…and make what Vig was about to do pointless.

But it would also almost guarantee *Pegasus* would lose the battle…and Vig would die along with the rest of them if that happened.

She could see the hold was at one hundred forty percent of normal pressure. She wasn't sure how high it could go. She'd never tried to bring it above normal levels before.

The main hold door was jammed, but there were two smaller hatches. Vig had never said what he was planning, but Andi knew with stone-cold certainty. He was going to blow the smaller hatches, and bank on explosive decompression forcing the main doors open. It might work or it might not, and even if it did, if it damaged the sensitive setup Vig and Lex had built, it would all be for naught.

But she knew it was the only way.

It had been the proudest moment of her life when she'd discovered that Captain Lorillard had left the ship to her, left her in command of the family they had all become. But sometimes she detested being the leader, and she longed for someone else to take charge, to make the hard decisions.

Like letting Vig carry out his plan.

His nearly insane plan.

"Go, Vig…and good luck…" She wasn't sure if he had cut off the comm, or if he could hear her and he'd just stopped replying.

She watched as the pressure gauge moved up. One sixty…one seventy.

Then, without warning, *Pegasus* shuddered hard, and she reached for the controls, desperately trying to stabilize the ship, as the vacuum of space sucked out the dense atmosphere—and anything else not securely fastened—from the hold.

She took a deep, ragged breath and hoped Vig Merrick was not one of those things.

Chapter Thirty-Six

Free Trader Pegasus
155,000 Meters from Planet Aquellus
Olystra System
Year 302 AC

Vig Merrick clung to the handholds, desperately trying to hang on as the high-pressure air inside the hold raced out into space, taking everything not bolted in place with it. For an instant, he thought his plan hadn't worked, but then, the immense force ripped the door free from whatever jam had held it in place, and the entire back of the hold was open to space.

Vig could feel his gloves slipping, and his body flew away, toward the open door, toward space. He sailed two-thirds of the way across the hold, and then he came to an abrupt stop, his tether line taut, straining...but somehow holding.

He floated about two meters from the deck for a few seconds, as the last of the air in the hold blasted out in a wild torrent. Then, he swung to the side, slamming into the wall. The only force affecting him now was *Pegasus*'s thrust, and along with whatever systems his stunt had damaged, the dampeners were no longer working. He felt the air driven from his lungs on the impact, and he floated there in his suit, still alive—miraculously—but barely clinging to consciousness.

He'd done it. His crazy scheme had worked, albeit at the cost of considerable damage to the ship. But he wasn't done. He still had one more thing to do. He reached around, checking to make sure the controller was still on his belt. For a few seconds, he felt cold panic, and he was sure it had come loose, that it was gone, out in the depths of space along with all the other debris.

Then he felt it. He was woozy, and he fumbled with it twice. *Careful, you fool…if you lose that thing…*

He knew he should check with Andi, synchronize the drop. But there was no time. He wasn't even sure his comm was still working.

He held the controllers tightly in his hand, and he brought his finger down. He could feel the blackness taking him, but he fought it off. He had to be sure it was working.

There was no sound, not across the vacuum of the shattered cargo hold, but he managed to turn his head just enough to see.

The device resembled a catapult, and even as his vision slowly blurred, he could see it doing what it had been built to do.

Hurling the remaining torpedoes out of the gaping hole that had been the cargo door…all along different trajectories, carefully defined vectors that would create something very much like a minefield right behind *Pegasus*.

A minefield directly in the path of the ship even then closing to finish them off.

* * *

"Commander! Multiple contacts ahead."

Boucher was already staring at the display. The data was still coming in, but there was no doubt *something* was out there.

Her first thought had been debris from the ship she was pursuing. There had been an explosion, or something of the kind, and there'd been some debris from that. But the eight contacts on the screen now were identical...and they were spread out in a pattern too regular to be random.

"Engine room, vector change, full power. Away from those contacts." Boucher's mind went back to the explosion that had cost her *Phantasia*'s two bombers. That had been a torpedo of some kind.

And the mass for the contacts up ahead was just about right...

She could feel the thrust shifting, hitting her in the second or two before the dampeners adjusted. *Phantasia*'s engines were firing at full...but the ship was moving at a high velocity, and it would take time to alter its vector enough...

She looked at the display again, and then down to her workstation. The AI was reworking the ship's prospective path, and that of the contacts up ahead. *Phantasia* would evade most of them, but it was going to be close with the two on the far end.

"More power," she screamed into the comm, even as the scanners finally confirmed what she already knew. The contacts *were* torpedoes. And they had activated their own drives. They were closing on *Phantasia*, vectoring in on the ship's course. That was going to make it even harder to evade them.

"Engine room, we need more power. Overload the reactor, do whatever you have to do...but get us away from those torpedoes."

The ship was rattling all around her, shaking wildly as her people pushed the reactor and engines to their limits and beyond. The thrust was considerable, and the ship's vector *was* changing...but the torpedoes were reacting, even as *Phantasia* made its desperate run.

Boucher gasped for breath, struggling to maintain some

level of calm as she waited.

Waited to see if her ship could escape the net of death her adversary had lain for her.

The trap…the trap I walked right into.

She checked the screen again, reran the calculations. It was going to be close.

* * *

"Vig? Vig…can you hear me?" Andi was hunched over the comm unit, screaming loudly as she tried to cling to some hope Vig had made it. He'd saved them all, or at least he'd given them a chance. It remained to be seen if their sparse and makeshift minefield snared its prey.

She hadn't heard from Vig.

He'd activated the catapult…that had been after he'd blown the doors. So, he hadn't been blasted out into space. At least that logic made enough sense for Andi to convince herself it was true.

Most of her thoughts, were devoted to Vig just them, but her eyes were glued to the screen. The torpedoes—her minefield—were chasing down the Union ship. The vessel had managed to elude six of the weapons, or at least gotten far enough away from their vectors that it was clear they would be able to escape any damage.

But two were still close.

She could let the torpedoes try to close, to impact with the enemy ship and obliterate it. That would be ideal, but it was also the least likely occurrence. Naval ships had almost given up using torpedoes in the last fifty years, at least physical ones. Modern ships had too much thrust, and energy weapon ranges had steadily increased over the last century. Andi figured she had one chance in three for one of the warheads to actually hit the enemy ship. Maybe one in four.

But she didn't need a direct hit.

"I want the engines ready…and Barret, you make sure the lasers are charged."

She could bet everything on destroying her enemy in one stroke…or she could hedge her bets. She tracked the likeliest vectors for the ship and the two pursuing torpedoes. If she detonated them at just the right instant, she might damage the enemy ship, even cripple it.

But she had to time it perfectly. Her mind raced, calculating the exact moment for the explosion, and even adjusting for the time it would take to transmit a destruct command. It was tight, difficult, maybe as much of a longshot as hoping for an outright hit. But she'd already decided, and Andi rarely second guessed herself.

She watched, tense, holding her breath…and then she pressed the button, sending the command to the two warheads, just as they were both passing within a kilometer of the Union ship.

*　*　*

Phantasia shook hard, and she spun around, gyrating in a wild roll. Boucher was strapped in, but even so, she could feel the pain as two of her ribs snapped. Her body had been thrown hard forward, and even as she tried to remain focused on the battle, she could see the damage all around.

The bridge was filled with smoke, several different shades of toxic fumes from various damaged systems swirling around her. The reactor was down, the ship's power limited to emergency battery stores. She could see Drusus Olivetti sprawled across the deck, the grotesque angle between his head and his neck making it immediately clear he was dead.

Phantasia was crippled, helpless. She'd screamed desperately into the comm unit, ordering her people in engineering to report, to get her ship functioning again. But all she'd heard was static. She didn't know if her people on the lower decks were all dead, or if the intraship comm was just out.

It didn't matter. She was beaten, finished. It didn't seem possible. How could that ship, that small, insignificant ship, have thwarted her at every turn, bested all of her people?

She looked across the bridge at the display, one of the few systems still functioning. The enemy ship was there, coming around, closing on *Phantasia*. If she'd had anything, a laser, or some engine power, Boucher could at least fight back.

But she had nothing.

Her ship was crippled, dead in space.

She felt the panic rising up inside her, the cold feeling of approaching death. She'd sent others to their ends, as often as not, in suffering and agony, with little sympathy and no remorse. But now that she faced death, all she wanted was to escape, to find the mercy that she had so often refused her own victims.

Surrender was forbidden, of course, against every mandate that directed the actions of Sector Nine operatives. The penalty for cowardice, for yielding to the enemy was death. But she faced death if she *didn't* give up.

Maybe she'd faced it anyway, even if she'd escaped the system, returned to Montmirail with the mission she'd commanded a total shambles. Perhaps it was better, for her, for all her people. The Confederation was the enemy, but their ways were different. She would be imprisoned at first, almost certainly, but she could make a deal, offer information in return for leniency.

Yes, perhaps she could make it work, build a new life. It seemed a better choice than dying in the depths of the Badlands.

She reached out, activated the comm. "This is Sector Nine ship *Phantasia* to the unknown vessel out there. We are crippled and defenseless, and we yield. We ask for mercy, and we surrender to you."

*   *   *

Andi started at the speaker, her face twisted in a nasty scowl. She heard the sounds of the Sector Nine commander, the Union killer who now sought mercy. She could see Barret across the bridge, looking on with some level of confusion.

Andi returned her comrade's gaze, but there was no uncertainty in her eyes. The mines had worked, they had crippled the enemy ship, rendered it harmless. But they hadn't destroyed it utterly, and they'd left it there…for Andi to decide its fate.

She could see Barret's discomfort. He despised the Union as much as anyone else, but even after the dishonor that had seen him expelled from the service, he still carried far too much navy honor with him, at least for Andi's tastes. And the Confederation navy did not refuse surrender requests, no matter how horrible the yielding party's crimes.

Andi turned back and stared at the comm again. The surrender was no trick, no deceit, she was sure of that. The scans left no doubt. The Union ship was utterly helpless. Likely, if left on its own, its remaining power would eventually fail, and it would lose life support. A terrifying, lingering death for everyone onboard.

Andi knew she couldn't allow that. She couldn't let cold and lack of air do what she had to do herself.

She reached out, flipped on the comm. "Sector Nine vessel, this is *Pegasus*. We have received your surrender request." She stared straight ahead, not a hint of emotion in her expression.

"Yes, *Pegasus*…thank you for responding. I am Commander Boucher. We have eleven survivors, and we all wish surrender. We request rescue and transit back to the Confederation, where we will cooperate with all authorities."

"That is good to hear, Commander Boucher. There is just one thing I must do first. I have to obtain approval from the surrender committee. Fortunately, on this ship there are only two members. Their names are Gregor and Jackal."

Andi got up from her chair and she walked across the bridge, carrying the portable comm mic with her. "Unfortunately, I can't seem to find them, Commander...no matter how hard I look."

She walked over to Barret's station, and she put her hand on his shoulder, pushing him gently from his seat. "I'm not sure where they can be..." She sat at the just-vacated position, and her hands moved over the controls. "They must have been killed, Commander...slaughtered by your murderous cutthroats." Her emotionless tone was gone, replaced by the sound of pure venom. "That is too bad, Commander...it leaves me no options."

Her hands gripped the gunnery controls, and she opened the power flow, charging up the topside turret. "Too bad for you. I'm afraid without my two friends, there is no way for me to accept your surrender. So, I guess I don't have any choice."

Andi could feel the discomfort from Barret, hear his breathing. Her friend knew she was going to do, and while she doubted he would try to stop her, he was clearly on edge.

"I'm terribly sorry, Commander." Andi brought up the scope and finalized the fire lock. The enemy ship had no thrust, no evasive capability. A child brought in from the street could have aimed the guns. Opening fire on a helpless vessel, one that had surrendered, would be nothing short of murder.

But Andi didn't care. Not one bit.

"Yes, I'm terribly sorry, Commander...sorry that this will be so quick, so relatively painless. Given time and opportunity, I would relish taking longer, looking into your eyes as the life fades from them. But circumstances allow us what they do. Goodbye, Commander Boucher. I called ahead and saved your place. You will get to see hell before I do."

Andi's fingers tightened, and *Pegasus*'s lasers fired…once, and then again, a few seconds later. She imagined the beams ripping into the damaged ship, slicing open its hull. She closed her eyes for a second, seeing the Sector Nine operatives running, screaming, lost in panic as the frigid vacuum of space tore into their ship, as they gasped for air and froze or died in the agony of the flames.

And then she saw the ship—*Phantasia*, her counterpart had called it—vanish from the scanner display.

The fight was over, and Andi felt a brief spark, a passing second of elation at the victory…and at what she saw as final justice meted out. But it was gone almost at once, and all that remained was a yawning pit of pain and loss, and the faces of two comrades, friends and brothers…gone.

Chapter Thirty-Seven

Samis Station Three
Orbiting Ventica VII
Year 302 AC

"I am sorry about your shipmates, Andi." There was genuine remorse in Durango's voice, Andi was sure of it. She rarely believed anything she heard, or took anyone's word. But she believed the shipyard manager, and whatever else he was, was reliable in his own way. "You were true to your word. You had to know the artifacts you brought back were worth more than the half million credits I promised you. Much more. Yet, you brought them back and honored the agreement. That is a rare thing, Andi. You are hard, cold—sometimes, I suspect, cruel and merciless—but at your core, you are an honorable warrior. You will always be welcome at Samis, for whatever you may need. Which, at this moment, appears to be significant repairs to your ship.

Andi nodded. She wasn't sure what she thought of Durango's words. She gave credence to flattery and kind words even less than she believed people's claims and promises. But again, there had been a sincerity to what he'd said. She nodded. "Yes, my ship needs…significant repairs."

Pegasus was battered, the entire rear of its cargo hold gone, the hull dented and pockmarked in a dozen placed and hastily patched in a dozen more. She'd barely gotten the ship back to Samis, and she hadn't dared to estimate the costs of making the vessel truly spaceworthy again, much less bringing it back to top condition. Half a million credits sounded like a lot of money when she'd accepted it for the mission, but now she figured she'd be handing most of that right back to Durango. She could live with that, for her part, at least. She'd never had much—for most of her life, she'd had nothing at all—but the thought of her people coming away with almost nothing for the second mission in a row was painful. Her mind was working, trying to decide what repairs could wait, how much she could leave undone and still take *Pegasus* on a couple milk runs to work her way through repair costs.

"We both know what you brought back is worth many times what we are paying you. I can't change that…I am not the ultimate decision maker. But I do have some authority…and I will repair *Pegasus* for you, back to tip top shape…at no charge.

The words hit Andi like a hammer. *This* was completely unexpected.

"I'm sorry, Durango…thank you for that offer…but I can't accept charity. Maybe we can sit down and shave off all the nonessential…"

"It is not charity. I am almost stealing from you on this. And, I know your ship was in top condition before you left, because I put it there myself. So, let me pay your fee, and let me fix the damages you suffered on the mission." A pause. "I can't do anything to bring back your lost comrades, of course, but I will provide annuities for their next of kin. It's the least we can do for those who served us so well."

Andi was dumbstruck. She'd wallowed so long in the sewers of humanity, she could hardly recognize someone dealing honorably with her.

"I don't know what to say, Durango."

"Don't say anything. You've got to be exhausted…and

you need some medical care yourself. Leave *Pegasus* to me. You will find your half million in the system AI. That's more convenient right now than a crate of platinum...but when you leave, it is instantly convertible to hard currency at the purser's office."

"Thank you again, Durango." She extended her hand. "Now, I have to find a way to sneak back to Dannith. I have some business there, and some considerable...complications...to deal with."

"I am sure you will find a way, Andi...after you visit the infirmary." Durango smiled, and he reached out and grasped her hand.

* * *

"We will have to keep an eye on her. I am quite impressed." The man stood in the shadows at the rear of the room, looking down at the small row of crates. "These artifacts are of considerable value. They will go a long way in sustaining our superiority over the Union."

"Two of her people died to bring these to us."

"People die in our line of work, Durango, and in hers. There is no way to avoid it. We have treated her fairly. I wholeheartedly agree with your addition of the annuities and your waiver of the repair costs for her vessel. Andi Lafarge has proven to be an asset of considerable value, and it is in our interests to ensure she remains active...and enhance her loyalty to you. We will very likely want to use her again."

"She is in serious trouble, sir...you know that. That, more than the damage to her ship, endangers her future prospects. And she is insistent on going back to Dannith to attend to...some business. We both know what that means."

"Perhaps we can help her with her problems with the authorities. I am not without influence. I believe we might get the case against her closed, the unfortunate damage done to the spaceport facilities classified as accidental...or caused in the act of self-defense. Her people were under attack there, after all, regardless of how many police and spaceport cronies Carmichael bribed to state otherwise."

"Is that really possible?" Durango was a gritty veteran of the rough and tumble frontier, a man who had dealt with every manner of rogue. But in that moment, he sounded purely earnest.

"Yes, Durango, I believe it is. I will see to it at once. By the time Andi Lafarge gets out of the infirmary and hops a shuttle back to Dannith, she will be an upstanding citizen...or at least the closest facsimile thereof."

The man stepped forward, coming out of the shadows. He was tall, handsome, every centimeter of him the picture of what all the Confederation believed him to be, the scion of a vastly wealthy family, one of the most well known throughout Confed space.

What few of those vast billions, almost none, in fact, knew was that Gary Holsten was also the head of Confederation Intelligence.

"She has served us well, Durango, served the Confederation well. And we take care of our own...even when they don't know they're ours.

*   *   *

Brewer walked into his office. He appeared to be a somewhat successful frontier merchant, dealing in various and sundry exotic merchandise. Under that veneer, he was a notorious black marketeer, a buyer of almost any old tech artifacts that could be had.

And under *that* cover, he was Sector Nine's station chief, the Union's senior operative on Dannith.

Aimee Boucher's mission had been overdue for weeks, and now he was getting scraps of intel, nothing reliable, but repeated rumors that Andi Lafarge and *Pegasus*—the hated

Nightrunner renamed—had returned with artifacts from Aquellus. He didn't know if it was true, but some nagging thought at the back of his mind told him it was.

"Curse that Andi Lafarge and her pack of pirates." The words echoed softly in the nearly dark room. He was alone. He'd left his guards outside. All he wanted was a drink, maybe two or three, and then to go home and get some sleep. In the morning he would try to find out more about what had happened to Boucher and her expedition...and he would commence a new operation, one that would finally rid him of Jim Lorillard's despised ship, and his handpicked successor. They had been a thorn in his side for too long, and it was finally time to do something about it.

He walked over to the bar and poured himself a drink. He lifted it to his lips and took a deep gulp. He felt the smooth brandy sliding down his throat...and something else. He set the glass down and stepped back from the bar. The drink tasted...strange.

"You needn't worry, Brewer. That one drink is quite enough, I assure you."

The Sector Nine operative put his hands to his neck, and he opened his mouth to scream for the guards. But nothing came out.

Then he fell to his knees as his body convulsed in pain. He could hardly move, and he rasped to suck in the smallest breaths of air.

"How much do you know about Blast, Brewer? I had a friend once, who was addicted. It's nasty stuff, really...but if it is dissolved into water with a handful of other, very easily obtained, chemicals and then distilled, it becomes quite a potent poison. And a fast-acting one, I might add, at least to the point of incapacitation." Andi Lafarge stepped out from the dark side of the room and started at the dying man. "But where are my manners, Brewer? Allow me to introduce myself. I am Andromeda Lafarge. I believe you know who I am, and while we are together, let me add to my resume for you. You needn't be concerned for the ship you sent to Aquellus. It is gone, along with everyone you sent out there."

Andi knelt down in front of Brewer, and her hand moved slowly, pulling her knife from its sheath. "The poison will certainly kill you, but it will take some time. Normally, I'd let you suffer, but I'm not sure I can lived with myself if I don't get to feel my knife sliding between your ribs, ridding the universe of one of its vast legion of parasites." As she spoke the words, she jammed the blade into Brewer's abdomen, and she shoved it upward, slicing into his lungs and his heart. She held it for just a second, feeling the blood pouring out, the hot warmth dripping down, over her knife and her hands."

She waited just a few seconds, and then she pulled the knife out as Brewer's body fell with a cold thud. She wiped off her blade on the side of his shirt, a largely pointless effort to clear away the mess. Then she stood up and slipped back into the shadows, and on to her next destination.

She uttered one sentence, a rushed whisper whose meaning only she knew, and then she was gone.

"One down…"

* * *

Carmichael walked into the room, each of his arms extended and wrapped around a buxom, and scantily clad woman. The three of them had been downstairs, but now, the gangster had decided to retire to a more private place, for a little one on two recreation.

His tastes in such areas were rather perverse, and even violent at times, but the women had been well-paid, and if either of them complained, well, the District had no shortage of such professionals, and another body or two found in some garbage strewn lot somewhere wasn't going to trigger any kind of red alert among the authorities.

"Over there." He pulled his arms free, and he gestured toward a very large piece of furniture, some kind of strange combination of a bed and a massive sofa. "Undress."

The two women walked across the room, and after the third step, the one on the left winced and crumpled to the ground.

Carmichael scowled. "I knew you had too much to drink. Now get back on your feet, unless you want a real beating this time." Even as he was finishing his drunken rant, the other woman dropped like stone. The gangster turned around, reaching for the weapon he suddenly realized he'd left on his desk. Then he felt something, a sharp pinprick...and he collapsed next to the women.

"I always suspected you were a sick and twisted piece of shit, Carmichael, but you're more disgusting than I'd even imagined."

The voice was familiar, and the gangster's stomach shriveled inside him. He struggled to move, putting everything he could muster into the effort. But to no avail.

"It's a very good paralytic, wouldn't you say, Carmichael? All the more intriguing because, while it renders the victim completely helpless, it does nothing at all to dull the pain centers of the brain. In fact, there are those who claim it enhances such feeling." Andi paused, and then she added, "It's a derivation of the Blast narcotic. I was just explaining to your friend, Brewer, how to make a highly effective poison from that banned substance. The paralytic is quite close chemically to the pure toxin, and it is made in almost the same way. But it is entirely harmless, and it wears off without effect in several hours."

She turned and looked down at the two woman. "I must apologize to both of you...but I couldn't have you running downstairs and giving alarm. I'm afraid your...date...and I have some things to discuss. You'll both have to be satisfied to sit and watch...and I fancy that you might just enjoy the festivities." She reached in her pocket and pulled out a handful of coins. "These are platinum Confederation credits…enough for you both to crawl out of these pathetic lives you seem to live. I have no moral problems with any trade, as long as it's conducted fairly, but seriously ladies…choose your clients with better care than this." She gestured toward the man who had now fallen to the ground and lay in an almost fetal position looking up.

She looked down at Carmichael, and she set a small tablet on the floor in front of him. "Do you see these images, Carmichael? They're my friends, Gregor and Jackal." She sat down next to him, slowly drawing a long knife from behind her. "I thought we could talk about them for a while. They are—were—very important to me."

Carmichael stared at the knife, and he flailed around wildly, but only in his thoughts. His body was immobile, rigid…and the only thing he could do was look up at Andi's blade, and at the horrifying glint in her eyes as she moved closer.

Chapter Thirty-Eight

Golden Strip
Port Royal City
Planet Dannith, Ventica III
Year 302 AC

Andi Lafarge sat in one of the two plush chairs overlooking the street below. She'd intended to find some District dive to stay in...something that would have itself been a significant step up from the abandoned ruin where she'd originally intended to hide from the authorities. But she'd received a communique from Durango just before her shuttle docked, one that told her she could abandon her disguise, and throw away whatever fake travel documents she'd acquired. The unfortunate situation at the spaceport had been resolved. She wasn't sure how that was possible, but as with everything else he'd promised her, Durango's word had proven to be good. She passed through the arrival checkpoint with her own ID, verifying that Andi Lafarge, wanted fugitive, was now Andi Lafarge, upright citizen.

She'd also found out that a hotel reservation was waiting in her name, not at one of the District's seedy dives, but for a suite at the Grand Royale, right in the middle of Port Royal City's Golden Strip. Another gesture of appreciation from Durango, and whoever he worked for.

She appreciated the gesture, but truth be told, she found the luxury to be a bit uncomfortable so soon after Gregor and Jackal had died. She'd come to Dannith on business—personal business—and she'd settled some scores. The revenge had felt good, as such things always did at first. But when the initial satisfaction dissipated, she had been left with two cold realizations. First, her friends were gone, and no amount of vengeance would bring them back.

And second, she had led them to their deaths.

What the hell was Captain Lorillard thinking? I'm not ready for this. I'm not capable.

She wanted to quit, to walk away from *Pegasus* and never turn back. She didn't care about the pursuit of wealth, not as she sat there…hell, she'd have gladly gone back to the Gut and dug for food in the garbage the rest of her life if it could have brought back Gregor and Jackal.

But she knew she couldn't quit. There was another ghost in her mind, standing in the way, staring at her with disapproving eyes. Captain Lorillard. She didn't know why, but he'd left the ship to her. More than that, he'd left his people to her care.

And you just got two of them killed…

She wasn't sure if the thought had been hers, from the depths of her own self-loathing, or if it had come from the ethereal lips of her lost mentor…but she was sure it didn't matter. She had led them all deep into the Badlands, and she'd come back without two of them. She would never forgive herself. She could blame the Foudre Rouge, Sector Nine, even Durango for not being clearer about what her people had been up against. But those were all excuses, cop outs. Andi had been in command. *Pegasus* was hers, and its crew had followed *her*. The blood of those who had died was on her hands. Their ghosts would haunt her until she closed her own eyes for the last time.

She would suffer, she would torture herself. But she wouldn't quit. *That* would be the ultimate breakdown, a failure to those who remained, and to the memory of the captain. And no matter how much pain she bore, she knew she could never do that. Andi Lafarge would never let anything defeat her. Not the deaths of her friends, not the guilt even then hollowing her out like a rotten tree trunk. Not the dangers that awaited, nor District gangsters and Badlands rivals. Not even Sector Nine, and all the Foudre Rouge the Union cared to throw at her.

She might fail, she might be beaten, she might die…but she would never quit.

Never.

* * *

"Andi, do you have a minute?" Lex Righter stood in the open doorway of Andi's cabin, looking like he'd rather be anywhere else.

"Sure, Lex…what's up?" Andi had been unpacking a few things. Durango had made good on his word, and *Pegasus* looked almost new. Every bit of damage, every scarred wall, was smooth and freshly polished. Andi couldn't even comprehend what the repair job would have cost…assuming Durango had accepted any payment. Which he hadn't.

"Sure, Lex…come on in."

"I wanted to tell you something…something I've never told anyone else. What I told you…about Maria, about how I lost control, it wasn't true." He paused, standing, looking very uncomfortable. "I mean, it was true about the relationship and how it ended…but it wasn't why I…had the problems I did."

Andi looked back, quiet, listening. She nodded gently, but she didn't respond. She knew Righter had more to say.

"I was on a ship's crew, Andi, one a lot like *Pegasus*. It was before I worked for Durango, about five years ago."

"I thought you seemed used to the Badlands. I've seen

people out there for the first time. It gets to them, almost always…but not you. I'm not surprised to hear you've been there before." Andi tried hard to keep any anger or judgment from her voice. She didn't like being lied to, especially by one of her crew, but she could tell Righter was telling her something he rarely spoke about.

Perhaps never spoke about.

That was difficult honesty…the most valuable kind, and a building block of loyalty.

"Yes, I spent a considerable amount of time in the Badlands, though most of it is a blur now. All I can remember clearly is…the last expedition." He paused, clearly struggling to continue.

"Lex…you don't have to talk about this. We can just start over, move forward from here."

"No, Andi…I have to tell you. *Pegasus* already feels like home to me, and you've got to know the truth. Now." He hesitated and sucked in a deep breath. "I have to tell you about *Serpent*, and about its crew. About my friends, my comrades…who all died out there because…" He paused again, and Andi could see tears streaming down his face. "…they all died because I couldn't save them. Because I failed. And I was the only one who came back."

Andi listened to Righter's story, and then she reached out and put her arms around him. Offering comfort wasn't the easiest thing for her, but she understood the kind of guilt that had broken the engineer.

"It's okay, Lex…I blame myself, too…for Gregor and Jackal. For so many things. But we have to go on. For the others who remain…and for the memories of those no longer with us. And for ourselves."

She sat quietly for a moment. She'd visited Yarra Tork in the hospital. Her friend was recovering, but she faced a long road of therapy before she was back on her feet…and she'd told Andi she needed some time after that. They'd both agreed, nodded and promised each other they would be together again on *Pegasus*. But Andi knew it would never be. All people had their limits, and Yarra had reached hers. The fire inside her, the power that drove her into the deadly emptiness of the Badlands, had gone out. Andi wished her friend well, with all her heart, and Durango had extended his annuity grant to Yarra as well as the families of the lost crew members. She would be okay. Between Durango's bequest, and the share of the payday Andi had insisted she accept, Yarra would live well, almost anywhere in the Confederation she chose.

Andi was happy for her comrade, and yet to her, it was the loss of yet another friend.

She spoke with Lex for a long time, hours, and she found some catharsis in it for herself. And when they were done, Lex Righter had found a new home, a permanent one...and Andi had accepted a new friend into her inner circle.

And *Pegasus* once again had an engineer.

*   *   *

"I'm sorry, I really am, but the data chips are too badly damaged. It's almost as though they caught a heavy dose of radiation...but of course, three centuries *is* a long time, and who knows what happened to these imperial ruins during the Cataclysm. It's beyond me to pull anything off these. I don't know if anybody else could, but I doubt it. Still, they're worth something as a curiosity. Maybe even worth a good bit. You want me to try to find a buyer?"

Andi looked down at the folio. She'd found the box of data chips in the imperial facility, and she knew they had been fully readable when she'd taken them. It was the antimatter explosion that had damaged them, she was sure of it. *Pegasus*'s data banks were shielded, but the folio had been in her bag during *Pegasus*'s flight from the planet, tossed on the floor of the ship's infirmary when her people had carried her back aboard.

"No, I don't think so. I'm going to hold on to these, I think. A souvenir of sorts." There was something about the small leather case that intrigued her. She'd tried to translate the writing on the cover, but with no success. It was Old Imperial, almost certainly, but nothing she'd been able to find in any database. "Before you go…do you have any idea what this writing on the cover says?"

The man looked down at it for a few seconds. "It looks like some kind of proper name to me. Let me see…" He pulled out a small analyzer, and he ran it across the smooth leather. "This has a pretty good database…a lot of rarely seen words and names." A couple seconds later, the man stared at the small screen with a puzzled look on his face. "Well, I'm not sure this is going to mean anything to you. It certainly doesn't to me."

"What does it say?"

He looked back at her for a few seconds, then his eyes went back to the screen on the device.

"It says, 'Chronicle of the Highborn.'

The Andromeda Chronicles Will Conclude With
Into the Badlands
Coming Soon

For Those Who Haven't Read Blood on the Stars,
it Begins with
Duel in the Dark

Appendix

Free Trader Pegasus (formerly Nightrunner)

Pegasus is a *Veritas*-class light cargo ship designed for long-run hauls of valuable freight.

Veritas-class vessels are sought after for illegal prospecting operations in the Badlands, mostly because of their extremely long cruising distances, often expanded further by the addition of secondary fuel tanks occupying part of the cargo hold. With the extreme value of even small amounts of imperial contraband, cargo space is far less crucial to such operations as extended cruising range.

Veritas-class ships are an outdated but extremely successful design, with more than nine hundred vessels delivered before production ceased in 261 AC. With the increasing age of ships remaining in service, spare parts have become increasing rare and difficult to obtain, resulting a wide variety of customized modifications and adaptations.

Pegasus was launched by Devellian Shipyards in 243 AC, and operated by Quincy Freight Lines for approximately forty years as *Gretel,* before being decommissioned and sold several times (records of these transactions are spotty and incomplete), ultimately being purchased on the secondary market by James Lorillard in 294 AC and rechristened, *Nightrunner.*

The specifications listed below are for standard *Veritas*-class vessels, plus known improvements installed in the ship. There are significant rumors of atypical, and often illegal, enhancements to *Pegasus*, especially in the early years of the fourth century AC, when the ship passed to the ownership of Captain Andromeda Lafarge. Previous owners had often skirted regulations, but none had shown Captain Lafarge's utter disregard for 'inconvenient' rules.

Engines:
One Enigmatic Industries 80-megawatt, dual cone engine.

Reactor:
One General Power Systems 125-megawatt tritium/helium-3 fusion reactor (with several unspecified upgrades in the case of *Pegasus*).

Weapons:
Top and bottom dual 30-megawatt laser turrets. There are rumors these weapons have been uprated beyond legal levels for civilian craft, and also that unidentified imperial artifacts have been installed to increase the hitting power of *Pegasus*'s weapons.

Cargo Capacity:
One thousand eight hundred tons.